From just behind Caitlin, a human voice moaned.

She jumped, her heart pounding, and whirled around, turning the flashlight like a weapon. "Who's there?" she cried.

The beam of the flashlight bounced and came to rest in the spot where she had heard the sound. At first Caitlin could not tell what she was seeing. And then, as her eyes adjusted, she recognized it. At the base of the hedge, propped up by the roots, its face turned into the leaves, was a body. A man lying on the ground.

"Oh, Jesus!" Caitlin cried. She wanted to run screaming, but instead she screwed up her courage and stepped closer.

"Noah?" she whispered, fearing what she might see. She pushed away the branches of the hedge and looked down.

His eyes were closed and his face was obscured by dark rivulets, his hair matted with blood. The body looked gray and limp, even in the flashlight's glare. She wanted nothing more than to look away, to run. Instead, she turned her flashlight full on the face.

Caitlin screamed. . . .

PATRICIA MACDONALD'S
suspenseful tales have captivated readers
across America, as well as in France, where
she is a #1 bestselling author. Her previous
novels include the Edgar Award-nominated
The Unforgiven. She currently resides with her
husband and daughter in New Jersey, where
she is working on her next novel.

PATRICIA MacDONALD

MISSING CHILD

W⊕RLDWIDE®

TORONTO • NEW YORK • LONDON
AMSTERDAM • PARIS • SYDNEY • HAMBURG
STOCKHOLM • ATHENS • TOKYO • MILAN
MADRID • WARSAW • BUDAPEST • AUCKLAND

Recycling programs
for this product may
not exist in your area.

ISBN-13: 978-0-373-06290-4

MISSING CHILD

Copyright © 2012 by Patricia Bourgeau

A Worldwide Library Suspense/November 2013

First published by Severn House Publishers Ltd.

www.Harlequin.com

Printed in U.S.A.

MISSING CHILD

To our dear friends and neighbors,
Karen and Yogi Kurtz .

PROLOGUE

CAITLIN STOOD UP and shook hands with the long-haired Asian girl in black-rimmed glasses who had been seated in front of her desk. 'Giang,' Caitlin said, 'I think we are going to be a very good fit for you.' Caitlin handed her a business card.

'I want you to call and make an appointment for your parents with this gentleman in the financial aid office. He will be able to help you sort out an aid package.'

Giang looked uneasily at the card. 'My parents don't speak any English,' she said.

'You can sit in on the meeting and translate for them,' said Caitlin. 'Brunswick University needs students of your caliber. We'll do all we can to make it work for you.'

Giang beamed. 'Thank you, Mrs Rogers,' she said.

'It's Miss,' said Caitlin. 'And trust me, the pleasure was mine.'

Caitlin watched as the petite, blue jean–clad high school senior left the minority recruitment office. She had given a presentation at Giang's inner-city school in Philadelphia recently, and had spoken to a number of likely prospects from that disadvantaged environment. Caitlin was the director for diversity recruitment at Brunswick University, and it was her job to seek out and encourage low-income minority students to fulfill their dreams of college at Brunswick. Sometimes she saw herself as a one-woman rescue operation, helping kids find a way out of poverty and into a brighter future. She felt lucky to have work that was meaningful to her.

'She was a cute one,' said Beverly, Caitlin's receptionist. Beverly had four kids of her own, and a heart big enough to accommodate every student at Brunswick, and then some.

'I hope she decides to come here,' said Caitlin. 'I sent her to financial aid. She needs help applying for scholarships, but I think it will work out for her. She's very motivated.'

'We like them motivated,' said Beverly. 'Speaking of motivated, how's your brother doing with that therapist?'

Caitlin sighed. Her brother James was, at sixteen years old, twelve years Caitlin's junior and had been assigned to therapy by family court. He had lost his provisional driver's permit for being caught trying to buy beer in a convenience store. He was suspended from school for fighting and he had a problem with prescription drugs—for which he had no prescription. She did not know where he got his supply, and he denied ever using the drugs she found in his room.

She tried not to judge him too harshly. She and James were still reeling from the death of their parents, who had both succumbed to illness in the past two years. Caitlin, who had been on staff at an Ivy League school in New England, had been forced to come home, move into her parents' house and assume the role of her brother's guardian. It had turned out to be a heavy responsibility. 'Well, this is only the second visit. Last week was mostly filling out paperwork and family history. We'll see,' she said.

'Sixteen is such a tough age,' said Beverly. 'And he is really kind of isolated around here.'

'I know,' said Caitlin. 'He hasn't made any friends yet.' Their parents had raised them in Coatesville, Pennsylvania, a blue-collar suburb of Philadelphia, and they had bought the house in among the marshes and inlets of South Jersey as a retirement home. But they decided to make the move early when James began getting into trouble in high school. In Coatesville, James had a girlfriend named Karla, a girl who ended up busted for drugs and serving time in a juvenile facility. Caitlin's parents had hoped that by removing James from Coatesville, they would get him away from Karla and his other troublemaking friends. Instead, James managed to get into even more trouble on his own.

'It's hard on you,' Beverly said sympathetically. 'How are you supposed to have a life of your own when you're running around from counselors to lawyers to school? You're a young woman. You need to meet somebody and have some fun.'

'One of these days,' said Caitlin.

'Well, you can't wait too long,' said Beverly. 'Not if you want to have kids.'

'I'll tell you something. After this business with James, I'm not sure kids are for me.'

'Oh, don't say that. It's different when they're your own. Speaking of which,' said Beverly, gathering up her purse and shopping bag, 'I've got to go pick up my youngest and get home. It's pizza night.'

'Probably pizza night for us, too,' said Caitlin. She waved to her assistant as Beverly left the office. Then, with a sigh, Caitlin filled out the paperwork about her last interview, and closed up her office as well.

The fact was that Beverly was right, Caitlin thought as she got into her car in the waning light of the November afternoon. She felt as if she had no life here, other than trying to deal with her brother's issues. When their mother died, leaving James alone, Caitlin had considered moving her brother up to where she lived in New England. But she hadn't wanted to relocate him again after all the loss and change that he had been through. Sometimes, she was not sure if she had made the right decision. She had made a life for herself and friends in New England. Here, she felt completely isolated.

The deserted marshes and pine forests of South Jersey under a melancholy gray, salmon and lavender sky reflected her mood. This whole part of South Jersey was, at once, scenic and down at the heels. She drove past a lovely field with horses grazing on the brown grass. But there was a rusted-out car beside the barn, and the barn had a hole in the roof.

When her father took early retirement, he had planned to hunt and fish and her mother was looking forward to taking a book to the beach on nice days. They had hoped that perhaps James would abandon his bad habits and start again. And they could enjoy their hard-earned free time. That was their plan, but they miscalculated. Now, they were both gone, and Caitlin had inherited their retirement cottage and their problems. If only, she thought, James would show some improvement, it might not seem like such an uphill battle. But most of the time he was depressed and didn't talk to her. It was as if she was living with a wraith who silently inhabited the house, drifting from room to room.

Caitlin pulled into the driveway of the neat, square little home that her parents had furnished and cared for with such high hopes. All the lights were out and the house looked forlorn. Her father's pick-up truck, normally kept in the garage, was parked in the driveway, and Caitlin instantly felt angry and anxious. James's driving permit was suspended. *He had better not have been out driving,* she thought.

Don't jump to conclusions, she told herself. *You asked him to clean out the garage while he was suspended.*

Maybe he moved the truck out to get easier access to the jumbled mess in there. She didn't feel very optimistic about the possibility, but she reminded herself to try to be patient and not jump to the worst conclusion.

Caitlin walked into the house and was startled by James, who was sitting in the living room without a single light on. She turned on a lamp and frowned at him. 'What are you doing sitting here in the dark?' she asked.

He looked at her, grave and hollow-eyed. 'Nothing,' he said.

'Do you want to tell me what Daddy's truck is doing in the driveway?'

'I just…moved it,' he said.

'You weren't out driving, I hope. You know you have no permit.'

'I know,' he said.

'OK,' she said. She decided not to make an issue of it. 'As long as you know.' She set her briefcase down on a chair, took off her jacket and hung it up. 'I'm going to see what I can put together for us for supper. You better go get a shirt on over that T-shirt and put some shoes on.'

'What for?' he asked.

'James. The therapist. That's tonight.'

James did not reply.

'Go on. Go get ready,' she said. She glanced at the clock. Too late to wait for a pizza delivery. She opened a can of soup and began to heat it on the stove. She pulled out plates and put sandwiches together.

'Caitlin?'

She looked up and saw him standing in the doorway to the kitchen. 'What?'

'I don't think I can go tonight,' he said.

'Why not?'

'I don't feel well,' he said.

In the bright, overhead light of the kitchen, she could see that he did indeed look ill. His skin was white and his eyes were sunken in his head. She put a hand on his forehead beneath his shock of greasy hair. He was not feverish. If anything, his skin was cold and clammy.

'You don't look too good,' she admitted.

'I have to go lie down,' he said.

Caitlin sighed. 'All right. I'll call and cancel.'

James disappeared from the doorway, and Caitlin called the therapist's office.

'If you cancel,' said the receptionist, 'you'll still have to pay for the session.'

'OK, fine,' said Caitlin. 'Send me the bill.'

She hung up the phone and called out to her brother. 'Do you want some soup? Or a sandwich?'

'No,' he said. 'I'm not hungry.'

Caitlin exhaled, and turned on the television to keep her company while she ate. On the news, the anchor was recounting the death of a young mother, the victim of a hit-and-run driver on Route 47, about ten minutes from where they lived. Caitlin was too distracted to pay much attention. As usual, she was worrying about James and wondering how she was ever going to get through to him. After she finished her supper, Caitlin switched off the television, and washed up her few dishes. She looked out the kitchen window at the truck, which was still in the driveway. She wondered if James had made any attempt to clean out the garage. She went through the hallway off the kitchen and called out to him.

'James? Did you get to work on that garage today?'

He did not reply.

What's the use? she thought. She knew the answer. *Might as well put the truck away,* she thought. She grabbed the keys off a hook by the kitchen and went outside. She entered the garage by the side door and flipped on the lights, hoping against hope that he might have made a start on the project. Nothing had been moved. The garage was as full of junk as ever. She sighed and shook her head. What had he done all day? He hadn't moved the truck to work on the mess in the garage. He said he hadn't been out driving, but she felt queasy, realizing that she didn't really believe him. It would be just like him to go out joyriding without a permit. *Tomorrow,* she thought, *I'm going to take the keys with me to work.*

She opened the main garage door from inside, walked out and stopped short. In the glow of the spotlight above the garage door, she instantly saw the damage. The truck was dented in the front. Seriously dented. *Goddammit,* she thought. *First he lied about not driving. His permit is suspended, and now this. No wonder he doesn't feel well,* she thought angrily. The closer she got to it, the more severe the damage looked. This was not a tap. It looked like he'd run into a tree. The whole front of the truck was pushed in.

'James!' she yelled, not caring if he was sick or not. 'Goddammit.'

She bent down to examine the damage and saw something dark and shiny on the imploded bumper. She reached down to touch it, and her fingers came up wet and sticky. Caitlin held up her hand and stared at it. There was no mistaking the substance on her fingers. Heart pounding, she jumped back away from the truck.

All of a sudden she realized that James was standing there in the darkness, just out of the arc of the garage floodlights. He was watching her intently. She looked from her own sticky fingers to his haunted face.

'What the hell happened here?' she whispered.

'I'm sorry, Caitlin,' he said. 'I'm sorry.'

'James. I asked you what happened. There's blood all over this bumper.'

James stared back at her. 'There was an accident,' he said.

ONE

'THIS IS GONNA be the best party ever,' Geordie declared.

Caitlin attached the last of the streamers and carefully dismounted the rickety stepstool. 'Well, I hope so.' She looked fondly at Geordie. 'It's not every day you turn six years old,' she said.

'Yesterday I turned six years old,' he reminded her.

Caitlin nodded. 'I know.' They had held off on having the party until Sunday because Geordie's only cousin, ten-year-old, had Boy Scouts on Saturday, and his mother didn't like for him to miss a meeting. 'It was nice of you to put off the party until today so Travis could come.'

Geordie nodded gravely. 'No one wants to miss my party,' he said. Geordie was a wiry little boy with a missing front tooth, buzz-cut brown hair and large glasses. Tucked under his arm was Bandit, a shabby stuffed Dalmatian with one ear hanging on by a thread and black rings around its eyes. 'Is the cake here yet?'

'Aunt Haley should be here any minute.'

As if on cue, the front doorbell rang. 'That's probably her,' said Geordie.

Geordie scampered off toward the front door while Caitlin made a mental inventory of the party goods she had set out. Cider and soda and paper cups, plates for the pizza and for the cake. Plastic forks. Noah was outside putting up the last of the games on the front lawn. They were pretty much ready.

'Caitlin, look!' Geordie cried.

He came dancing into the kitchen ahead of a round-faced, blond-haired woman carrying an enormous cake shaped to appear like a medieval castle with Playmobil knights tucked into the ramparts.

'Oh, Haley,' Caitlin exclaimed. 'That is fantastic.'

Haley Jordan smiled proudly. 'He asked for a castle.'

'I didn't know you could make gray icing.' Caitlin laughed.

'Oh, sure. There's just not a very big demand for it.' Haley owned Jordan's, a bakery in downtown Hartwell. She was the ex-wife of Geordie's uncle Dan, who now lived in Philadelphia. In the two years that Caitlin had been married to Geordie's father, Noah, she and Haley had become friends. Caitlin suspected that Haley still carried a torch for Dan, although they were now ostensibly just friends.

'So, who all is coming?' Haley asked casually.

'Well, everybody,' said Caitlin. 'Half a dozen kids from Geordie's class. Emily's parents, of course, and Dan.'

'It's really good of you to have Emily's family,' said Haley. 'I know they appreciate it.'

'Well, they're Geordie's family. They always will be,' said Caitlin, gazing down at the little boy who was trying to resist poking a finger into the gooey icing.

The doorbell suddenly sounded. 'Hey, you,' she said to Geordie. 'You better go out there and greet your guests.'

He looked up at her, his innocent eyes magnified by his glasses, overcome by a sudden attack of shyness. 'Will you come with me?'

'Your dad's out there,' Caitlin reassured him.

'OK,' he said, popping up.

'Hey,' she said, 'why not leave Bandit here in the kitchen? You're gonna need both hands for presents.'

Geordie looked reluctantly at his beloved toy. He clearly

did not want to part with him. 'No. Someone might sit on him,' said Geordie.

'You're right. You know what?' said Caitlin. 'I have got to sew that ear of his back on. I promised you I would. Before the party gets underway, why don't you run and put him in my room on the bureau. That way I won't forget and I can sew his ear on tonight.'

Geordie hesitated, and then nodded. 'OK.' He skipped out of the room and down the hall clutching the shabby toy.

Caitlin turned back to Haley. 'Let's see. Where was I? Noah's sister and his mother. And...' Caitlin rolled her eyes. 'Travis, of course. If he sees Geordie carrying Bandit around, he'll start baiting him about how he has a real dog and Geordie doesn't. And how only babies carry stuffed animals. Why should Geordie have to put up with that at his own party?'

'Hey, if Emily were here, she'd agree with you,' said Haley.

Caitlin felt her cheeks redden when Haley equated her with Geordie's real mother. It was two and a half years ago at a charitable event commemorating Emily's death that Caitlin had first met Noah. The event was announced in the paper. A year after her death, Emily Eckhart's family was going to plant a garden in her honor at the Pediatric Cancer Center in Vineland. The public was invited to the planting of the garden, which was a fundraiser, as well as a day of remembrance. Caitlin had debated with herself a hundred times whether or not to go. She knew that she needed to introduce herself to Emily's family, to tell them the truth. On the day of the actual event she felt physically ill, and almost talked herself out of going, but then she summoned all her courage and went.

The day did not turn out at all as she had planned. She met the late Emily's husband, Noah, and instantly there was a connection between them. Caitlin hesitated and, to her shame, kept her secret. Noah called her the next day for a date. Their courtship lasted all of six months. Geordie was four years old when Caitlin married Noah, moved into Emily Eckhart's house and became her son's stepmother.

The first year had not been easy. Geordie was never a cranky child, and Caitlin naively assumed that they would all adjust smoothly. But instead of the blissful honeymoon period she had hoped for, Caitlin found her every night's sleep rent by Geordie's cries as he immediately began to suffer from night terrors. Noah would go to him, and soothe him back to sleep. No sooner would they get back to sleep, than Geordie would wet the bed and call out for help. Together, Caitlin and Noah would strip the bed and remake it with clean, dry sheets.

In the morning, bleary-eyed as she washed the sheets before she left for work, Caitlin would force herself to think about the loss of his mother and all the changes that Geordie had endured. She would remind herself to stay on his side. Little by little, her patience was rewarded. Little by little, it got better.

'Thanks,' said Caitlin. 'I'd like to think so.'

CARRYING A TRAY of paper cups filled with cider, Caitlin stood on the lawn in the lovely September sunshine and paused to enjoy the shrieking of happy six-year-olds as they tussled with one another over the games in the yard. Noah came up on her from behind and slipped his arms around her waist.

'Yikes,' Caitlin said, 'the cider.'

Noah took the cider tray from her hands and set it down on a nearby table.

Then he resumed holding Caitlin around the waist. 'This is a nice party,' he said. 'You did a great job.'

'Geordie seems happy.'

'Which is all that really matters. Because for his father, it will, no doubt, be the longest afternoon of the year,' he said.

Caitlin smiled. 'Oh, stop it.'

'Children's birthday parties are just slightly more pleasurable than a toothache.'

Caitlin took his grumbling with a grain of salt. He was the most devoted of fathers. He just couldn't pretend to enjoy the commotion of the birthday party. Truth be told, she would also be glad when it was successfully completed and the last guest had left. All that really mattered to her was that Geordie should be happy with his party.

A well-worn Volvo pulled in and parked behind the last car of the many assembled in their long driveway. Noah let go of Caitlin. 'Let me see if Naomi needs help with my mom.'

'Sure,' said Caitlin. She watched as Noah loped toward the Volvo. He was a tall, broad-shouldered man with a wide face and wavy, light brown hair. She knew that Geordie resembled his late mother more than Noah. All the photos of Emily around the house showed a slim, dark-haired woman with shiny brown eyes and an oval face.

Noah opened the passenger door of the Volvo to help his mother, Martha, get out of the car. She was an otherwise healthy woman in her sixties, but she suffered from the effects of macular degeneration. Her eyes seemed to tremble behind the thick lenses of her glasses like two gray egg yolks. Martha, widowed at an early age, had lived a very independent life, but now, because of her condition, she was completely reliant on Naomi. Noah helped them financially but his sister, Naomi, was Martha's caretaker.

Naomi, her ten-year-old son, Travis, and Travis's dog, an ill-tempered mutt named Champ, got out of the car as well. Champ began to yip in a loud, frantic tone. Travis, pudgy and scowling, walked with his head bent, fiddling with his Game Boy.

Why did Naomi let him bring Champ? Caitlin thought. She didn't want a dog running loose among all these children. She was reluctant to complain, for she knew how attached Travis was to Champ. Travis's father, Rod Pelletier, had been killed in Iraq when Travis was small, and Naomi had let him get a dog shortly thereafter as a way to console him. But Champ was cranky and highly strung and Caitlin didn't trust him around all these kids.

Noah's family ambled in Caitlin's direction, Martha resting her hand on Noah's arm. Naomi was carrying two wrapped packages. Plain and overweight, Naomi dressed for comfort and never bothered with makeup. She worked at the county recycling center, where she had created and ran a free bookstore organized from salvaged books which people had discarded.

'Welcome,' said Caitlin. 'Glad you could be here.'

Martha gazed in Caitlin's vicinity. 'It's a nice day,' she said.

'It's a beautiful day,' Caitlin agreed. 'Travis, there're so many kids here. Maybe you should put Champ back in the car.'

Travis glowered at her. 'No. Mom, tell her. You said it was OK.'

Naomi seemed oblivious to the exchange. 'Is there somewhere I can put these presents?' she asked.

Caitlin took a deep breath. 'Inside,' she said. 'I'll show you.'

Noah put a hand on Travis's shoulder. 'Caitlin's right. Champ's going to have to wait in the car. We don't want any of these kids upsetting him. Don't worry. I'll roll the windows down and we'll give him some treats. I'll take him. Why don't you go play with the other kids? They're playing space ship.'

Travis shook off his uncle's hand. 'I don't want to play dorky games with first graders.'

'Come get something to eat then,' said Caitlin. She led the way across the lawn, up the front steps and into the house. It was a comfortable house with new construction in an old, farmhouse style. It had been Emily's house, and from time to time Caitlin wondered what it would be like to have a house that was only hers, but then she would banish that thought, ashamed of herself.

As she climbed up onto the porch, she saw Haley gamely making conversation with Emily's brother, Dan, and the woman he had brought along, a lovely, long-limbed girl in Jimmy Choo stilettos named Jillian. Caitlin had been at the door when Dan arrived with Jillian. The expression on Haley's face, when she saw the honey-haired beauty on Dan's arm, had been painful to behold. Of course, their marriage had been over for years, and each of them had had other lovers, but Caitlin suspected that, for Haley, no one compared to Dan.

Caitlin opened the front door and pointed to an oak sideboard in the dining room. She looked back at Naomi. 'You can put the presents there,' she said. 'There's snacks everywhere and there's pizza in the kitchen.'

'I want pizza,' said Travis, pushing past her.

She followed him into the kitchen. Emily's parents were manning the kitchen activities. Paula Bergen, who had worked her way up from file clerk to director of operations for the electric company, was helping in the kitchen by cutting up pizza and putting it on paper plates, while her husband, Westy, was creating balloon animals for a small but rapt audience of children at the kitchen table.

'Now this is what I call a birthday party,' Paula exclaimed. 'Where is Geordie? I want him to see what his grandfather is doing,' she said, smiling indulgently at Westy, a balding man in a blue shirt. Westy never shared his wife's ambitions. 'One executive in the family is enough,' he liked to say. He had inherited family money, and spent his working life in the local hardware store. Now retired, he could build or fix anything.

'Westy,' said Naomi, 'you have hidden talents!' Westy looked up at Noah's sister, and Naomi pointed to the turquoise-blue dachshund which was taking shape in his gnarled, arthritic hands. Naomi gave him a thumbs up.

Westy beamed.

Caitlin felt, not for the first time, a certain admiration for these two families, related by marriage. They seemed to have bonded over the tragic deaths of Rod and Emily to provide some continuity for the children. 'Pizza, Travis?' asked Caitlin kindly, sliding a plate across the counter and handing it to the stocky boy who suddenly grew quiet in the company of so many grown-ups.

'You can take it out in the yard with the other kids.'

Travis grabbed the plate of pizza in both hands and headed for the yard. He encountered Noah, coming into the kitchen. Noah ruffled Travis's hair as they passed in the doorway.

Noah came up to Caitlin and draped an arm around her shoulders. Caitlin smiled and grasped his hand. As always, she felt a little self-conscious when Noah showed her any affection around Emily's parents. But if Paula and Westy had any resentment of Caitlin taking their late daughter's place, they didn't let it show. On the contrary, they always seemed grateful that their grandson had a stepmother who cared so much about him. Paula was humming and wiping the counters as if she were at home. Seated at the kitchen table, Westy took orders for balloon animals and exhorted the children to be patient, that he was twisting balloons as fast as he could.

Haley came into the kitchen and looked around anxiously. 'Is it time to serve the cake yet?' she asked.

All the children at the table forgot about balloon animals. 'Yes. Cake!' they cried.

THE CUTTING AND serving of cake was followed by the opening of presents. Geordie sat perched on a chair above a colorful mountain of ribbon and wrapping paper. Many parents had already come to collect the pint-sized guests, but there was a knot of unclaimed children remaining.

Geordie's uncle Dan came up behind Caitlin and Noah. He wore a Ralph Lauren polo shirt and smelled of expensive aftershave. Dan had a life, Caitlin mused, that any man might envy. He lived in a townhouse in the city, wrote a popular sports blog and worked as a sportscaster for a satellite radio station in Philly. He traveled to every stadium in the country, watched games and got paid for it. His new girlfriend was young and beautiful—one of several such women he had brought around. Dan spoke quietly. 'Has he opened my gift yet?'

'What'd you get him?' Caitlin asked.

'That set of Pixar DVDs he wanted.'

'Yeah, he opened them,' said Noah.

'Does that mean we can leave?' Dan asked hopefully.

'No. If I have to stay, you have to stay,' Noah said to his former brother-in-law with cheery malevolence.

'Oohs' and 'aahs' erupted from the remaining kids as Geordie listlessly held another stuffed animal aloft. Westy presented him with another package, this one in a square box. Geordie tore off the wrapping and then looked puzzled at the result. 'What is it?'

'It's binoculars,' said Westy. 'Your very own. So we can go birdwatching!'

'Birdwatching! Westy, for heaven's sake,' Paula chided him. 'I told you to get him sports equipment. That's a sport for old people.'

Westy's blue eyes widened and a hurt expression crossed his face. 'I saw a bald eagle last week. I'll bet he'd like that. And there's ospreys and herons down by the lake. We can take the canoe!'

The confusion in Geordie's eyes turned to delight as he opened the box and pulled out the binoculars. 'Cool! Can I, Dad? Can I go birdwatching with Grandpa?'

'Sure,' said Noah. 'Look, finish up there, son. People have to leave.'

Geordie looked cursorily for another unopened package. 'I don't see any more,' he said. He slid off the chair and picked up a package of laser light swords. 'Can I take these outside and play with them?'

'Sure,' said Noah. 'Why don't you? Take these kids with you.'

Geordie ran screaming through the house, the few remaining kids in tow.

Caitlin got a big garbage bag and began to stuff it with wrapping paper and ribbons. Haley stood there awkwardly, trying to avoid glancing at Dan. 'Can I help?' she asked.

Caitlin pushed her hair out of her eyes. 'Oh, that's all right. You've done enough, bringing that cake. We'll just clean it up as we go. I'll bring that tray the cake is on back to the bakery.'

'No hurry,' said Haley. 'I've got lots of them.'

A sudden, terrible noise erupted outside the house. Caitlin instantly recognized the sound of Geordie's crying. She ran toward the front yard. Geordie was in tears, holding the remains of a broken laser sword in his hand. Travis was watching him furtively.

'What happened?' Caitlin demanded.

Geordie could barely sob out the words. 'Travis broke it.'

'I didn't mean to,' Travis protested in an unconvincing tone.

'You did it on purpose,' Geordie insisted.

'You're just a crybaby,' Travis sneered. The other six-year-olds cowered, not wanting to come between the warring cousins.

Naomi sighed. 'All right. Come on, Travis. Time to go. Mom, are you ready to go?'

'I'm ready,' said Martha brightly.

Caitlin tried to catch Noah's eye, hoping he would take the opportunity to chasten his nephew, but Noah was looking the other way.

Dan walked up to Caitlin, Jillian trailing behind him, her high heels gouging holes in the lawn. 'We're gonna have to leave too,' he said.

Paula, who also had rushed outside when she heard Geordie crying, peered at her grown son. 'Dan, what's the matter with you, now?'

Dan rubbed a hand over his forehead. 'We have to go. I'm getting…a headache.'

'I've hardly seen you,' Paula cried.

'I know, but my head feels like it's in a vise,' said Dan. 'Really.'

He put an arm around Jillian and directed her toward the waiting car. 'Can you drive, babe?' he asked.

'I told you. I don't drive,' said Jillian.

'I guess I'll go too,' Haley said to Caitlin in a defeated tone.

Caitlin gave her a hug. 'Thank you so much. That was the best cake in the world.'

'All right. Party's over,' Noah declared, scooping up his crying son in his arms.

All the fight seemed to have gone out of Geordie, and he suddenly lay his head on his father's shoulder. An occasional shuddering sob passed through him. He was too young to be ashamed of his tears.

Paula and Westy approached their grandson on either side. Westy rubbed his little back and Paula kissed him on the cheek. 'I guess we'd better be going too, Geordie. If you want me to take those binoculars back and get you something else…' said Paula.

'Hey,' Westy protested. 'My buddy and me are going to check out the swamp birds, right?'

Geordie nodded wearily and yawned.

'You are a nice little boy,' said Paula, shaking her head.

Caitlin smiled at them, happy that Geordie had saved the day with his sweet enthusiasm over their gift. Westy now seemed positively proud of his choice. 'Thank you for everything, you two.'

Caitlin and Noah waved goodbye to Geordie's grandparents. They watched as Paula and Westy walked arm in arm down to their car. After they left she turned to Noah. 'Noah, you know Travis broke that sword on purpose.'

'Oh, I know it. I just didn't want to get into it with my sister. Not at the party. She has a lot on her plate.'

'I know that. And I know you feel guilty about her taking care of your mother. I understand that. But you might want to mention it to her at some point. Travis really has a mean streak.'

Noah rearranged Geordie against his shoulder. 'Where'd Dan go?'

'He left. He said he had a bad headache.'

'Yeah, right,' said Noah, chuckling.

'What?' said Caitlin.

'Not exactly Dan's idea of fun.'

'It was fun,' Caitlin insisted.

'Did you enjoy your party?' Noah asked the child on his shoulder.

Geordie nodded without lifting his head.

'Thank God you only have one birthday a year,' said Noah.

'I know,' Geordie murmured solemnly.

'You're terrible,' said Caitlin good-naturedly. 'Both of you.'

Noah whispered in Geordie's ear.

'Thanks, Mom,' Geordie said and reached out a little hand to her.

Caitlin took it and squeezed it in her own. 'You're welcome, sweetie,' she said. She turned her face so he would not see the tears which sprang to her eyes. She wiped them away and cleared her throat. 'Well, I better get some of this stuff put away,' she said. She started back up the lawn to the house, trying to think about what she needed to do next. But as she walked, her heart was singing, and all she could think about was that Geordie had called her Mom. He had made it official. He belonged to her.

TWO

THE FOLLOWING MORNING, Caitlin stood at the sink and felt the sun on her face as it streamed through the kitchen window. The morning sun also filtered over the breakfast table where Geordie rested his cheek on one hand and played with his cereal. Caitlin cast a sympathetic glance at the listless child. The post-birthday let-down seemed to be hitting him pretty hard.

Noah came into the kitchen carrying his briefcase and set it down beside the table. He picked up a piece of toast and took a bite. 'Hey, you better eat that cereal, buddy,' Noah said. 'You didn't have any supper last night. All you ate was junk food and birthday cake.'

'I'm not hungry,' said Geordie. 'I think I'm sick.'

Noah frowned. 'Sick how?'

Geordie shrugged. 'I think I caught it from Uncle Dan.'

'Uncle Dan had a headache. You can't catch a headache.'

Geordie was undeterred. 'Can I stay home?'

'You don't look sick.'

'I want to stay home with you,' Geordie said plaintively.

'Can't. I have to be in court this morning,' said Noah, taking a bite out of a piece of toast. 'And you, my friend, have school. Now hurry up and finish. Caitlin will take you today.'

'But it's Fall Festival,' Geordie protested. 'You have to come and see my project. The one we did about the leaves.'

Noah grimaced. 'I thought it was on all week.'

'You have to come today,' Geordie exclaimed.

Noah pondered the problem. 'Tell you what. How 'bout if I pick you up after school and you show it to me then?'

'That's no good. Everybody's coming this morning,' Geordie insisted, slumping over, his head resting on his skinny little arms on the tabletop.

Noah finished his toast. 'This afternoon. That's my final offer,' he said.

'Come on, Geordie,' Caitlin said. 'I'm going to come in and look at your project. And if you hurry, we can drive by that barn with the horses.'

Geordie looked up, his eyes wide behind his glasses. 'Will the horses be outside?'

'Probably,' said Caitlin.

That was all the encouragement that Geordie needed. His ailments and disappointment forgotten, he hopped up from the table and started for his room.

'Hey. Bowl,' said Caitlin.

Geordie turned back without protest, collected his bowl and spoon and brought them to the sink where Caitlin was rinsing the dishes. Then he ran off to get his backpack.

Noah sighed. 'Thanks. You saved my butt. You're good at this, you know.'

'Good at what?' Caitlin said.

'Kids. You're good.'

Caitlin did not reply.

'You are,' said Noah. 'You're a natural.'

'Not really,' said Caitlin.

Noah frowned at her. 'Thinking about your brother?' he asked.

Caitlin sighed and shook her head, even though he had read her mind.

'Look, by the time they get to be teenagers, it's too late. You can't really change them,' said Noah.

This was a subject Caitlin avoided. Noah knew the outlines of her history. He knew that after her parents had died, Caitlin had moved back to the family home in South Jersey to take care of her teenage brother. He also knew that James had been in and out of trouble and had died of a drug overdose. That was all. 'I know that,' she said irritably.

'What happened to James was not your fault. Believe me. I see these kids in court all the time. It's beyond what even a parent can do. Never mind a sister.'

'I'm sure you're right,' she murmured.

'I know you tried your best,' said Noah.

'It wasn't enough,' she said.

'Look, you may not believe me,' said Noah, 'but I meant what I said. You are good at this.'

'Good at what?' a small voice piped up from the vicinity of their hips.

Noah turned, looked down and saw his son's upturned face. His big glasses. The space between his teeth. He grabbed Geordie up in a hug. 'Good at eating you up,' Noah proclaimed.

Geordie let out a shriek of laughter as his father made juicy gobbling noises against his downy cheek.

NORMALLY THE SCHOOL parking lot was an orderly procession of cars stopping to discharge kids, and then pulling away. Today, because of the Fall Festival, adults were looking for parking and accompanying their children inside. Usually, Caitlin dropped Geordie at the front of the school, but this time the door outside the entrance to the auditorium was open, and it was closer to the parking lot.

She drove around to it, keeping a careful eye out for little ones who might absent-mindedly dart into her path, and parked the car.

Geordie ran ahead, disappearing into the crowd flowing through the open doors to the auditorium. Caitlin went in behind him. The school auditorium had a proscenium at one end, and an open kitchen at the other. The auditorium doubled as the cafeteria at lunchtime and the gymnasium at others. During Fall Festival all the gym classes were held out of doors in the mild, autumn sun, and the kids ate lunch as usual among the exhibits which lined the walls.

Caitlin walked into the crowded auditorium and looked around for Geordie. The room was filled with moms and dads either being dragged or ignored by their kids. She did not know many of these parents, other than by sight, although they all seemed to know one another. Many of them had known Emily. Since marrying Noah, Caitlin had deliberately tried to keep a low profile so as not to be seen as disrespecting Emily's memory. Caitlin didn't see Geordie, but suddenly she spotted Naomi, and felt a sudden pleasure at the sight of a familiar face.

'Naomi!' she called out. Naomi, who was deep in discussion with another mom, turned and frowned at her. Then she raised a hand in greeting. Caitlin went over to her. 'Hi,' she said.

'Hi, Caitlin. You know Janice?'

Caitlin shook her head and Naomi introduced her to the other mom, who then said she had to slip away.

Caitlin looked around the noisy auditorium. 'I'm looking for Geordie. He ran in here before I could tell him to wait.'

'I haven't seen him,' said Naomi. 'I'm just leaving. Who's his teacher?'

'Mr Needleman,' she said.

'I'm sure Mr Needleman's flitting around here some-where in his ballet slippers,' said Naomi.

'He seems like a very good teacher,' said Caitlin, a note of reproof in her tone.

'Oh, yeah. He's capable,' said Naomi. 'I just think it would be helpful for these boys to have a more…tradi-tional role model.'

'Traditional?' said Caitlin.

'Masculine, I mean,' said Naomi. 'That's why I like Travis to go to Scouts. One of Rod's old army buddies is the Scout leader. I like him to have that kind of influence. Life is confusing enough these days.'

Caitlin didn't want to get into an argument with her sister-in-law. 'I think it's good for kids to know all kinds of people,' she said diplomatically.

'I suppose,' Naomi sighed. 'Well, I've got to get to work. If I see Geordie on my way out I'll tell him you're looking for him. You should check out Travis's project. He did it on recycling,' Naomi said proudly.

'I'll look for it,' Caitlin promised.

Naomi headed for the door and was swallowed by the crowd.

Caitlin made her way over to the display from Mr Needleman's class and began to look for Geordie's proj-ect. Every so often she glanced around, looking for Geor-die, but there was no sign of him. She went through every student's project until she found Geordie's and then she took it in, trying to memorize everything about it, so she could describe it to him when she saw him.

'Geordie did a good job,' said Alan Needleman, com-ing up beside her.

Caitlin turned and looked at the teacher. He was young—not much more than thirty—but his blond hair was already thinning. He had pale eyelashes and dimples. He wore an argyle vest over his shirt, the latest in running shoes, and exuded a kind of positive energy which made Caitlin smile every time she saw him. Rumor had it that he lived with a male partner who worked at the fire department in Deptford County. 'He's very proud of it,' Caitlin admitted.

'He told me that you helped him collect the leaves and look up the Latin names.'

'I did,' said Caitlin, beaming. 'We went over to the Arboretum. It was fun. I love doing things with him.'

'He's a very special boy,' said Mr Needleman.

'We think so,' said Caitlin, scanning the room again for a sign of Geordie. 'Have you seen him, by the way?'

'Oh, I'm sure he's running around here somewhere.'

Caitlin looked at her watch. 'I hate to leave without telling him myself, but I've got to get to work. Will you let him know that I saw his project?'

'Sure,' said Mr Needleman.

'It's not like him to miss out on a chance to be praised,' said Caitlin, frowning as she glanced around the hectic scene.

Alan Needleman rolled his eyes. 'They're all the same that way. Don't worry. I'll tell him.'

CAITLIN PARKED IN her space at the college, went into the building and unlocked the door to her office. August and September were usually a nightmare of students changing schedules, changing their majors, changing their minds in general. But, to her surprise, the last week or so had been quiet. She even had a little time to catch up on her paperwork in the mornings before her first student appointment. She went out into the reception area to say good morning to Beverly. Angelic pictures of Beverly's four kids were lined up on her desk. But this morning a stranger sat in Beverly's seat.

'Good morning,' said Caitlin.

'Hi, Dean Eckhart,' she said. 'I'm June. I'm filling in for Beverly. One of her kids fell off the deck and broke his wrist.'

'Oh, no,' said Caitlin.

'She'll be in tomorrow.'

'Thanks,' said Caitlin. 'Do you know what to…'

June held up a hand. 'Beverly briefed me. All's well.'

'Thanks,' said Caitlin, pointing back toward her office. 'I'll be in there.'

June nodded and picked up her phone, which was ringing. 'Dean Eckhart's office.'

Caitlin went back into her small but comfortable office and waited for her phone to ring. But whoever the caller had been, June did not put them through. Caitlin frowned. It could have been some matter that wasn't in Caitlin's purview. Of course, she would expect Beverly to be able to screen her calls, but how could June be expected to know which ones to put through? *Stop micromanaging,* she thought. *Enjoy the peace and quiet.* 'I'm sure she knows what she's doing,' Caitlin said aloud to no one in particular. Suddenly, Caitlin's cell phone rang and she jumped. She fumbled to pick up the phone which she had not expected to ring.

'Mrs Eckhart?' said an unfamiliar voice.

'Yes.'

'This is Miss Benson. I work in the office at Geordie's school. I tried to reach your husband but his phone seems to be turned off.'

'He's in court. What is it?' Caitlin asked. She thought about Geordie's complaints of illness this morning. Maybe he wasn't faking. Maybe he really wasn't feeling well. 'Is Geordie sick?'

There was a silence at the other end of the line. 'I was just calling to ask *you* that,' the woman said slowly.

Caitlin frowned, instantly wary. 'What do you mean?'

'Well, he is not in school today. It's our policy to check on all absent students.'

Caitlin could hear the thudding of her own heart in her ears. 'There must be some mistake. He is in school. I took him there myself this morning.'

There was another silence. Then Miss Benson said, 'I will double check this and call you right back. It will only take a moment.'

'Wait a minute. What's going on?' Caitlin cried.

Miss Benson hesitated. 'Geordie's teacher reported him absent to the office.'

'Mr Needleman? That's got to be a mistake. I talked to Mr Needleman at the Fall Festival this morning.'

'I'm sure it is. I'll call you right back after I check.'

'No. Wait. Don't hang up,' Caitlin pleaded.

'I won't. I'll call on the other line.'

Caitlin's hands were sweating on the phone. She wiped them on the pants of her suit.

The woman came back on the phone. 'I'm sorry. There's no mistake. Geordie did not show up in Mr Needleman's class. We are going to make an announcement and search the building. I can call you right back.'

'No. No. I'm coming over there right now.'

Before the woman could reply, Caitlin ended the call and scooped up her purse and her jacket. She felt dazed, as if she had just been punched in the face. She stopped by June's desk just long enough to say that she didn't know when she would be back. Ignoring June's protest and questions, she headed out the door.

THREE

As she raced up the school steps two at a time, Caitlin prayed. 'Let it all be a mistake. Oh, please, God. Let it be a misunderstanding.'

A big, colorfully painted sign announcing the Fall Festival was set up in the school lobby. Caitlin rushed past it, threw open the door to the office and saw the knot of people standing there. Before anyone spoke a word, she knew.

Mr Needleman approached Caitlin directly. 'Mrs Eckhart. We are combing the school.'

Caitlin shook her head. 'I told you at the festival. He was here.'

'I know. I know. But he never turned up in my classroom,' Mr Needleman said.

'I don't understand…'

Mr Needleman looked pained. 'As soon as I realized…'

The principal, a stout, middle-aged woman named Mrs Hunt, stepped forward and spoke soothingly. 'Let's not panic. There's any number of possible explanations. His father may have picked him up. So far we have had no luck reaching him.'

'He's still in court. I called the court house on my way here,' said Caitlin. 'I told them to send his father over here right away.'

'Good. Hopefully, he may know something about where Geordie is. But we don't want to waste precious time, just in case. I've called the police and they are on their way.

Meanwhile, the entire school is being searched. He could be hiding somewhere. Kids do that sometimes.'

'Oh, my God,' said Caitlin. 'The police?'

'Just a precaution. Here, sit down,' said Mrs Hunt, offering her a chair. Caitlin wanted to refuse, but her knees were shaking uncontrollably. She sank down onto the seat. She could hear phones ringing in the office and voices talking excitedly. A murmuring crowd was gathering in the foyer, outside the office. Someone in the office offered Caitlin a glass of water, which she declined.

In her mind's eye she went over the events of the morning. Cereal, a quick stop to see the horses and then the drive to school. She could see Geordie, darting through the crowd, eager to get to the Fall Festival. But he wasn't there when she went into the auditorium. *Why didn't I look for him?* she thought. *I shouldn't have left until I saw him, and told him that I'd seen his project. Why did I just leave?*

Mrs Hunt came over to Caitlin and rested a cool hand on her forearm. 'Your husband just called. He is on his way.'

'He hasn't seen Geordie?' Caitlin asked fearfully, knowing the answer. And her next thought made her stomach churn, as if she were going to throw up. He had entrusted Geordie to her. It was her fault.

Mrs Hunt tried to smile encouragingly.

Caitlin couldn't summon any words to speak. *Geordie.*

Outside she heard the sound of a siren. The police were arriving. A clammy chill coursed through Caitlin's body. Where could he have gone? Had someone… Her mind could not bear to rest on the possibilities.

Through the glass outer wall of the office, Caitlin could hear the thud of footsteps, and the front doors opened. It was not one policeman, but about a half a dozen who rushed in. Two of them entered the office while the others waited in the foyer, ignoring the questions they were being peppered by from the curious knot of students and teachers who were gathering there.

The first officer, a bald, strong-featured man in his early fifties with graying fringe and dark eyebrows, wearing a tie and jacket, introduced himself curtly. 'I'm Detective Sam Mathis,' he said. 'Any sign of the missing child since we spoke?'

Mrs Hunt shook her head grimly.

'All right,' said the detective. 'Do we have photos of him?'

Caitlin hesitated and then said, 'Yes.' She stood up unsteadily, fumbling in her bag.

Detective Mathis turned and frowned at her. 'Are you the child's mother?'

'Stepmother,' she whispered, pulling out her wallet with the school picture of Geordie taken last year.

'Where is his mother?'

'She is…she died,' said Caitlin, handing him the photo from the plastic sleeve in her wallet. 'This is Geordie.'

Detective Mathis gazed impassively at the photo. 'How old is Geordie?'

'Six,' said Caitlin. 'He just turned six. Yesterday was his party.'

'What was he wearing this morning?' His tone was abrupt, but not unkind.

Caitlin tried to think. 'Um. A sweatshirt. One of those hoodies. A gray one. A T-shirt with some crazy picture on it.'

'What kind of crazy picture?'

Caitlin tried to visualize the shirt. 'One of the *X-Men*. Wolverine, I think.'

Detective Mathis turned and passed the photo to the secretary behind the desk. 'Does he always wear glasses?'

'Yes, always,' Caitlin whispered.

'Did you get that?' Detective Mathis asked the secretary.

Miss Benson, the young secretary, nodded apprehensively.

'Type it out, scan this photo to the page and make me a hundred copies. Can you do that? Right away?'

The young woman nodded and rushed to comply.

'Who reported him missing?'

Alan Needleman stepped forward, raising a hand half-heartedly. 'I'm…Geordie's teacher. My name is Needleman. Alan Needleman. The morning was somewhat chaotic. We have the Fall Festival going on…' He waved his hand in the general direction of the sign in the foyer.

The cop frowned at the slightly built man in his colorful argyle vest. 'And?'

'And so, I didn't get to take attendance right away. But when I did… Geordie wasn't there. I'd seen his mother at the festival this morning, and she told me that she brought him to school today. So I…got worried, of course.'

Detective Mathis turned back to Caitlin. 'All right. I need to know exactly what happened. You drove him here today?'

'Yes.'

'Where was his father?'

'He…Noah…is an attorney. He had court this morning.'

'So you drove him from your home directly to school?'

'Yes. I mean, no. We stopped…along the way…'

'Stopped for what?'

'To pet some horses. He likes to do that. Then we came to the school.'

'And you took him inside?'

'Yes.'

'You physically took him in. By the hand?'

'Well, no. I mean, he was excited about the festival.

But I saw him go in. He ran ahead. But I watched him go inside.'

'You didn't go with him?'

'I was behind him. Just a little bit behind him,' said Caitlin.

Detective Mathis had cool, gray eyes which were unreadable. 'This front door here?' he asked.

'No,' Caitlin admitted, her face flaming. 'There's a door down by the auditorium that was open this morning for the Fall Festival. People were going in to look at the projects.'

'What is that?' Detective Mathis demanded of Mrs Hunt.

'Well, we have it every year,' said Mrs Hunt. 'The kids do autumn-related projects, and it's all set up in the auditorium. The families can come in and look at them before school. Everything's set up in there.'

'You went in to look at the projects?' he asked Caitlin.

'Yes,' she said.

'Did you see anyone else as he went in? Did anyone pass him coming out?'

'There were lots of people,' said Caitlin miserably. 'Coming and going.'

Detective Mathis looked at the principal.

'I'm afraid that's true,' Mrs Hunt agreed.

'Anyone you recognized?'

Caitlin thought for a second. 'Yes,' she said. 'Yes. His aunt. She was there to see her son's project. He goes to the school.'

'I'll need those names,' said Detective Mathis.

'Naomi. Naomi Pelletier. And Travis.'

'Who else?'

Caitlin grimaced. 'I talked to his teacher. Mr Needleman.'

While she was talking to the detective, Caitlin saw the

front door open. Noah stood in the doorway, stopped cold by the sight of all those police uniforms.

'That's my husband,' she said. 'Can I…'

'Stay right here,' said the detective.

Noah saw her in the office and rushed in. 'What's going on?' he cried. 'Where is Geordie?'

Caitlin burst into tears. 'I don't know. They can't find him.'

Noah steepled his hands over his nose and mouth as if to muffle a scream.

Detective Mathis gazed at Noah, recognition dawning in his eyes. 'You're the boy's father?' he asked.

Noah lowered his hands. He nodded.

'We've met before. I… My team investigated the hit-and-run when your wife was killed.'

'I remember,' said Noah with a trace of bitterness. 'You never got the guy.'

'I'm sorry to be meeting you again under these circumstances,' said Detective Mathis.

Noah's face was cold and white, like marble. 'Where is my son?' he asked.

'That's what we're trying to determine,' said Detective Mathis brusquely. 'Does Geordie have a cell phone?'

Noah shook his head. 'No, he's only six.'

'Lots of kids that age have cell phones,' said Detective Mathis.

'Well, not Geordie,' said Noah.

Detective Mathis nodded. 'When was the last time you saw your son?'

'This morning. At breakfast. He…' Noah pressed his lips together.

'Go on.'

'He complained he didn't feel well. He wanted to stay home. I had to be in court,' he said apologetically.

Detective Mathis looked thoughtful. 'Is there anyone he might go to if he wasn't feeling well and decided to leave school?'

Noah shook his head. 'I don't know. My mother. My in-laws,' Noah said miserably. 'His grandparents. He would have had to ask someone to call them. Another kid, maybe. He knows their phone numbers by heart.'

'Give them to me.'

Noah complied. 'I can't imagine it, though. My mother can't drive. She couldn't have picked him up. And my in-laws…they wouldn't have taken him out of school without telling anybody.'

Detective Mathis was dialing the number. 'What is their name?'

'Bergen,' said Noah acidly. 'Don't you remember?'

Detective Mathis nodded gravely. 'Yes. Now that you say it, of course I do.' He held up a finger to silence Noah. 'Yes. Mr Bergen. My name is Detective Sam Mathis…'

Just then the secretary came out from the inner office with a sheaf of papers. Caitlin caught a glimpse of Geordie's small, bespectacled face pale against the blue sky background used for student photos. Detective Mathis took the papers from her and left the office, even as he continued to talk on the phone. He distributed them to the cops in the foyer, who scattered like birds off of a wire.

Noah turned to Caitlin. 'My mother will be frantic. Emily's parents, too.'

'There's got to be some explanation,' Caitlin insisted.

Noah ran a hand over his face. 'Oh, my God.'

Caitlin slipped into Noah's arms. He squeezed her tightly and she could feel him shaking. His breathing was short and labored, as if he were lifting a heavy weight.

'They'll find him,' she whispered.

'Where could he have gone?' he cried.

Detective Mathis returned to the office. 'My officers have Geordie's picture now. They will question everyone at and around the school to see if anyone saw your son leaving the grounds, either by himself or with someone else. I've sent an officer to talk to your mother. Your in-laws are on their way. I told them to meet us at the police station. Is there any chance that your son might have run away? Does he have any history of running away?'

Noah shook his head and lifted his hands helplessly. 'No. He's six years old. He doesn't even…know where anything is.'

'Sometimes small children act impulsively. Was he unhappy about anything?'

'No,' Noah insisted. He looked at Caitlin with bafflement in his eyes. 'He wasn't, was he?'

'No,' she said, shaking her head. 'He was fine.'

Noah looked at his phone for the thousandth time, as if he were hoping for some clue to Geordie's whereabouts to magically appear on the screen. 'He said he was sick, and I didn't believe him.'

'He wasn't sick, honey,' Caitlin insisted. 'He wasn't. He was fine.'

Alan Needleman edged up to them. 'Mr Eckhart?' he said. 'I'm Geordie's teacher.'

Noah sighed. 'Yes, Mr Needleman.'

'I'm so sorry. I don't know how this happened. I called the office the minute I realized…'

'It's not your fault,' said Noah.

'Was your son upset about anything that you know of…? Any reason why he might leave school without saying anything?' asked Detective Mathis.

'No,' Noah said. 'Nothing.'

Needleman grimaced and held up a hand as if he wanted to be called on in class. Detective Mathis stared at him.

He lowered his hand. 'Some of the older kids picked on him sometimes. He's…a small boy. Slight. They teased him about that. They called him four eyes and so forth.'

'Travis,' Caitlin blurted out angrily.

'Who is Travis?' asked Detective Mathis.

Noah glared at Caitlin. She looked down and shook her head.

'Travis is Geordie's cousin,' said Noah. 'My sister's boy. He's had a very hard time. His father was killed in Iraq.'

'He bullies your son?'

Noah sighed. 'Not bullies. Look, this has nothing to do with Travis.'

'Detective Mathis,' Mrs Hunt called out from behind the desk.

'Excuse me,' said Detective Mathis. He left them sitting there.

'So sorry,' Needleman whispered. 'If there's anything I can do.'

Noah sat scowling, unresponsive.

'Thank you,' Caitlin said, nodding.

Needleman backed away from them.

In the office, the teachers clustered together speaking in low voices. The principal conferred with Detective Mathis. Officers were re-entering the school, reporting to another detective in the foyer. The detective came to the door and hailed Detective Mathis. The two men spoke quietly, intensely, together.

Caitlin clutched Noah's hand and prayed, though her lips were dry and no sound issued forth.

After a few minutes, Noah pried her hand loose from his, stood up and began to pace, running his hands through his hair. Finally, he could stand it no longer. He interrupted the two men who were talking. 'What's going on? What are you doing?'

Detective Mathis turned back to Noah and the rest of them. 'All right, look,' he said. 'I'm going to leave a number of my men here to question students, teachers and the staff. Geordie may have told someone where he was headed or asked someone to make a call for him. There are still many possibilities. Meanwhile the rest of us are going down to the station. You need to tell us everything you can think of. Everywhere that Geordie might have gone. And, just to be thorough, we have issued an Amber Alert.'

Noah groaned.

Caitlin wiped her eyes with the back of her hand. 'What's that?' she demanded.

'It's a nationwide alert that is put out for a missing child,' said Detective Mathis. 'Missing children are treated differently than missing persons, or even missing teens. There's no waiting period. The search begins immediately.'

Noah stared at him. 'You think someone took him?'

Caitlin let out a cry.

'We don't know that,' said Detective Mathis. 'He could have left on his own. That does happen. Kids get an idea and off they go. Or he could be hiding somewhere right here in the school. It could be any number of things. But we have to…assume the worst. Hope for the best. But assume the worst.'

'That someone took him?' said Noah, his voice shaking.

Detective Mathis looked back at him, and there was a glimmer of sympathy in his businesslike expression. 'We have to go on that assumption. Yes.'

FOUR

THE ATMOSPHERE IN the police station was electric. Every available officer had been called in. The desk sergeant was assigning tasks, and officers were leaving in pairs, armed with the flyer of Geordie's picture. For a moment, all activity stopped as Caitlin and Noah, shocked and shivering, followed Detective Mathis into the room.

Paula and Westy were already there. Paula let out a cry and ran to Noah, who embraced her briefly. 'I was working from home today. When you called, when Westy told me what you said…'

'We came right away,' Westy said, tears standing in his eyes.

'Thanks,' said Noah.

'That little boy is everything to us,' Paula cried. 'We love him so much. He's all we have left of Emily.'

Westy lowered his head and put his arm around his wife to comfort her. Caitlin could see that his lips were trembling. Just then the door to the station house opened and Naomi walked in, accompanied by a police officer.

'Noah,' Naomi called out, waving. She spoke to the officer, who nodded. Naomi came over to where they stood. 'Noah, what is going on? The police showed up at work and said I needed to come in. They wouldn't tell me a thing.'

'Geordie has disappeared,' said Noah.

Naomi clapped a hand over her heart. 'Oh, my God! Disappeared? But he was at school.'

'No one has seen him since…Caitlin took him to school.'

'How can that be?' Naomi cried.

'And you are…?' Detective Mathis asked.

'This is my sister, Naomi Pelletier,' said Noah.

'Thanks for coming in,' said the detective.

'No problem. But what do you want from me?'

'Mrs Pelletier, we need to ask you a few questions,' said Detective Mathis. 'Mrs Eckhart said that she saw you at school this morning.'

Naomi's eyes widened. 'Yeah, I was at school. Of course I was at school. I went to see my son's project.'

'Your son is Travis.'

'Yes. I'm a single mother. His father was killed in Iraq.'

Detective Mathis ignored this reference to her sympathetic status. 'We're questioning anyone who might have seen Geordie this morning.'

Chief Burns hung up the phone and came out of his office. He was a ruddy-faced, silver-haired man nearing retirement age. He was dressed in his uniform, and exuded an air of calm and competence. He shook hands gravely with the family as Detective Mathis introduced him. When he came to Paula he stopped and peered at her. 'Mrs Bergen. We've met before.'

Paula blanched. 'We certainly have. When my daughter was killed.'

'Right,' said Chief Burns, grimacing.

Westy's eyes flashed. 'You can't have forgotten our daughter, Emily. She was killed several years ago by a hit-and-run driver.'

Chief Burns looked embarrassed. He cleared his throat and avoided Paula's stricken gaze. 'Of course I haven't forgotten. Unfortunately, we never were able to find the driver.'

'It's a cold case,' said Westy angrily. 'Isn't that what they call it?'

Paula took his hand as if to restrain him. 'Please. Just find our...grandson.'

Chief Burns spoke gravely. 'We will. I promise you. Now folks, I know how difficult this is for all of you. Your cooperation will be a great help to us. You've already met Detective Mathis. He will be the team leader on this case. He and all my officers will move heaven and earth to get Geordie back to you. I just got off the phone with the FBI. I am keeping the Boston office current with the situation.'

'Are they getting involved?' asked Noah.

Chief Burns rubbed his hands together. 'Right now, Mr Eckhart, we don't know for sure that any crime has been committed. But I have alerted them. They are aware of the situation. All we can say for certain is that we have a missing child and, as Detective Mathis told you, we have issued an Amber Alert. That means that Geordie's picture and information will be broadcast at frequent intervals both on radio and television.'

'Wait till Travis hears this,' said Naomi. 'He'll be all upset.'

I'll bet, Caitlin thought, and then chided herself for her unkindness.

The chief continued: 'It would help if we had a description of a car, or someone who might have been seen with Geordie this morning. We're still trying to locate a witness. The problem is that there were a lot of people coming and going this morning because of the Fall Festival. A lot of unfamiliar faces in the school. Now, it still could be that Geordie ran away or is hiding somewhere in the vicinity of the school. We have not ruled that out yet as a possibility.'

Oh, please God, Caitlin thought. *Let him be hiding in the school.*

The chief looked at Noah. 'I am going to have the phone tapped at your home, Mr Eckhart, in the event that there is a ransom call. I've already been in touch with the judge and the warrant has been obtained.'

'How likely is that?' Noah asked.

Chief Burns exchanged a glance with Mathis.

'A ransom call?' Detective Mathis asked. 'Well, the fact that Geordie disappeared from school makes a ransom demand less likely.'

'Why do you say that?' Westy demanded.

'Kidnappings for ransom are usually planned pretty carefully. Unless he's really stupid, the abductor would know that the school has protocols and they must contact the police immediately if a child is missing. There's little possibility of the silence preferred by the perpetrator in a ransom situation.'

'So you think it could be…random?' Noah asked.

'We don't know. Until we have more information it's useless to speculate,' said the chief severely.

'What do we do now?' Noah asked in a shaky voice. His skin looked clammy and there were beads of sweat on his forehead.

'Right now,' said the chief, 'we need to fingerprint all of you and take your DNA, just for purposes of elimination.'

'Elimination from what?' Noah demanded.

'The CODIS database,' said the chief evenly.

'I can assure you, Detective,' said Noah, 'none of these people are in the CODIS database.'

'What's that?' Caitlin whispered.

'The national clearing-house for sex offenders,' said Detective Mathis, who had overheard her question.

'You should fingerprint that Mr Needleman, Geordie's teacher,' said Naomi. 'I've heard he lives with a man.'

'That doesn't make him a pedophile or a criminal, Naomi,' Noah said impatiently.

'I'm not saying it does,' said Naomi. 'But he does spend all his time around little kids.'

'He's a teacher for God's sake,' Caitlin exclaimed.

Naomi looked at Caitlin with raised eyebrows. 'I'm trying to think of every possibility,' she said indignantly.

Detective Mathis interrupted. 'Geordie's teacher had to be fingerprinted and cleared before he could be employed by the school,' said Mathis evenly. 'Every teacher is required to do that. If he is employed in this county as a teacher, he is not in the database. We know that for a fact.'

'Just trying to help,' Naomi insisted.

Chief Burns continued: 'Detective Mathis and these other officers will accompany you back to your home, Mr Eckhart. We want you to be there in the event that anyone tries to contact you. Or, in the happier event, that Geordie is simply lost and manages to find his way back to you. I know this is very difficult, but try to keep your hopes up. It's early yet, and no reason to despair. We'll find Geordie for you. We won't rest until we do.'

'Thank you,' said Noah weakly.

Detective Mathis ordered two waiting officers to take them all to be fingerprinted and have their DNA taken.

'I'll go first,' said Naomi, seemingly still stung by everyone's reaction to her suggestion about Mr Needleman. 'I have nothing to hide.' She followed the officer down the hallway.

Detective Mathis turned to Paula and Westy. 'If your grandson has run away,' said the detective, 'is it possible he could find his way to your home? I assume he's been there many times.'

'Ever since he was born,' said Paula. 'Although I doubt he could find his way on his own.'

'We'll send an officer home with you, too.'

'Whatever you need to do,' said Westy. 'Come on, darling,' he said to Paula. 'Let's get swabbed or whatever, and then go home. Maybe our little boy will somehow find us.'

Paula nodded and then looked anxiously at Noah. 'We should be with you.'

'No, he's right,' said Noah. 'You go on. In case Geordie... Besides, once this goes out on the television, people are going to be calling. It would help if I could tell them to call you.'

'We'll take care of all that,' said Westy. 'Anything you need.'

Noah hugged his in-laws again. Then Paula turned to Caitlin. Her eyes were filled with sorrow and concern. 'I know how much you care for him. Try to be brave, dear. They'll find him.'

Caitlin felt as if she might fall apart in Paula's embrace. It felt so good to have someone acknowledge her loss.

'You'll see,' Paula crooned. 'He'll come back to us. He has to.'

'Come on, now,' Westy urged his wife gruffly. 'Let's get on with it.'

Paula and Westy went first toward the room where the fingerprinting and testing would be done. They were in and out in a few minutes. They waved as they left the station, accompanied by an officer.

Noah and Caitlin were next. They were swabbed, fingerprinted and sent back out into the corridor to wait.

As they sat back down, Noah's phone rang, and he answered it.

'Hey, Dan, hi,' he said. 'Yeah. How did you know? Really. Already? Man, that was fast. Yeah. We're still in the police station. It's a fucking nightmare. No. Caitlin took him to school and that was it. He vanished into thin air.

The police are looking for him.' Noah listened for a minute. 'Well, if you want to come back up here, sure, but there's nothing you can do. I'm sure your parents would appreciate it. No. Really. I'd tell you, but I don't know anything. But thanks. Yeah. That might be a good idea. We'll keep in touch. Thanks, buddy. Bye.'

'Emily's brother?' asked Caitlin dully.

Noah nodded. 'He's at work. He found out about it when they received the Amber Alert at the station where he works.'

'Does Haley know?' Caitlin asked.

Noah sighed. 'I imagine Dan will call her.'

An officer leaned in and spoke to Caitlin and Noah. 'Mr and Mrs Eckhart, Detective Mathis will be here shortly to accompany you.'

'I feel like we're wasting time,' Noah said bitterly.

'I promise you, sir, no effort is being spared.'

'I know. I just keep going over this in my mind. What happened this morning?' Noah turned to Caitlin. 'What happened exactly?'

Caitlin looked back at him. 'What do you mean? I told you.' She could tell that the officer was listening. 'I drove him to school and he went running into the building. I saw him go in.'

'You didn't go in with him?' Noah demanded.

'I went in,' said Caitlin. 'Of course I went in. I wanted to see his project. But he was ahead of me. He was impatient to get inside.'

'Because of the festival,' said Noah.

'That's what I thought. But…'

'But what?' Noah stared at her.

'Well, I went over to his class's display. I saw Mr Needleman. And I looked at his project.'

'Geordie was there,' Noah prompted her.

'No. The kids weren't necessarily stationed by their projects. They were running around. They were all excited,' said Caitlin.

'Where was Geordie?' Noah asked.

'I don't know,' said Caitlin quietly.

'Did he show up? Did you see him before you left?'

'Stop it,' said Caitlin. 'You sound like you're cross-examining me. I waited for him. I looked for him…'

'And then?'

'He didn't come by the class display. I was surprised he wasn't there, too. You know how he loves to show you what he's done. Get a compliment about it. I thought he'd be there any minute. I waited as long as I could…'

'And then you left,' said Noah. 'Without seeing him.'

'I assumed that maybe he ran into a friend and got distracted…'

'So you just left,' Noah said.

Caitlin did not reply.

'Why didn't you go and find him?' Noah cried. 'He's only a little boy. Why didn't you make sure…?'

'He was in his school. I assumed he was safe in his own school,' Caitlin cried.

'You assumed.'

'I thought he was fine. I watched him go into the school,' Caitlin protested. 'I don't know what happened.'

'He could already have been taken. While you were standing around over there making small talk,' Noah cried.

'I'm sorry,' Caitlin beseeched him.

'Sorry doesn't do me any good. Sorry doesn't bring him back,' Noah snapped.

Caitlin absorbed his anger like a punishment and felt a wave of guilt wash over her like a filthy tide. And then, to her own surprise, she emerged, sputtering, from the wave, and was suddenly furious. He didn't seem to realize or care that she was suffering just as he was. 'How dare you say that to me, Noah? It could have happened to anybody. You would have done the same thing in my place, and you know it,' Caitlin accused him.

For a moment they glared at one another.

Then Noah turned his eyes from her angry gaze. He frowned, and seemed to think over what she had said. Finally, he sighed. 'You're right. I know you're right,' he said. 'I probably would have done the same thing.'

All her anger melted away. 'Noah,' she pleaded, reaching for his hand.

Noah shook his head.

'What?'

'He's my child,' Noah moaned. 'He's my son.'

Caitlin was shivering, although the station house was overheated. 'I know that,' she said. She thought about Geordie after the party, resting against his father's shoulder, reaching out his hand to her. Saying, 'Thanks, Mom.' *He's my son too,* she thought.

But she didn't dare to say it.

FIVE

CAITLIN STOOD IN their front yard, her gaze focused on Geordie's bike, training wheels attached, which was parked where Geordie had left it, at a crazy angle under a tree. Noah, accompanied by Detective Sam Mathis, opened the front door of their house and stepped inside. 'Geordie, are you here?' She could hear her husband's breaking voice echoing through the rooms. There was no answer. 'Geordie. Answer Daddy. Where are you?' Noah cried. Other police officers followed as Noah and Detective Mathis went inside.

Caitlin turned her back on the house. Geordie was not inside. Of course he was not there. If someone drove him home, he probably wouldn't even be able to recognize their driveway from the street. Their house, like all the others in this wooded area, sat on an acre lot, and had been built far back from the dangerous two-lane highway at the foot of their drive. The house was not visible through the wall of trees, not even in the dead of winter, and they never heard the sound of passing traffic.

Along the treacherous curves of Route 47, their neighborhood appeared to be a forested area, interrupted only by the occasional barn or a series of large, placid lakes. The only sign of the homes along the route were the mailboxes on the side of the road, and the mouths of driveways that disappeared into the trees.

Even if, by some miracle, Geordie found his way to a

place nearby, Caitlin could hardly bear to imagine him walking along the side of that deserted highway where cars whizzed past the deer peeking out of the woods and there was no path or sidewalk to follow on foot. It was on this road, at the end of their driveway, that Geordie's mother, Emily, had died. Caitlin could not prevent herself from picturing that terrible scene—Emily's lifeless body lying in the road, the bills and flyers she had just collected from her mailbox strewn around her, while the panicked, reckless driver sped away.

Caitlin closed her eyes, trying to force the grisly scene from her mind. But it was no use. She had to live with it. Every single day. She started up the lawn to the front steps, pushed the door opened and walked into the house.

Noah was seated on the sofa in the living room to the left of the entrance hall.

He was clasping his head with both his hands. Caitlin turned on a lamp in the corner and then went over to the sofa where he sat. She could hear the voices of the police officers in another part of the house.

Caitlin sat down beside Noah. Noah wiped his eyes. 'How could this have happened?' he asked.

Sam Mathis came back into the living room. He pulled a chair up close to where Noah sat beside Caitlin on the sofa.

'All right, Mr Eckhart,' said Sam.

'Noah. Call me Noah.'

'Now, Noah,' said Sam. 'I need to be very blunt with you. Even though we are prepared here for ransom demands, the least likely thing that could have happened to Geordie is that he was taken by a stranger. In most of these cases, a child is taken by someone he knows.'

Noah shook his head. 'Who would take him?'

Sam frowned. 'Well, our first thought is always a parent in a custody dispute, but obviously in this case...'

'Geordie's mother is dead,' Noah said.

'I know. What about her family? You seem to have a good relationship with them. Are they allowed to see your son when they wish to? These days there are issues with grandparents sometimes…'

Noah waved the question away. 'They see him whenever they want.'

Sam waited for him to elaborate.

Caitlin hesitated. Then she said, 'Noah makes sure that Geordie knows his grandparents. He spends lots of time with them. Yesterday was Geordie's birthday party. We invited the whole family. Grandparents. Aunts and uncles. Friends. Girlfriends…'

'One big happy family,' said Sam skeptically.

Noah looked at him indignantly. 'Yes, actually. A kid needs an extended family. When my wife died…' Noah's voice cracked.

Caitlin took his hand and kneaded it in her own.

'My wife's family. My family. They helped us to get through it. We helped each other,' said Noah.

Sam turned to Caitlin. 'What about you, Mrs Eckhart? Was your family invited to this party?'

Caitlin looked up at him, startled. She had been thinking about the fact that in moments of stress, Noah still referred to Emily as 'his wife.' As if she were still here, still living in this house with him. 'Excuse me?' Caitlin asked.

Sam Mathis looked at her steadily. 'I asked you if your family was at the party.'

'I don't really have any family anymore,' she said. 'Other than Noah. And…Geordie. My parents died a few years ago. I had one brother but…he died, too.'

Noah had recovered himself. 'I just want to be clear, Detective. My wife's parents have been a godsend. When Emily died, I promised her parents that I would never move away from this area until Geordie grew up. I want him to have that consistency in his life. A sense that he belongs somewhere.'

Sam turned to Caitlin. 'How long have you two been married?'

'Two years,' said Caitlin.

'So you have no…family ties here.'

'No. I work here. I'm the director of the diversity office at Brunswick University.'

'Have any ambitions to move to a bigger school?'

Caitlin started to answer, and then realized that it was a loaded question. 'I came from a bigger school. I'm very happy with my position here,' she said.

'But even if you had a better offer, you wouldn't be able to move away from here,' said Sam. 'Because of Geordie.'

'I don't want to move away from here,' said Caitlin. 'And I agree with my husband. Geordie needs to have his family nearby.'

Sam turned back to Noah. 'As I recall, this is the very same house that you lived in with your first wife. Am I right about that?'

'Yes,' said Noah.

'Does that bother you?' he said to Caitlin.

'No, it doesn't bother me,' Caitlin snapped. 'Why are you asking us all these questions? Why aren't you out looking for Geordie?'

'What about you and Geordie?' Sam persisted, ignoring her outburst.

'What about us?' Caitlin asked.

'How do you get along with Geordie?'

It was not a question you would ask a child's mother, Caitlin thought bitterly. The truth for her was that she loved him so much, sometimes she actually forgot that she was not his biological mother. But the world did not forget. *We get along like any mother and her son,* she wanted to say. But she felt as if she couldn't.

'Geordie is...a wonderful little boy.'

'No arguments?'

'No. Well...' Caitlin glanced at Noah. 'I mean, yes, of course, the usual things,' she said uncertainly.

Sam Mathis detected her hesitation. 'Like?'

Caitlin threw up her hands. 'Nothing. I don't know. Bedtime, food preferences, manners. The day-to-day things.'

'Detective,' Noah interrupted. 'You're barking up the wrong tree. Caitlin loves Geordie as if he were her own.'

As if he were mine, Caitlin thought. *Even Noah says, as if...*

'The reason I ask,' said Sam, 'is that sometimes a disagreement, even when an adult doesn't think it's important, it can cause a child to run away. They tend to exaggerate everything in their minds.'

Caitlin looked at him levelly. 'I know that. There was nothing.'

'Do you ever strike your son, Mr Eckhart?'

'Spank him, you mean?' Noah asked.

Sam nodded.

'No,' said Noah wearily. 'I don't believe in spanking.'

'What about you, Mrs Eckhart?'

'No, I don't hit Geordie.'

'Even when he's acting up? He's not your child, after all. Sometimes it's hard not to get angry.'

'I didn't say I never got angry,' said Caitlin. 'I said I never hit him.'

'You can corroborate that?' Sam Mathis asked Noah.

'Yes, of course,' said Noah. 'You're wasting your time here, Detective. My wife and I love Geordie more than anything. No parents ever loved their child more.'

'That's really true,' said Caitlin fiercely, her voice

choked with tears. She and Noah had their hands locked together.

Sam Mathis was moving on. 'What about friends—anybody whom Geordie sees on a regular basis. Is there anyone he sees regularly who has been in trouble with the law? That you know of.'

'No, of course not. That I know of,' said Noah.

'What about in your work?' Sam asked. 'You're an attorney. Do you have any enemies as a result of cases you've been involved in?'

Noah shook his head. 'I do mostly contracts, business law. I rarely do criminal and almost no family law. The odd divorce.'

Sam Mathis sighed. 'If a stranger tried to take Geordie out of the building, would Geordie know enough to resist? To try to fight back?'

Noah nodded. 'Oh, yes, definitely. He knows about strangers. I can't imagine he would ever go willingly with a stranger.'

'You'd be surprised. Tell a kid you need help finding your puppy and watch everything they've ever learned about strangers go right out the window.'

'That's really comforting,' said Noah.

'Sorry,' said Sam. 'But it's true. We are scrutinizing the background of every teacher in the school, everyone who lives or works near the school, including the crossing guards and the janitors.'

'You already said these people have to go through clearance before they can work in a school,' Noah said.

'Yes,' said Sam. 'But things get overlooked. It happens all the time.'

'Great,' said Noah. He leaned forward and put his head back in between his hands.

'Our problem is that the general public was invited to

this Fall Festival today, so there could be any number of people who came and went and we have no idea who they are.'

'Don't they have security cameras?' Noah asked.

'At the front door,' said Mathis. 'They have a camera there, but not on the other doors. Those doors only open from the inside, and they are normally kept locked. They don't usually leave the door by the auditorium open.'

Caitlin understood what he was saying. The camera would be no help. 'It's almost as if someone chose this day on purpose, knowing the security would be lax. Or non-existent,' she said.

'That's a possibility,' said Sam. 'Maybe now the school will get serious about it.'

'Too late,' Noah said.

THE EVENING WAS long and miserable. No ransom call came, though everyone jumped when the phone rang. Mostly it was other people in town who had heard the news on television or through the grapevine. A child had gone missing from Hartwell Elementary School. That information spread from one home to another in no time, and there were a lot of people who sincerely wanted to help. Their calls were dispatched instantly to keep the line free.

At around nine o'clock, Paula and Westy arrived, driven over by one of the officers assigned to their house. Paula announced that she had made food.

'She couldn't help herself,' Westy explained. 'It's how she deals with stress.'

Paula took the lid off her casserole and began dishing it out of plastic plates.

Noah just stared at it, as if the very sight of food was sickening. On the other hand, the police officers who were coming and going did not need to be asked more than once to take a plate and the serving dishes were empty in no time. The coffee pot held only dregs. Westy sat with Noah, who sat staring blankly ahead, while Caitlin joined Paula in the kitchen and helped her to clean up and organize her kitchen gear.

'I wish I could do more to help,' said Paula.

'Bringing all this food was a help,' said Caitlin.

'Haley called. She talked to Dan.'

'Noah did, too,' said Caitlin.

'I thought Naomi would be here,' said Paula.

Caitlin shrugged. 'She called to say that Travis was too upset about Geordie to come over.'

Paula looked skeptical. 'Really?'

'Probably feels guilty for having picked on Geordie so much,' said Caitlin, putting Paula's casserole dish back in her carrier bag.

'Well, that boy hasn't had an easy time of it,' said Paula. 'Losing his father in the war like that. And then his mother was depressed for such a long time. All she ever did was sit with her nose in a book.'

'I know. But sometimes I get so mad because Naomi won't scold Travis no matter how badly he treats Geordie,' said Caitlin. 'Noah won't either. He feels too sorry for him.'

'We've all tried to help Naomi out with that child. It hasn't been easy for them,' said Paula. 'We try to include him whenever we can.'

Caitlin felt as if she had been unkind. 'I know you have. And Noah really appreciates it.'

Paula suddenly lifted a soapy hand from the dishwater and patted Caitlin on the forearm. 'Thank heavens Noah has you,' she said.

Caitlin tried to smile as Emily's mother looked at her with such kindness in her gaze. 'That's really nice of you,' said Caitlin. 'I mean, especially because…because of Emily.'

'Well, it's not as if it's your fault. It was just a horrible, horrible thing that happened to my Emily. But I know my girl is up in heaven, and I'm sure she's happy that Noah and Geordie have someone like you in their lives. I just feel it.'

'I hope you're right,' Caitlin whispered. She could barely speak. *Paula is right,* she reminded herself. *It's not your fault.* But it didn't matter what she told herself. She felt as if guilt was rising in her throat and choking off her breath.

SIX

GEORDIE WAS RUNNING down a strand of sunny beach. The water was silvery and calm. The sand was a shade of dusty bisque but, as he ran, his heavy sneakers did not kick up a cloud of it. His backpack bounced against his hoody as he went. 'Geordie,' Caitlin whispered. He did not turn around to look at her, but kept on running. She tried to call out to him but her voice, no matter how she tried, would make nothing more than a squeak. She tried to run after him but she was frozen in place, and he was disappearing into the distance.

Caitlin awoke. Gray light was filtering through the space between the curtains. Day. As soon as she woke up, she remembered. No word from him. No ransom demand. No sightings of him. Nothing. Nearly twenty-four hours had passed. Geordie was still gone. He had vanished completely, as if he had never existed.

Caitlin rolled over in bed and saw that Noah's side of the bed was empty. She was not surprised. Still in her clothes, she had succumbed to exhaustion at about five o'clock in the morning. Obviously, he did not join her. She could hear voices in the other room.

There was no excited note from those voices. No one had come to wake her. That had to mean that there was no news. By yesterday afternoon a search had been mounted with volunteers from all over Hartwell willingly giving up their time. It had gone on late into the night. The leaders of each group of searchers reported in at regular intervals. Noah and Caitlin had wanted to join the search. Sam advised them that they needed to stay right there in the house.

Caitlin let herself think about Geordie. Yesterday, of course, she spent the whole day thinking of Geordie. But that wasn't exactly true. They all spent the whole day thinking about what might have happened to Geordie. Going over mugshots and surveillance footage and teacher's statements and neighbor's statements. It was like an invisible puzzle that the police were trying to reconstruct out of thin air. They thought about different aspects of the puzzle. But they tried not to think about Geordie.

At one point she went into Geordie's room and stood there, gazing at his belongings. Noah angrily told her to get away from the door. 'Why?' she had demanded.

'You look as if you're…remembering him,' he said. She understood his anguish, and closed the door to the room. Geordie existed somewhere out there in the wide world. Not in memory. He wouldn't allow it.

Now, lying there, looking at the band of gray light at her window, Caitlin allowed herself to think of him. His small, earnest, bespectacled face. His high voice. His giggle. The way he concentrated. The way his teeth, present and absent, took up all his mouth when he grinned. As she pictured Geordie, tears seeped from her eyes and ran down her face into the pillow. She began to gulp back sobs until it was becoming difficult to breathe.

'Caitlin,' Noah's voice called out. 'Are you awake?'

'Yes,' she called back, her voice thick.

'Haley's here.'

Haley. Caitlin could picture her friend's sweet, earnest round face, her blond hair, her clothes dusted with flour. *It would be good to see Haley,* she thought. *Get out of bed,* she told herself. *Change your clothes. Go out there.*

She forced herself out of the bed. She went to her closet, took off yesterday's rumpled suit and silk shirt and left them where they fell on the floor of the closet. She pulled out leggings, knit boots, a sweatshirt tunic. Clothes for warmth. Clothes for comfort. She put them on, brushed her hair up into a loose ponytail and looked at herself in the mirror over her dresser. Her face was gaunt and gray, her cheekbones jutting out from beneath her dark eyes. Her hair, normally coffee-colored and shiny, looked dull and lifeless. Caitlin turned away from the mirror. With an effort, she opened the door and left the bedroom.

Noah was seated at the kitchen table with Haley. He looked up at Caitlin, who had appeared in the doorway. 'Hi, sweetheart,' he said. Haley got up from the chair and came around to where Caitlin stood. The two women embraced, and Haley rubbed Caitlin's back briskly, helplessly.

'How are you holding up?'

'One foot in front of the other,' said Caitlin.

'I brought sticky buns,' said Haley, pointing to her gooey confections on a doily-topped plate sharing space with paper coffee cups, notepads and newspapers on the surface of the kitchen table.

'Thanks,' said Caitlin. 'You're so good.'

'I didn't know what else to do.'

'That was exactly what we needed. They'll all get eaten, believe me,' said Caitlin, thinking of the cops who were coming and going from the house.

'Well, I know everybody says this, but if there's anything more I can do…'

Caitlin hugged her friend again. 'I know you mean it.'

'I'm gonna go but…' Haley made a phone receiver out of her hand and held it to her face.

Caitlin nodded. 'I'll walk to the door with you.'

Caitlin led Haley through the house, past the two cops who were poring over computer printouts in the living room. 'Good morning,' she said.

They nodded gravely as Caitlin walked by. She and Haley stopped at the front door as Caitlin held it open.

'I can see you've been crying,' said Haley sympathetically, squeezing Caitlin's hand.

'I was dreaming of Geordie,' she said.

'They'll find him, Caitlin. They have to.' The two women embraced again, and then Haley headed out to her delivery van, passing Sam Mathis who had just arrived in the driveway and was coming up the walk.

'Anything?' Caitlin asked him.

'Maybe,' said Sam.

'Really?' Caitlin cried. 'What?'

Sam did not reply but walked through the house to the kitchen. Caitlin followed him, and sat down beside Noah at the kitchen table. Caitlin pulled her folded legs up to her chest and rested her feet on the chair seat beneath her.

'They might know something,' she said to Noah.

Noah looked up. Before he could blurt out his question, Sam raised his hands as if to calm their expectations.

'A teacher's aide who is new to the school came forward. She's young—just out of college—and she doesn't know Geordie so she couldn't be sure. But she was coming out of the ladies' room on the morning of the festival and she saw a boy matching Geordie's description—a boy with glasses, skinny, wearing a hoody, leaving the auditorium with a man in a ball cap.'

'Oh, my God,' Caitlin gasped.

'What do you mean?' Noah demanded, jumping up. 'Was he being dragged away? Why didn't she stop him?'

Sam shook his head. 'The child appeared to be accompanying the man willingly. It seemed perfectly innocent.

She thought it was a parent, walking the child back to his class.'

'And she's sure it was Geordie?' Noah demanded.

'As I said, she doesn't know Geordie, so she couldn't be sure.'

'Jesus,' said Noah.

Caitlin briefly rested her forehead on her knees.

'What did the man look like?' Noah demanded. 'Young, old, what?'

'She only saw them from behind,' said Sam.

'Did she see them leave the school?' Noah persisted.

'No. She said the only reason she noticed them at all was because the man was wearing an Eagles cap, and she's an Eagles fan. She just noticed it in passing.'

'She and every other football fan in South Jersey,' Noah said disgustedly.

'I have to ask,' said Sam. 'Do you have an Eagles cap?'

'Do I?' Noah cried, his eyes widening.

Sam's gaze did not waver.

'Yes. Of course I have an Eagles cap,' said Noah. 'Don't you?'

Sam did not reply. 'We've asked the witness if she is willing to be hypnotized to see if she can recall any more details. She said she would be.'

'Does that work?' Caitlin asked.

'In some cases, it's been helpful,' said Sam.

'And in others, it's a complete waste of time,' Noah said in a hopeless tone.

'Testimony under hypnosis isn't even admissible in court.'

'We're not in court,' said Sam. 'We're trying to find your boy.'

Noah sighed. 'I know, I know. I'm sorry. I'm just so frustrated.'

'Someone took him,' Caitlin whispered. The idea of her son being led off by a stranger to God knows where… Her heart felt like it was being crushed by fear. She glanced at Noah, her eyes wide. She saw the answering fear in his gaze.

'We don't know for sure that it was Geordie,' Sam cautioned them. 'I have my detectives checking to see if any kids were taken out of school that morning by a parent for any reason. Meanwhile,' said Sam, 'I was talking it over with the chief and we think it's time to make a direct appeal.

'One, or both of you, can prepare statements to read in front of the television camera. Basically, you'll be asking for anyone who might know anything to come forward. All you want is your child back. No questions asked.'

'Like hell there'll be no questions asked,' said Noah.

'We're trying to lure anyone who may know something out of the shadows,' said Sam.

'I know, I know,' said Noah. 'I understand.'

'Also, you want to appeal to Geordie, in case there is a TV on wherever he is being held. Urge him to call you. The numbers will run constantly on the screen.'

'He knows our numbers,' said Caitlin.

'Just in case,' said Sam.

'We'll do it,' said Noah grimly.

'Caitlin?' Sam asked.

'Of course.'

'When can we do this?' Noah asked.

'As soon as possible,' said Sam. 'The sooner the better.'

'Make it happen,' said Noah.

'All right then,' said Sam, getting up from the table. 'I'm going to set it up. Excuse me.' He pulled out his phone and began to tap in numbers.

Caitlin looked at her husband. He had not shaved, and

he was wearing a sweatshirt over the dress shirt he had worn to court yesterday, before their world collapsed. His cheeks were sunken and his complexion had a yellowish cast.

He smelled stale, like sheets left too long on the bed.

She reached her hand out and put it over his. Their eyes met briefly, and then he shook his head and looked away.

At that moment, Sam Mathis came back into the room. 'All right. It's all set for…' He glanced at his phone. 'Two hours from now.'

'Do these appeals ever work?' Noah asked angrily.

'Well, there's no guarantee. But you never know what you're going to shake out with one of these,' said Sam.

'We have to try,' said Caitlin.

'Anything,' Noah agreed.

SAM MATHIS HAD warned them that the TV studio would be crowded with police and reporters, but they were unprepared for the crush of people who had assembled to hear them plead for information. Sam instructed them not to speak to individual reporters, but to simply deliver their prepared statements.

Caitlin held Noah's hand as they sat down behind the bank of microphones at the cloth-covered table. The lights all around them were blinding. Noah was asked to sit in the chair beside an easel bearing an enlargement of Geordie's photo, and Caitlin was directed to the seat on his left. Sam Mathis stood at the microphone and called the noisy crowd to order.

'As you all know,' Sam said, surveying the room with his gaze, 'George Eckhart, six years old, known as Geordie, disappeared from the Hartwell Elementary School yesterday morning. He was last seen entering the school that morning by his stepmother, Caitlin Eckhart.' At this

Sam nodded in Caitlin's direction. She wasn't sure how to respond. A wave? A smile? Nothing could seem less appropriate, she thought. She licked her lips and stared straight ahead.

'We've asked his parents to address you all today to ask the public for some help with this baffling disappearance. If you have seen George Eckhart, there is a number on your screen for you to call. Please don't hesitate. Even if you're not sure, we welcome any tips you might be able to provide for us. Anything at all. Call the number on your screen. Write it down. Geordie's life may depend on it.' He turned to Noah. 'Mr Eckhart? Would you like to speak first?'

Noah nodded and cleared his throat. He had showered, shaved and put on a clean shirt and a tweed jacket. He looked almost presentable, but for the circles under his eyes and the lack of color in his skin. Caitlin was glad he was speaking first. She was not normally shy, but today her stomach was in spasms, and she wasn't sure that any sound would come out when she opened her mouth.

That would not be a problem for Noah, she thought. He was used to being in court, speaking to crowds. He never had a moment's stage fright. He would speak calmly, persuasively. But when he opened his mouth, she felt almost alarmed by the halting way he began. It seemed to be torture for him to release each word of his statement. 'My son, Geordie,' he said, 'is only six years old. He is a wonderful little boy who never hurt anyone in his life. I'm speaking now to the…person who took my son from me. From us. Please, I don't know why you took him, but if you have any human decency, I beg you. Let my son go. Let him come home to me. To…us. To his…to Caitlin and me. We love Geordie more than we can say. I don't care about punishing you for what you've done. Just…let

Geordie go. Let him come home. Leave him somewhere. Anywhere. I'll come and get him. Please don't hurt him. He never hurt anyone. Please.'

Noah drew back from the microphone and covered his eyes with one hand.

Sam nodded to Caitlin.

She wrapped both hands around the microphone, as if it were going to jump up and try to escape. She put her mouth close to it, and she looked straight ahead into the camera, as Sam had told her to do. Her whole body was shaking.

'Thank you,' she whispered. 'Geordie, if you are listening to this, if you can see me, I want to tell you something. You are a very brave boy, and a strong boy and I want you to stay brave and try not to be afraid. We're going to find you. I promise you. Daddy and I are going to…bring you home. You just keep remembering that. We love you more than anything, and don't you forget that. If you can hear me.

'As for the person who took Geordie…' Her voice trailed off, and she averted her eyes. Sam bent down to her.

'Are you OK?' he whispered.

Caitlin nodded and continued: 'I assume there is something terribly wrong with you, to take an innocent little boy like that from his family. To take him from his school. All I can ask of you, from the bottom of my heart, is that you don't hurt Geordie, and that you let him go so he can come home. He's only six years…old.'

Her last words came out in little more than a squeak, like in her dream, when she was trying, in vain, to call out to Geordie. She let go of the microphone and sat back, drained by the effort. Noah put his arm around her, and pulled her to him.

A voice from the crowd called out, 'Caitlin, you were the last one to see the boy alive…'

The camera caught the startled look on her face.

Sam Mathis shook his head at Caitlin. Then he turned back to the audience of reporters. 'No questions. We can't take questions. But we do appreciate your efforts to get his parents' plea out to the public in the hope of finding this child and possibly saving his life.'

Caitlin stared straight ahead into the glare of the lights, while she and Noah gripped one another's hands. Was he hurt? Or hungry? Was he frightened? She tried to imagine Geordie looking into her eyes on the television screen.

Don't be afraid, she thought. *I love you. We'll find you. Try not to be afraid.*

SEVEN

EXTRA PERSONNEL WERE put on the police department phones, and three officers took turns manning the phones at the Eckhart home. For the first twenty-four hours, the results from the televised plea seemed promising. Many tips came in, and all were checked out. Some were soon discounted. One woman who called the hotline claimed that she had heard whimpering cries in her building coming from the super's locked workroom in the basement. The police went to the building and ordered the super to unlock the door. The super, it seemed, was concealing a litter of newborn pups in a building which allowed no pets. Another caller was a woman who said that her son claimed to have talked to Geordie at school on Monday morning. When two officers arrived to question the boy, his story became vague and more disjointed, until the boy admitted that it must have been the week before. A male caller with a slurred voice suggested that Mr Needleman was to blame, and that everybody knew it at the school. Mr Needleman broke out in hives, but insisted that he would not be intimidated.

One lead was promising. A caller said that he saw a man and a boy walking away from the school that morning. This seemed to confirm what the teacher's aide had witnessed. According to this man, who worked for a cable TV company, he was sitting in his truck when he saw them walk by. The cable guy was pretty certain that the man whom he saw was not wearing an Eagles cap, or any other kind of hat. The boy was crying and protesting. The cable TV man assumed it was a father and son. This morning, Sam was questioning the man himself. He promised to let the Eckharts know if this lead seemed to offer a direction to the investigation.

The morning passed with agonizing slowness. Caitlin was alone in the house. Noah's secretary, Lois, had called, apologizing for the fact that Noah was urgently needed in the office. An out-of-town client was only going to be in for a couple of hours and insisted on seeing his attorney. Noah was reluctant, but Caitlin told him to go, smiling bravely and telling him to take his time. But as she watched his car disappear down the driveway, Caitlin felt suddenly, unaccountably abandoned. She and Noah had not been apart since the moment at Geordie's school when they learned that he was missing. They buoyed one another up through the day, each one offering hope when the other was low. Suddenly, without him, Caitlin felt the full weight of her loss.

It wasn't, she thought, as if she were actually alone. There were two officers arriving in the driveway, even as she looked out on the dreary, interminable morning. They greeted her as they came up the walk and entered the house. 'There's coffee inside,' she said.

'Any more of those cinnamon rolls?' asked the younger officer named Jack.

Caitlin nodded. 'They arrived this morning. Help yourself.' Haley had left another sack of rolls on the front porch before they had even awakened. Caitlin felt overwhelmed by the kindness of people. Her kitchen counters were covered in plates of food but there was nothing which tempted her in the least. The desire to eat had left her, as had the ability to sleep. She could sleep for what seemed like minutes at a time, and then she would wake up, stricken, remembering. This morning, after Noah left, she had thought about taking a shower, but realized that she was too afraid. What if the phone rang while she was in the shower? She knew that her fear made no sense. She could always check to see if she had missed a call. But, still, she did not shower. She felt filthy and exhausted. Any task which flitted into her consciousness was immediately dismissed as impossible to even begin. She was paralyzed, and could not do the slightest thing.

Suddenly, as she stared out at the gray day, Caitlin saw Sam Mathis's car pull into the driveway. Her heart leapt up. She ran out to meet him in the drizzle. Sam rolled down the window.

'What happened?' she cried. 'The teacher's aide. Was she hypnotized?'

'Last night.'

'And?'

Sam shook his head. 'Nothing useful.'

'Nothing?' she asked. She could feel the frustration rising in her throat, choking off her breath as if she had eaten something she was allergic to. 'How about the guy from the cable company?'

'He wants to help,' said Sam. 'He really does, but the guy has no kids. I have found, over the years, that men with no kids barely even notice children, much less what they look like. I'm on my way to the school to get an array of photos of the kids in Geordie's grade to try to jog his memory. I just stopped to give you a progress report. I'm afraid I can't stay.'

'No, wait,' Caitlin said. She wanted to grab the sleeve of his jacket and cling onto it, to prevent him from leaving her there alone with her obsessive fears.

Sam looked at Caitlin. 'What?' he asked.

'I can't bear this,' she said.

'I know,' said Sam. 'We're doing everything we can…'

'I know. I know that,' said Caitlin. 'I just feel so useless.'

'It's a terrible situation,' he said.

'Let me come with you,' Caitlin blurted out. 'I can do something. I can join the search.'

Sam frowned at her. 'I'm sorry. I know you're frustrated,' he said. 'But it's better if you just stay here at home.'

Caitlin shook her head. 'You don't understand. I can't,' she said. 'I just can't. I've done everything exactly as you've asked. But I can't spend the day just waiting around here. I want to go and look for Geordie with the other searchers. Let me do that at least. What harm would there be in that?'

Yesterday, after their televised plea, she and Noah had been allowed to visit the church which served as the command center from which the teams of searchers started out or returned for a break. Sam had ordered one of the younger officers to bring along the blown-up display photo of Geordie to the church with them, probably to inspire the volunteers there. Concerned parents and senior citizens who had gathered there produced flyers and plates of cookies and urns of coffee for the search teams of ordinary citizens. Touched by the community support that they received, Caitlin and Noah had shaken hands with people and accepted their blessings and good wishes. Then the police had whisked them away.

'I know this is difficult,' said Sam. 'But there's a reason for these procedures. It's difficult to control the situation if the parents get involved in the search. Reporters can harass you, and important information can inadvertently leak out. We can't have that.'

'I wouldn't talk to anyone, I promise,' Caitlin pleaded.

'All those nice people who have volunteered to look for your boy? You wouldn't want to speak to them?'

'I know how to speak to people without running at the mouth,' she said indignantly.

'For all we know,' he said, 'the kidnapper could be among the volunteers. Sometime these perps get their thrill from being on the scene, seeing the suffering up close and personal.'

Caitlin shuddered. 'What a thought. How sick would you have to be?'

'You don't want to know,' said Sam.

'I've got to tell you,' she said. 'This is some special kind of hell, sitting around watching the rain and looking at the clock all day long. Is that what you'd want to do if it were your child?'

Sam frowned and sighed. Finally, he said, 'All right. I know you're getting stir crazy. If you like, you can ride along with me.'

'Thank you,' Caitlin sighed. 'Oh, thank you.'

'Don't make me regret this,' he said.

'Just let me run in and get my rain jacket.'

CAITLIN FELT WOBBLY, like a patient who was finally allowed to leave the hospital. She sat in the passenger seat of Sam Mathis's SUV and felt almost dizzy with the air and the change of scene. For a moment, she didn't think about Geordie. But only for a moment. Then she sighed.

Sam glanced over at her. 'There's nothing worse than this,' he said kindly. 'The not knowing.'

'That's the truth. Do you have children, Detective?'

Sam nodded. 'Two teenagers. A girl and a boy. They worry me half to death.'

'I know,' said Caitlin. 'I remember.'

'Being a teenager?' he asked.

'No, I...I was thinking of...my younger brother. Those are difficult years,' she added hastily.

They rode in silence for a moment, the only sound the rain thrumming on the roof of the car. Then Sam said, 'So, were you acquainted with your...Geordie's mother?'

'No,' said Caitlin, shaking her head. 'I feel like I know her, though. I think she must have been a wonderful woman.'

Sam nodded thoughtfully. 'And how did you and Noah meet?'

Caitlin's face burned, remembering. 'Um, we met at a charity event,' she said offhandedly.

'Was this before or after his wife was killed?'

Caitlin swiveled in the seat and glared at him. 'After, of course. Is this why you let me ride along? Are you accusing me of something?'

'Just making conversation,' said Sam smoothly, but clearly noting her discomfort. 'I've gotten to know and like you people since this happened. I was curious about what brought you together.'

'Well, sorry to disappoint you, but I never had any interest in married men,' said Caitlin. 'I always figured, if they would cheat on their wives, what would prevent them from cheating on me?'

'A good point,' he said.

'Besides, as I understand it, Noah and Emily were very happy together.'

'Yes,' said Sam. 'I remember when she died. Your husband was just completely distraught. I always felt badly that we weren't able to apprehend the driver who killed her.'

Caitlin was silent, staring through the windshield.

'Your husband has had unbelievable misfortune. First his wife dies in a hit-and-run accident. Then his son is kidnapped. It seems like more than a person should have to endure in one lifetime.'

'Luckily, he is a very strong person.'

Sam turned right, and then right again into a familiar parking lot.

'We're at the school,' said Caitlin.

'You don't have to come in if you don't want to,' said Sam.

Caitlin hesitated, her heart pounding. 'I do want to.'

Sam put the SUV in park and turned off the engine. 'All right, but please, don't answer any questions. Just keep to yourself.'

THE PEOPLE IN the main office looked stricken and uneasy at the sight of Caitlin. Caitlin knew that the secretary and the principal and many of the teachers had joined the search parties leaving out of the Presbyterian Church. She was grateful, and she felt as if she ought to try to put them at ease, but there was a part of her that was just too weary. She stood quietly by, avoiding their anxious gazes, while Sam Mathis signed them in and announced that he was here to see Mrs Hunt. He then gave Caitlin a visitor's badge to wear. As she pinned it on her T-shirt she thought about Monday. If they had only been so careful on Monday... What's the use? she reminded herself. The school prided itself on being welcoming to the public when there were programs. They wanted to encourage community participation. It was something she had liked about this school.

'I'll be right out,' said Sam as he was ushered into the principal's office.

Caitlin sat in a chair beside the door, feeling conspicuous. She could tell that the secretaries behind the desk were stealing glances at her, as if she were some kind of circus freak. She wanted to yell out, 'What are you looking at?' but she knew better. The office door opened and she heard a man laughing. She turned to look and saw Mr Needleman talking to another young man who waved as he walked on down the hall. Mr Needleman entered the office, calling out, 'Hello, my fair ladies.' The secretaries behind the counter gave him a warning look. Mr Needleman turned to see what they were warning him against. When he saw Caitlin, he let out a cry. All the color drained from his face.

'Hello, Mr Needleman.'

'Mrs Eckhart. I didn't know... Is there news about Geordie?'

Caitlin shook her head.

'I'm sorry. I didn't mean to be laughing just then,' he said, pointing vaguely in the direction of the hallway. 'I was just talking to the music teacher...'

Caitlin's face reddened at his words. It was as if all happiness was forbidden in her presence. 'Don't be silly,' she said softly, avoiding his gaze.

There was a brief, awkward silence. 'So, no word yet?' he asked.

'No. Nothing,' she said. She could tell that he wanted to flee from her. She felt like someone with a contagious disease.

Mr Needleman hesitated, and his complexion turned from pallid to pink. He took a deep breath. 'Look, Mrs Eckhart, I can't imagine anything worse than what you're going through. I just wish I had been more alert that day. I wish I could have done something—anything—to prevent it.'

'It's not your fault. I was there too, remember? How could we have known?' She hesitated, and then she added, 'I hear you've been harassed. I'm sorry about that. People can be vicious.'

Needleman smiled wanly and shrugged. 'What's a few eggs cracked on your windshield? I can take it. Just so long as you understand, I love kids. All kids. I would never do anything to harm a child.'

'Don't,' said Caitlin. 'You don't have to defend yourself.'

'I pray for Geordie's safe return every single day,' he said earnestly.

'Thanks,' said Caitlin. 'Keep doing that.'

Mr Needleman nodded and approached the counter solemnly, ready to transact his school business in a hushed tone.

Caitlin got up from the chair and left the office to wait for Sam in the hallway. She couldn't stand to sit there any longer, under all that sympathetic scrutiny. She leaned against the wall and closed her eyes so that she wouldn't have to meet the pitying glances of those who came and went in the hallway.

EIGHT

OUTSIDE THE PRESBYTERIAN CHURCH, high school students who had volunteered to give up a study hall were standing in the drizzle handing out flyers with Geordie's picture on it to passing motorists who slowed down to rubberneck. A uniformed officer, his hat covered with plastic shower cap-type protection from the rain, was stationed at the outer door of the church basement, and a couple of reporters and photographers were huddled under the overhanging roof, buttonholing those who came and went from the search headquarters within.

The officer at the door nodded briskly to Sam, who spoke to him briefly before entering the huge meeting room. Caitlin, her hands jammed in the pockets of her rain jacket and her hood pulled up to cover her face, came in behind him.

The basement of the Presbyterian Church had seen many a genial gathering for a chicken dinner, church bazaar or men's club meeting, but today it had a grim atmosphere, unusual in that gently weathered space.

The first thing Caitlin saw when she entered the room was the easel with the enlarged photo of Geordie in Tigger's embrace which stood at the front, beside three long tables which had been pushed together. Behind the tables was a bulletin board with a map attached to it. The areas which had been searched were marked as well as how many times they had been searched.

A cluster of volunteers in rain gear sipped coffee, ate from plates of sandwiches and wiped off their rain-spotted glasses as they conferred. As Caitlin scanned their faces for some hint of hope, she suddenly recognized two of them. Naomi, dressed in heavy-duty coveralls, her wet hair plastered to her head, was talking to an elderly man in corduroys. Martha sat beside them, her quivering eyes averted, occasionally interjecting something into their conversation. Caitlin walked over to them.

Naomi looked up at Caitlin and then turned to her mother. 'Mom. It's Caitlin.'

They did not have a demonstrative relationship, but Caitlin felt a surge of affection for her sister-in-law, obviously here to search for her nephew. She reached out to hug her and Naomi awkwardly returned the embrace. Caitlin reached for Martha's hand and squeezed it. 'Good to see you, Martha.'

'Wish I could say the same,' said Martha. 'That's a joke.'

'I know. Were you out on the search today?' Caitlin asked Naomi.

Naomi shrugged. 'Things were quiet at the recycling center. The free bookstore doesn't get too many customers when it's raining. I decided to try and do something useful and take a shift on the search.' She nodded toward her mother. 'I left her here to talk to people. She's better off sitting here talking to people than sitting home alone worrying. Paula and Westy were just leaving when we arrived. They were on the early shift.'

'Everyone is helping,' said Caitlin.

'Where's Noah?' Martha demanded in a loud voice.

'He had to go into work for a little while,' said Caitlin. 'I decided to come down and join the search. Detective Mathis didn't want me to, but I can't stand the waiting.'

'No kidding,' said Naomi, shaking her head. 'The time just drags.'

'I guess there was no sign…' said Caitlin.

'No. Not where we were. Well, I'm gonna take Mom home and get back out to the center. Call me if you hear anything. Come on, Ma. I'm taking you home.'

'We're praying for Geordie night and day,' said Martha.

'I know,' said Caitlin. 'Thank you.'

At the front table, Sam Mathis was speaking to a middle-aged woman in an Eagles ball cap. Caitlin walked up to them.

Sam Mathis introduced Caitlin as Geordie's mom. Then he turned to Caitlin. 'Mrs Eckhart, do you know Madelyn Crain?'

Caitlin nodded. She recognized the woman who, along with her husband, Burt, was the de facto civilian coordinator of the search. 'We've met before. Thank you so much, Mrs Crain, for all you and your husband are doing for Geordie.'

The woman in the ball cap enveloped Caitlin in a motherly embrace. 'Don't you worry. We won't stop till we find him. One party just came in, and we've got another getting ready to go out.'

'I thought people might have lost interest by now,' Caitlin admitted.

'Lost interest? In a child who disappeared from school? We've all got kids or grandkids in that school. No one is going to lose interest,' said Madelyn.

'Well, I can't tell you how much it means to me and my husband. You know,' said Caitlin, avoiding Sam Mathis's gaze, 'I thought I might go out with them today.'

'Oh, dear, is that a good idea?' asked Madelyn. 'If those reporters outside see you going out on a search they'll be chasing after you.'

'It's not a good idea,' said Sam.

'I'll keep my hood up and my head down,' said Caitlin stubbornly. 'They didn't notice me coming in.'

Madelyn looked at Sam. 'You can't blame her.'

'I'd prefer you didn't,' Sam said firmly.

Caitlin looked at the cadre of women of varying ages in sweatshirts and slickers, the fit young construction workers and the stooped, white-haired men who were assembling at the front of the room, all of them giving their time to search for her son. 'I have to,' she said.

THE TEAM LEADER, a young police officer wearing a yellow plastic vest over his black rubber raincoat, gave them instructions before they set out. 'My name is Ralph,' he said. 'I'm wearing this vest so I'm easy to spot in those marshes. You need to keep one eye on me when you're out there.' Ralph showed everyone the area on the map that they were searching.

'This is going to be messy, people,' said Ralph. 'I want you all to pay attention. I don't want anybody ending up in the bog. Just keep one eye on me and the other eye out for any sign of our victim.'

Caitlin winced at the term and immediately understood another reason Sam had discouraged her from joining in. It wasn't possible to spare her feelings in all this. She had to be matter-of-fact like the rest of these people. They were searching for a kidnapping victim.

'Now, we know what he was wearing. Here's a picture,' he said, holding up a photo made of clothes similar to Geordie's. 'We're looking for clothing, anything from his backpack, any sign of the boy. If you find anything— whether you're sure it's important or not—do not pick it up or touch it. Is that clear? I have to emphasize that. Call for help immediately. OK? There will be half a dozen police officers out there on Goshen Hill Road to examine whatever you find. Let us make that determination. We can't take a chance on losing any possible evidence by mishandling. Does everyone understand?'

There was a murmur of assent from the group.

'OK, people. Let's get in our cars and get out there,' said Ralph.

Everyone trudged out the meeting room doors and into the parking lot. Caitlin was assigned to a car with a fire department license plate and a driver named Jerry. She pulled up the hood of her rain jacket and tied it, calling herself Kate when asked, and left it at that. Jerry was a nice-looking, stocky man with squarish hands, curly black hair and a gap between his front teeth. He drove a Subaru Forester. Caitlin got into the front seat with him and two elderly men in foul weather fishing gear got into the back.

The men bantered about the weather and fishing they had done in the marshes near Goshen Hill Road. Caitlin soon realized, from their conversation, that these men had met one another in the course of searching for Geordie. They had all been out several times during the week. Her heart swelled with gratitude toward them, though she couldn't say it.

'Yeah, they got muskrats out in that swamp,' said one of the men in the back.

'Tons of 'em. Ugly little creatures.'

'Are you kidding?' said Jerry. 'I've been to that muskrat banquet at the VFW Hall. They're pretty tasty if you cook 'em right.'

Caitlin thought she was going to be sick. 'Is it far?' she asked weakly.

'Right up ahead,' said Jerry. He stopped the car and put it in park. 'All ashore that's going ashore,' he said cheerfully.

Everyone piled out of the vehicle. The police were all in yellow vests, and two of the cops had German shepherd dogs on a leash. The dogs were growling and panting, as if they could not wait to get started. It seemed to take a fair amount of muscle to hold them in check. Caitlin saw one of the police officers offering a red rag under their noses for them to sniff. Suddenly Caitlin recognized the rag. It was a T-shirt she had taken from Geordie's closet when Sam Mathis asked her for an item of clothing which Geordie often wore. She felt faint when she realized what she was looking at.

'All right, people, listen up,' said Ralph. 'Follow your group leader and watch where you step. These marshes can look solid and then give way without warning. The boy has only been missing for four days now, so there is no chance that you will find a skeleton or bones belonging to him. If you find him, he's still going to be intact…'

Caitlin had to turn away and take a deep breath. He was talking about her son. *Get over it,* she thought. *Sam Mathis warned you not to come.*

'You OK?' asked one of the men in her party.

Caitlin nodded. 'I'm fine,' she said. 'Let's go.

Caitlin soon found that she had to watch every step she took. Staying near the trees was no guarantee of staying dry. The trees seemed to be rooted in the muck. Over and over again Caitlin slid in mud, or on slick leaves, and nearly ended up in the brown water which seemed to rise in pools around her boots. As they picked their way along, she and the others in her group found food wrappers and empty cups from what would seem to be every fast-food restaurant in South Jersey. They found nothing belonging to Geordie.

He's not here, she thought. *If he were here, I would know it. I would just feel it.* She kept her intuition to herself. These good people were enduring a fair amount of misery, and she didn't want to discourage their willingness to search.

All of a sudden, the dripping quiet of the marshes was rent by the anxious, high-pitched sound of the dogs barking. Their ferocious baying was incessant. Caitlin thought she had never heard a sound so terrible. Her heart began to hammer, and she felt all the blood drain from her head into her feet. She swayed as she stood in place.

'Don't fall in there, Kate,' said Jerry amiably. 'It's just the dogs.'

She looked up and saw him standing at the edge of the water, looking toward the clearing where the clamor was originating. 'Sounds like they've got something,' he said.

Caitlin did not reply. For a moment she stood frozen at the edge of the swampy water. Then, she turned away from the ooze where she had been searching, and began to run, slipping and sliding across the leaves, her face whipped by bare tree branches in her path. She ran in the direction of the dog's barking.

'Hey, take it easy,' Jerry called out. 'I think we're supposed to stay together.'

Caitlin ignored him. *Stop it. Stop it,* she thought. She felt furious at the dogs for their obvious excitement. As if something wonderful had happened. Like vultures. Like vampires. She emerged from a copse of trees and saw the cluster of police and searchers who had gathered around the dogs. No, she thought. NO.

Before she could get any closer, she heard one of the cops calling out in a loud, edgy voice. 'It's nothing, people. Forget about it. False alarm. They saw a muskrat and wanted to chase it.'

There was relieved laughter from the searchers, who turned back to what they were doing.

Caitlin doubled over, resting her hands on her thigh, as if she had just run a race, and tried to calm the thudding of her heart. It was nothing. They'd found nothing. *He's not here.* She knew now that she didn't want them to find anything in this desolate marsh. If Geordie had been lost or left here, he would freeze. He would drown. He could never survive it. She needed to go home. She needed to get away from this terrible place. She could not stand to imagine him here, alone. Afraid.

'Hey, look,' someone shouted. Caitlin straightened up shakily.

'Glasses. I found a pair of glasses!' the searcher cried out.

The police in their yellow vests began to converge on him as he pointed to the prize at his feet, but Caitlin got there first.

She came up beside the old man, and saw the reflection off a lens below the surface of the water.

Instantly, she bent down, plunged her hand into the water and pulled the broken glasses out of the muck.

'Do not touch anything you find,' the approaching officer scolded. 'I thought we made that clear. Ma'am, please do not pick anything up.'

Caitlin grasped the glasses in both hands, and tears rolled down her face. She began to shake her head. 'No,' she said. 'No.'

'What do you think you're doing? Give me those glasses,' the officer demanded. 'What's the matter with you?'

Caitlin continued to shake her head. 'No,' she repeated.

'No what?'

Caitlin clutched the glasses to her chest. 'They're not his,' she gasped.

The officer peered at her, while the other searchers

formed a jagged horseshoe around them. 'How do you know?' he said. 'Wait. Are you…' His voice faded away.

Caitlin did not lift her head. 'I need to go home,' she whispered.

CAITLIN SAT SILENT in the front seat while the young officer named Ralph drove her to the house. She was shivering from head to toe, and she could not stop the tears which continued to run down her cheeks. She wiped them away automatically.

The squad car pulled into the driveway behind two squad cars, Noah's car, and another beat-up car which she did not recognize. Caitlin turned to the officer. 'I'm very sorry, officer. I shouldn't have… I'm sorry I caused you so much trouble.'

'Probably best if you leave the searching to us,' he said gravely.

Caitlin nodded and thanked him again before she emerged from the car and walked up to the house. She thought about a hot bath and cup of tea with Noah.

She couldn't think past that right now.

She opened the front door and walked inside. Noah was seated at the edge of a sofa cushion, tapping the tips of his fingers on the arm of the sofa. His face was pale, and his eyes held a warning.

Seated opposite him in a sage-green rocking chair was an overweight, mocha-skinned young woman with a pitted complexion and a dried-out mop of frizzy brown hair. She was wearing a tight skirt, fishnet stockings with holes in them and a black pleather jacket. An oversized cross was hanging from a chain around her neck.

She looked up as Caitlin came into the room. 'Caitlin,' she said. 'How you doin', girl?'

Caitlin's heart skipped a beat. 'Karla!'

'I saw you and your husband here on the internet,' she said. 'I knew I had to come.'

NINE

KARLA STOOD UP in her wedge-heeled boots, walked over to Caitlin and embraced her. Then she pulled away. 'You're sopping wet,' she said.

Caitlin glanced at Noah who was staring at her, unsmiling. His body was rigid with tension. 'I went out on the search today,' Caitlin explained.

There was not a flicker of warmth in Noah's eyes. He did not ask if she or the other searchers had found anything.

'Karla, um…this might not be the best time for a visit,' Caitlin said.

'Why not?' Noah demanded.

Caitlin looked at her husband in surprise.

'Oh, I came all the way from Coatesville just to see you,' Karla said balefully. 'I guess I shoulda waited for an invitation, but I just felt so bad for you all. I didn't want to wait. As you know, I was in…rehab when James died. I wished I could have come then. But I'm here now.'

Caitlin was afraid to look at Noah. 'I really need to change into something dry. Did you want something to drink? There's probably soda or iced tea in the fridge.'

Karla made a smoothing motion with her hands. 'I'm fly.'

'I'll be right back,' said Caitlin uncertainly. She looked at Noah. 'Honey…?'

Just then, one of the officers who were forever with

them came out of the kitchen. 'Mr Eckhart. Can I have a word?'

'Sure,' said Noah, standing up abruptly. 'Nice talking to you, Karla.'

'And to you too, Noah,' said Karla. 'I hope everything goes good and you get your boy back.'

Noah scowled and followed the officer into the kitchen. Caitlin ducked into their bedroom, pulled off her wet things and threw on the first dry clothes she put her hands on. She felt as if she had to get Karla out of the living room and into some less public place, but judging by Noah's expression it was already too late. She ran a comb through her hair and returned to the living room.

She indicated a small, book-lined room off of the living room at the front of the house. 'Why don't we go into the den,' Caitlin said. 'It's...cosier.'

Karla nodded agreeably. 'Whatever,' she said.

Caitlin led the way into the den and indicated a crewel-work embroidered wing chair. Karla settled herself into it, and Caitlin curled up in the leather club chair opposite it.

'You seem different, Karla,' said Caitlin. It was true. The girl she remembered from James's junior high school days was sullen and monosyllabic. The crucifix was new as well. Karla's religion had been prescription drugs, mainly stolen, as Caitlin remembered it. That was why she got arrested just before Caitlin's family left Coatesville for South Jersey.

'I am different,' said Karla. 'Truly different. I have found the way, and the light.'

'Well, that's great,' said Caitlin.

'My Lord Jesus Christ,' said Karla unselfconsciously.

'That's good,' said Caitlin. 'I'm happy for you.'

'Would you like it if we said a prayer together? For your son?' Karla asked.

'That's all right,' Caitlin demurred.

'We all need the Lord's help,' Karla insisted. 'I'm just saying.'

'I know. There's been…quite a lot of praying going on,' said Caitlin.

'I'm glad to hear that,' said Karla. 'I figured as much. On the Net it showed a lot of people around here trying to help.'

'Everyone has been very kind,' said Caitlin. She pulled a knitted throw over her legs. She was still shivering. 'I must admit I…wasn't expecting to see you here.'

'Talk about the Lord working in mysterious ways. I was surfing the Net and I came across your video. It was getting a lot of hits 'cause people love to know about missing children. Me, too. I admit it,' she said, raising her hands as if confessing to a love for chocolate ice cream. 'Anyway, I wasn't even thinking about you and all of a sudden… Well, I could not believe my eyes,' said Karla. 'There you were, looking just the same as I remembered you. Not that I saw you all that much when I was with James. You used to work somewhere else… Where was it?'

'In New England,' said Caitlin. 'I was at a college in Massachusetts.' The shivering was getting worse. Her teeth were actually chattering. Karla did not seem to notice.

'That's right. I remember now. James always said you were the smart one.'

Caitlin nodded, pained at the mention of her brother.

'I wish I coulda been here when James died,' Karla continued. 'First they said I could go to the memorial, but when they found out it was out of state they said no. I cried and cried. It was like the worst day of my life.'

'I don't…like to think about that time,' said Caitlin.

Karla would not be deterred. 'When I got out, I organized a memorial service for him at my church. It wasn't anything big, but some of his old friends came. I sent you an invitation. Did you get it? I sent it to your parents' address. The house you were living in when James…you know…'

'No,' said Caitlin. 'I didn't. It was a very chaotic time. I'm sorry. That was very nice of you.'

'Well, it turned out very beautiful. My pastor let us play a lot of James's favorite music. A couple of people said stuff. I made a DVD. I'll send it to you.'

'That's really… I'm really glad to hear that,' said Caitlin. 'He would have liked that.'

'I know he wasn't a church person. Well, neither was I when I knew him. But I got involved with this church group while I was in rehab and it really changed my life. It's really opened my eyes, and I found my way.'

'That's wonderful, Karla,' said Caitlin, getting out of the chair. 'And it was nice of you to come here. I wish I could ask you stay to dinner or something but we are in such a terrible state because of…our son being missing.'

Karla nodded sympathetically. 'I know. How terrible for you. What happened to him? The little boy?'

Caitlin shook her head. 'I really…I can't get into it. It's been all over the news. He was…abducted from his school.'

'Well, I know that. I saw that when I saw you on the Net. I just meant, do you know why?'

'Why someone would take a little six-year-old boy? No, I have no idea.'

'I know it's sometimes hard to discern God's purpose,' Karla said solemnly.

Caitlin sighed. 'Yes. Indeed it is.'

'Like with James,' she said.

Caitlin stared at her. 'I'm sorry?'

'Well, suicide. I mean, that is the lowest depths.'

'Actually, he died of a drug overdose,' said Caitlin.

Karla shrugged. 'Well, that was just the way he picked to go.'

'I suppose that's true,' Caitlin said quietly.

'I wish I coulda been there for him during those dark days,' Karla continued. 'I mean, he and I… Our souls were very bonded together. I often think I could have saved him. But while I was in the facility there were strict rules about the phone and texting and I wasn't allowed access. He needed somebody he could talk to day and night. Plus, I was very involved in my own recovery and all. I didn't realize how that guilt was getting to him…'

Caitlin froze. 'Guilt?'

'And don't you blame yourself,' said Karla. 'I was telling your husband. I'm sure you did all you could, but James just couldn't live with it.'

The thought that Karla had told what she knew to Noah was enough to make Caitlin feel dizzy with anxiety. She grabbed the back of a chair to steady herself.

'You do know about it, don't you?' Karla looked up at her innocently.

'Know what?'

'About the accident.'

Caitlin answered with an edge of impatience in her voice. 'Yes. I know about it. I just don't want to talk about it, Karla. Right now, it's all I can do with Geordie missing…'

'James couldn't live with himself. He found out that woman had a child and everything. He kept seeing her every time he closed his eyes, running out in front of his truck like that. He literally couldn't live with it.'

Caitlin felt a sudden flash of anger, remembering James. He had begged her to understand and forgive him. He also begged her not to go to the police. He had been terrified of the consequences. 'Listen Karla, before you start polishing that halo for James, he wasn't all that concerned about the person he killed. He just didn't want to go to jail,' said Caitlin sharply. 'His permit was suspended. He was high...'

'I don't think he was,' said Karla.

'Oh, for heaven's sake,' said Caitlin in exasperation. 'I was there. I dealt with him every day. Believe me. I know what he was doing at that time.'

'He bared his heart and soul to me, Caitlin,' Karla insisted.

'Karla, I really can't talk about this.' She had to end this conversation. She glanced at the door, fearful that Noah might be listening.

Karla nodded sadly and stood up. 'All I'm saying is, knowing what I know now, I could have offered him some words of comfort that might actually have helped, but at the time...'

'It's too late now,' said Caitlin. 'There's nothing we can do. It's in the past.'

She said it firmly, as if to close a door. Then she walked out of the little den and waited for Karla to follow her. Karla came out into the living room, and reluctantly picked up her enormous pocketbook from beside the chair.

'Thank you for coming all this way,' said Caitlin stiffly.

'I just wanted to help,' said Karla.

'I know,' said Caitlin.

'Well, you take care. I hope you get your son back very soon.'

'Thank you,' said Caitlin. She walked the girl to the door and submitted to a brief embrace. As she ran across the yard to her car, Karla lifted her satchel over her head to keep off the rain, and her skirt rode up to the top of her thighs. The holes in her tights were visible as she picked her way down the path. Caitlin watched her get inside the car, make a K-turn and wave before she started back down the driveway. Caitlin kept her gaze fastened to the car until it disappeared. She wanted to be sure she was gone.

She could feel Noah standing behind her before he even spoke. Her mind was racing, and even though she had imagined this conversation a million times she did not know what she was going to say.

'Caitlin,' he said.

She turned and looked at him. 'She's quite a talkative girl, that one. My brother was crazy about her. I had no idea she was coming.'

'So she said.'

'If I'd known, I would have stayed home.'

'We had an interesting talk,' he said coldly.

'Has she been here long?'

'Long enough,' he said.

Caitlin nodded.

'Let's go out to the car.'

'What for? It's raining.'

'I want to talk to you, and I don't really want an audience,' he said, glancing at the two detectives seated in the dining room.

'We could go in our room,' she said.

'NO,' he barked. 'Definitely not.'

'Let me find my dry boots,' she said.

'I'll be in the car.'

SHE DID NOT ask him where they were going. She was afraid to start the conversation while he was driving for fear that he would not be able to concentrate on the road. He drove to a park not far from their house, which had been set up by the Lions club. It had a view of the nearby lake, and most days little kids were fond of climbing on the jungle gym or swinging as high as they could go. She often took Geordie here. She could picture him hanging upside down on the monkey bars, his glasses sliding down his nose, as he called out to her to watch him. The park was deserted today because of the rain.

Noah parked the car and they sat in silence for a moment.

'Geordie loves it here,' she said.

'I don't want to talk about my son,' he said. There was no missing the ominous note in his voice.

Finally, Caitlin spoke. 'Look, I don't know what she said to you but you seem very upset. I know I never told you all that much about my brother but...'

'Stop,' he said. He turned and looked at her, and the expression in his eyes was menacing. 'I want the truth.'

'I don't know what you...'

'Don't,' he said. 'I swear to God, Caitlin. Don't push me. I am at the end of my rope as it is. I just want to know the truth.'

How many times she wished she had told him on that first day. She remembered every moment of that day as if she had lived it in slow motion. She had gone to that garden planting for Emily for one reason only: to find the members of her family and explain to them what had happened. It had taken all her courage to go, but she knew that she owed them the truth. They needed to know what had happened to their loved one.

They needed to know that James had paid the price— the ultimate price—for his actions. It was only fair. Her hands shook as she got ready that day, but she forced herself onward, knowing it was the right thing to do. And then she met Noah, who was attractive and smart and made her laugh the first time he spoke to her. She hesitated, and was lost.

'About...'

'Your brother's accident. Almost four years ago, wasn't

it? He hit a woman in his car. A young mother. Killed her. And then he ran.'

Caitlin thought she could hear the blood pounding in her own ears. For a moment, in her desperation, she thought to deny it. Say that Karla had it wrong. But she could not bring herself to do it. It was one thing never to have confessed it. It was another thing to deny it. She could make up a name, another victim. But then, immediately, she knew that it was no use. He would be able to find out she was lying in no time. He was an attorney. He was used to researching crimes. And clearly, he already suspected the truth. He was not going to just let it go.

'Yes. That's true.'

'Who was it? Who was the woman?'

Caitlin took a deep breath. She wanted to start by making an excuse. By explaining. But it was too late for explanations. Hopelessness filled her to the brim. She really had no choice. 'It was Emily,' she said. 'It was your wife.'

TEN

Noah sat very still, staring through the windshield. 'I thought so,' he said.

'I wanted to tell you,' she said.

Noah turned his head and looked at her blankly.

Caitlin shook her head. 'I know how that sounds.'

'You can't imagine,' he said.

'No. But you have to believe me. I never intended to deceive you, Noah, the day we met. The day we were all planting the garden for Emily. I went there that day with one goal in mind. I knew Emily's family would be there, and I wanted to…tell everything I knew.'

'But you didn't,' he said flatly.

'No. I didn't. I met you and…I lost my nerve. I couldn't figure out… It was a stupid idea. I should have realized that that was the worst possible moment.'

'So, when I called you, and asked you out, you decided it would be better if I didn't know that it was your brother who had made me a widower. Took my wife. Took my son's mother from him…'

'It wasn't like that. You make it sound like I had some kind of plan. I tried so many times to find the words. But I never expected to become involved with you. I was in love with you before I knew it and I was afraid…'

Noah held up a hand as if to shield himself from her. 'Oh, please,' he said, his voice dripping sarcasm. 'The love defense.'

'It's not a defense. I'm not trying to defend myself. I just want you to know how this happened.'

Noah would not meet her pleading gaze. 'You knew this all along. From the day it happened…'

'Not…exactly,' she said. 'Not everything. I mean…I knew that he hit someone in the car… At first he wouldn't say where the accident happened. But I figured it out from what I saw on the news.'

'No. Stop. Let's not call this an accident, shall we? Let's call it what it was. It was vehicular homicide. It was a murder. The driver was going so fast that Emily was instantly killed. She was checking the mail. Our baby…Geordie was still in the car. Asleep in his car seat while his mother was killed. The driver never stopped. He never tried to help her. He left her to die in the street. That was your brother.'

Caitlin shook her head. 'I know. I'm so sorry… And I'm not trying to make excuses for him. There's no excuse. I told him that he had to turn himself in. He agreed that he would, but then he hid in his room. He wouldn't come out or speak to me.

'I knew I had to do something. I kept thinking about the family of the woman he hit. How they must feel. And what my own parents would have wanted me to do. I knew what was right, but it was so difficult. I made up my mind, though. I went to his room and I told him that we were going to go to the police in the morning. He was lying on his bed with his back to me. I told him that he had to face the consequences of what he'd done. That night he overdosed. The next morning I found him…dead.'

Noah's gaze was stony. 'Am I supposed to feel bad about that?'

Caitlin hesitated. 'No. No, I guess I wouldn't expect that.'

'You guess? You knew this all along. You knew this and you said nothing?'

'I'm not going to make excuses. I…'

'You knew this and you married me? You pretended to care for Geordie? Emily's son?'

Caitlin wiped away her tears. 'Don't say "pretended." That's not fair.'

'Fair?' he demanded. 'You have the nerve to talk about what's fair?'

'I'm just trying to explain, Noah,' she said. 'You know me. We've been together for two years now. Two and a half if you count our courtship. You must know I didn't do this to hurt you. I was a coward, I admit that. And it has been a form of torture to know this and not be able to tell you. Sometimes, I would see an opening and think, 'Now. Do it now.' But I didn't want to see the look in your eyes. That look. The one in your eyes right now. I couldn't bear it. I've been so happy with you. I thought maybe it would just…dissipate in time.'

'Dissipate,' he said.

'I don't know the word. Diminish, I guess. I hoped that in time the pain would diminish and I would find an opportunity to tell you.'

'Or not,' he said.

'Not?' she asked.

'Not tell me. Never tell me. That was your real plan, wasn't it?'

'I didn't have a plan. Like I said, I guess was waiting for an opening. A moment…'

'What were you expecting the perfect opportunity to be? Christmas? My birthday?'

'Don't say that,' she pleaded. 'Don't. You don't mean that. You make it sound like I was trying to hurt you.

Haven't you ever gotten into a situation that you just couldn't resolve? That just…got out of hand?'

'No,' he said. 'Frankly, I don't know what the fuck you're talking about.'

She felt the brutal force of his words like a slap across her face. She flinched, but she had no urge to retaliate. She deserved his contempt. It was her own fault. 'Look, I don't blame you for being angry. I'd be furious if I were you. But try to remember that it wasn't me that was driving that car. It wasn't me that killed Emily.'

Noah took a deep breath and stared at her. She hoped that he was hearing what she said, and considering the impossibility of the situation she had found herself in. She hoped, but she didn't really believe it. He was looking at her with a loathing she hadn't imagined was possible. Part of her wanted to blame Karla for blundering into a situation she didn't understand, but Caitlin knew better. It wasn't Karla's fault. Not any of this. She did this to herself. She should have spoken, and she didn't. She'd had a million opportunities, and she let them go.

'Noah?' she said. 'Say something.'

Noah shook his head, still gazing at her. 'How do I know this is true?' he said. 'How do I know anything you say is true? I only have your word for it. Now I see what your word is worth.'

'Don't say that, Noah. We need each other right now. We need to stick together. We're so frantic about Geordie…'

'There is no "we," Caitlin.'

'That's not true,' she whispered.

'Now I have to doubt everything you've ever said to me. I mean, did you take Geordie to school on Monday? Or was there an accident? Maybe you decided not to tell me. For my own good. Better to think he disappeared?'

'Noah.' She was stunned by what he was suggesting.

'I don't know you, Caitlin. I don't know what you're capable of.'

'Are you accusing me? Of…hurting Geordie?'

Noah stared at her. 'Well?'

'How could you?' she said.

'How could I?'

That's enough, she thought. *That's enough. I was wrong. I did the wrong thing. But to accuse me, to even suggest that I would hurt Geordie…* She didn't know what she was going to do. She didn't know where she was going to turn. She just knew that she wasn't sitting in that car with him for another minute. Caitlin opened the car door, slid out and slammed it shut.

He did not look at her or urge her to get back in. The drizzle was seeping under the collar of her raincoat and down her face. She turned away from the car and began to walk. He did not call out to her or come after her. She walked toward the entrance to the park and then, slowly, out to the street. She reminded herself to be careful on this road. It was the same road where Emily had died. Where James had run her down.

She shoved her hands into her pockets and began to walk back in the direction of the house. In a few moments, Noah's car emerged from the park. He drove past her without a glance in her direction.

WHEN SHE GOT back to the house, the door to their room was shut. She knew her face was swollen from weeping on the way home, but there was nothing unusual about that. The police in the house were used to seeing her like that. They hadn't seen her any other way. Still, she felt as if she had no refuge. She took off her wet coat and hung it on a hook by the front door. Then she went into the den and curled up on the leather chair. She pulled the knitted throw over her legs stared out the window. There were books and newspapers and magazines in the den. There was a television and a computer. None of it interested her in the least. She felt too weary to even expend the energy to stare at a screen.

She wondered how long it would be before they would be speaking to one another again. She didn't know how she could endure the fact that Geordie was missing without Noah to lean on. They leaned on each other. He was bound to realize that. She didn't expect him to forgive her right away. She had already forgiven him for his cruel accusation. She understood that he wanted to strike out at her because he felt betrayed. Every time she wanted to sob or be angry at his reaction, she stopped herself. He had a right to his anger.

She heard the door to their room open and she looked up hopefully at the door as she heard his footsteps coming down the hall toward the den. Noah appeared carrying two bulging suitcases. Her suitcases. Her mouth fell open.

He looked in at her. 'I'll put these in your car,' he said.

Caitlin scrambled to get up from the chair and came out into the living room. 'What are you doing?' she asked.

'What does it look like I'm doing? These are your things. Some of them, anyway. Take them and go. I'll send you the rest.'

'You're putting me out of my own house?' she asked.

'Your house?' he said.

'Oh, that's right,' she said. 'It's not my house. It's Emily's house.'

There was a flicker of guilt in his eyes, but it was gone in an instant. 'Please go,' he said. 'Let's not drag this out.'

'And Geordie,' she demanded, ashamed of the catch in her voice. 'What about Geordie?'

He looked at her coldly. 'Do you know something about Geordie? Because if you do, now's the time to tell it.'

She understood that he wanted to punish her. She didn't even blame him for that. But to continue to suggest that she was concealing some information about Geordie…that was more than she could stand. That was the limit. 'That's cruel, Noah. Worse than cruel. You know how I love him.'

'Do I?' he asked.

She pulled her coat and bag off the hook, snatched the suitcases from his hands and awkwardly pushed open the front door. The rain had let up a little. She lugged the bags across the lawn, threw them into the back of her car and slammed the trunk shut. She did not look back at the house. She got into the driver's seat and headed down the driveway. Out of sight of the house, she sat at the driveway's end and stared at the highway in front of her. She did not know where to go. She literally did not know which way to turn.

ELEVEN

CAITLIN STOPPED HER car beside the weather-beaten 'For Sale' sign, and sat staring at her parents' modest retirement home. Some houses seemed to be cursed, she thought. Her parents had bought this house full of hope for the future, and instead each had fallen ill and died within two years. James had killed himself in this house. And now, here Caitlin was, back here, exiled by her husband, her child missing. At least here she could call Geordie her child in her own mind. Her heart could not be any more shattered, she thought, if she had given birth to him.

She did not want to be here in this abandoned house which had seen so much sorrow, but she didn't know where else to go. Everyone she knew in this area, she either knew through the college or through Noah. She didn't want anyone at work to know about this fresh disaster, and anyone she knew through Noah would not want anything to do with her when they found out why she and Noah were estranged.

Caitlin pulled her cell phone from her purse and called the Realtor's number on the sign. She got the voice mail. 'Stephanie,' she said. 'This is Caitlin Eckhart. I'm going to be staying in my parents' house for…a while. So, if you have any prospective…lookers, please call my cell and let me know before you show up at the door. Thanks.' Not that lookers were much of a problem, Caitlin thought, throwing the phone back in her bag. The house had been on the market for two years now without a nibble. Because of the collapse in the housing market, it was the worst possible time to try to sell a house. Particularly a house as unexceptional as this one.

She chided herself for that thought. Her parents had been so pleased when they found this house. It was neat and tidy, and had only one story for easy access for the old age they did not live to see. The house was surrounded by trees and had a screen porch in the back with rocking chairs, where they had envisioned sitting during long, twilit summer evenings. Tears came to her eyes as she remembered her mother and father. Their dreams had not been extravagant. Peace. Quiet. A little well-earned leisure. It was not to be.

At least, Caitlin thought, she still owned this house. Right now, it would serve a valuable purpose. She could turn the key and go inside, and no one could throw her out, accusing her of terrible crimes. For that, she was grateful.

Caitlin sighed and got out of the car. She pulled out her suitcases and carried them toward the house. She passed the garage, where her father's damaged truck was rusting away in the darkness. Emily's blood had probably flaked off the smashed front bumper by now. Caitlin had parked the truck in there and never moved it. It was easier than trying to explain the needed repairs to someone at a body shop. As she passed it, Caitlin did not glance into the garage. Why look? If that truck had somehow vanished, she would be grateful.

Caitlin inserted the key in the front door and had to struggle to get the key to turn in the lock, which was stiff with disuse. She opened the door and walked into the dark, clammy house. *Home, sweet home,* she thought, and her heart sank at the thought.

She wanted to collapse on the sofa, curl up in a fetal position and not move, but she resisted the urge. She had to make sure the place was habitable before night fell. It had been empty for so long, except for the occasional quick visit from a Realtor, that she was not sure what she would find. She was up to date on the bills, so at least she knew the gas and electricity were still on. Was the water running? Were there sheets on the bed, or anything to eat?

Caitlin carried her suitcase past the doorway to her parents' bedroom. Though it was the largest bedroom, she couldn't bear to sleep in that room, which had been a sick room almost nonstop for almost two years. Her father's heart had given out quickly. Her mother had lingered. Each one had been carried to the hospital from that room to spend their final days. She moved down the hall past James's room, with only the briefest glance inside. More misery, she thought. The tiny guest room would do. She opened the door and placed her bags inside. It was a sweet-looking room, decorated in the country style her mother had favored. The bed was made. Caitlin ran her hand over the sheets. They were as clammy as the air in the house. She opened up the bed to air it. She would turn the heat on. Maybe that would dry it out before she had to lie down in those sheets. She hoped it would dry it out soon. But she was so exhausted that it almost didn't matter. She would sleep wherever she dropped.

She went back to the living room. There was no cable in the house so the TV didn't work. She turned up the heat and went into the kitchen. The heat made clanking noises, but it came on. The kitchen was dusty, but not dirty. She had paid a cleaning service to clean the whole place before she put it on the market. She opened the refrigerator door hesitantly. Fortunately, there was no food inside, and it didn't smell bad. She looked in the cabinets. There were still a few staples. Some cans of soup. Some boxes of stale crackers and pasta. There were cans of vegetables and jars of sauce. The water in the faucets ran. It was enough, she thought.

A sharp rap on the front door made her jump and clutch her chest. No one knew she was here. She went to the window of the kitchen door, pulled back the ruffled curtain, and peeked out down the driveway. Immediately she recognized the car. She had ridden in it just this morning.

Caitlin went to the front door and opened it. Sam Mathis stood on the front step. 'Geordie?' she asked.

Sam Mathis shook his head. 'May I come in?'

Caitlin's shoulders slumped. She stepped back so that he could come inside. 'How did you know I was here?' she asked.

'Your husband thought you might be here,' said Sam. 'He said he'd asked you to leave the house.'

Caitlin felt as if her face had been slapped. 'He didn't waste any time. Did he tell you why?'

'Yes. He said that you know who killed his first wife.'

Caitlin flinched at the word 'killed' but did not protest. She indicated that Sam should sit down. He took a seat in her father's old easy chair. Caitlin sat on the sofa. She knotted her fingers together and looked down at them. 'Did he tell you anything else?' she asked.

'I'll ask the questions,' said Sam brusquely. 'What do you know about Emily Eckhart's death?'

Caitlin stared at him for a moment. It was difficult to see his eyes in the gloom of the late afternoon. She got up from the sofa and went around the room, turning on the lamps. Then she sat back down. Sam was watching her coldly.

'I don't know where to begin,' she said.

'First things first,' said Sam. 'Does this have anything to do with Geordie's disappearance?'

'NO,' Caitlin exclaimed. 'No, it has nothing to do with Geordie. If it had, I would have told you right away.'

Sam looked at her coldly. 'You better tell me right now.'

Caitlin took a deep breath. She felt like someone who was about to fall off a cliff. 'OK. Just to explain… A girl named Karla saw our plea on the internet and came to see us today. She's my late brother's girlfriend. She was in touch with my brother at the time that he…killed himself. Well, it was a drug overdose, but I've never thought it was accidental. Anyway, Karla was in touch with my brother when it happened. He told her that he had hit a woman while he was driving my father's truck. Then he fled the scene. The woman died. James was distraught about it. This event actually precipitated his overdose.

'I wasn't home when Karla arrived. While she was waiting for me to return home, Karla explained all this to Noah. Noah's a very smart man. He figured out the rest. The person that my brother hit was Emily Eckhart.'

Sam grimaced.

'Yes,' she said.

'Your brother was Emily's killer?'

'That's right,' said Caitlin.

Sam recoiled. 'And you knew this? You knew it when you married Noah?'

'I knew it,' she said.

'No wonder he kicked you out,' said Sam disgustedly.

'Thanks,' said Caitlin.

'Well, come on, Caitlin.'

'I know,' she said. 'I brought this on myself.'

'Why didn't you turn your brother in if you knew he'd done something like that?'

'I threatened to turn him in. That's when he overdosed.'

'You still could have come forward so the family would have closure.'

'That's what I was trying to do when I met Noah. I sought out Emily's family to tell them the truth and, instead, I fell in love with her husband.'

Sam shook his head. 'And you never told him…'

'I never told him. I was too ashamed. I never told anyone.' Caitlin knew there would be consequences to this admission. She didn't care. 'I realize that by keeping silent, I may have committed a crime,' she said.

Sam frowned at her. 'What car was your brother driving when he killed Emily Eckhart?'

'He was driving my father's truck. It's…out there, in the garage, if you want to see it,' said Caitlin.

'Has it been repaired?'

Caitlin shook her head. 'I thought about taking it to a body shop. Telling them I'd hit a deer. I just didn't have the heart to tell any more lies about it. Would you like to see it?'

'Yes,' said Sam. 'I would.'

'Come with me,' said Caitlin. Part of her knew that it was foolish to offer this evidence of a crime up to the police. She should call a lawyer and cover her own interests. But she had brought this on herself by staying silent. All she felt now was the need to be shed of it. And, if necessary, to be punished for that silence.

She turned on the outside lights, slipped her coat back on and led the way out to the garage. She opened the garage door and they went inside. The battered pick-up truck sat where she had left it years ago.

Sam walked around the truck and looked at it. 'It's got a lot of dings,' he observed.

'This is no ding,' she said.

He had to wedge himself between the front of the truck and the wall of the garage to get a look. He frowned as he examined the damage. 'Was your brother high when this happened?' he asked.

'Probably,' said Caitlin. 'He usually was.'

Sam was studying the truck, his eyebrows knitted together in a frown. He bent over the front bumper and squinted at the rusted spot where it was bashed in. 'I'll need to impound this truck,' he said, 'so we can determine for certain if this is the vehicle that killed Emily Eckhart.'

'It is,' said Caitlin. 'Go ahead and impound it. I don't care. Just tell me what's going to happen to me.'

Sam shrugged. 'You withheld evidence in a homicide investigation. First we have to be sure that this is, in fact, evidence of that crime. If there is still blood on this grille, we should know in pretty short order.'

'And then?'

'You could be arrested.'

Caitlin wondered if she could feel any worse than she already did. She doubted it. 'Whatever,' she said. 'I don't want any more lies.'

Sam's icy expression thawed a little bit. 'You may be treated leniently, now that you've voluntarily given up the evidence. It all depends on the judge. In any case, I would suggest you engage an attorney.'

'You're not arresting me now?' she said.

'Not right this minute,' he said.

'Noah will be disappointed,' Caitlin said.

'Your husband understands legal procedure,' said Sam. 'Seen enough?'

'Yeah,' said Sam. 'I'll leave the closer look to forensics.'

He led the way out of the garage, and Caitlin snapped off the light behind him.

Out in the driveway, Sam made a phone call while Caitlin shivered in the chilly evening. She felt better somehow, just knowing that this truck would be hauled away from here. That she would not have to constantly be reminded of all that had happened. All the mistakes she had made.

Sam ended his call and turned back to her. They stood in the silvery circle that the outdoor halogen lights threw on the driveway.

'I heard you had a tough time at the search today,' he said.

'Once I got there, I understood why you didn't want me to go. I shouldn't have insisted.'

'Some things you have to leave to other people,' he said.

'When those dogs started to bark…' Her eyes filled with tears at the memory of her fear. She shuddered and shook her head.

'You should go inside,' he said.

Caitlin nodded. 'I think I will.'

'They'll be around for the truck in the morning. I told them there was no need to come get it tonight. I trust that you will not tamper with it.'

'Why would I tamper with it now?' she asked.

'I'll let you know what we find out.'

'I'd appreciate it.'

'Now that you and Noah are living in separate spaces, I've had to arrange for an officer to come by here. A squad car should be arriving shortly.'

'Thank you,' she said.

'For what?'

Caitlin hesitated. 'I'm glad to have it off my chest.'

Sam looked at her with a hint of kindness in his eyes. 'Try and get some rest.'

Caitlin raised a hand in farewell and started up the walk to the house.

She went inside, locked the door behind her and sank down on the sofa, still wearing her coat. She felt as if she might never be able to move again. She thought about what

Sam Mathis had said. An attorney. She and Noah used David Alvarez, a partner in Noah's office, as their attorney. Obviously, she could not call on him. There was the attorney who had handled her parents' estate. He was an older guy who probably didn't handle criminal matters. She could call him. But that implied that she was going to try to evade some responsibility and that was not her aim.

She heard the crunch of Sam's tires on the gravel driveway and then the sound of his car's engine faded away. She was all alone in the silence. Caitlin closed her eyes and rested her head on the back of the sofa, her hands still in the pockets of her coat. She heard her cell phone ringing in her bag which she had left on the coffee table. Her first thought was reporters. Could they know already? No, it was too soon. Sam wouldn't say anything to the press until the truck was known to be the vehicle which killed Emily. She had not given any thought to the publicity that would ensue when the truth came out. That would be another nightmare. She would probably lose her job at the college.

The phone kept ringing. She hoped for a moment that it might be Noah, but she knew better. Still, it could be news of Geordie. For that alone, she had to answer it. She rummaged for her phone and looked at the caller ID. Unknown name. She didn't recognize the number or the area code. A bad sign, she thought.

'Hello?' she said.

She heard a tiny, distant voice speaking hesitantly into the phone. 'Mom?' he said.

TWELVE

IF SHE HAD been zapped with a taser, she could not have been more shocked. 'Geordie,' she whispered. 'Oh, my God. Is that you?'

'Hi, Mom.'

Caitlin clutched phone, as if she could reach through it and seize him. 'Geordie,' she cried. 'Sweetheart, where are you? Are you all right?'

'Where's Dad?' he asked.

'He's…not here. Honey, talk to me. Where are you? Are you OK? Has…anyone hurt you?'

'I'm OK. But I can't tell where I am,' he said plaintively.

Before she could answer, or ask why, the call was ended. 'Geordie!' she cried into the dead line. 'Geordie.' She stared at the phone as if she could see his face in it. She pushed the caller ID number again. It was nothing she recognized. Her heart was thundering. Instantly, she pressed the button to return the call. The phone rang and rang. Nothing.

Despair rose in her like a tidal wave. He was gone. He had slipped away, and was once again out of reach. And she still knew nothing. Not where he was, or how he was. Nothing. But then she corrected herself. *You know the most important thing. He's alive. He is alive!*

A blast of the doorbell made her jump. She rushed to the door and jerked it open.

'Mrs Eckhart?' said the uniformed officer on the front

step. 'I'm Officer Wheatley. Detective Mathis sent me.' He suddenly seemed to notice the agitated expression on her face. The visible whites of her eyes 'Are you OK?'

'Yes,' she cried. 'Yes. Call him. Detective Mathis. Call him right now. Tell him my son just called me. Geordie called me!' She brandished the cell phone in her hand, as if the device itself were somehow proof.

'The missing boy?' the officer asked.

Caitlin nodded.

'Is he all right?'

'Yes. Well, I don't know. He wasn't allowed to talk. Look, I need your help. Please. I can't drive. My hands are shaking too hard. I need to tell my husband. Can we go to the house?'

'You want to go to your husband's house now?'

'I have to tell him. Please?' Caitlin begged him.

The young officer considered this request, which required a deviation from his orders. 'Let me call Detective Mathis.' The officer made a hurried call and spoke in a low, urgent voice. Then he turned to Caitlin. 'All right, come along,' he said. 'Detective Mathis and your husband are going to meet us at the station.'

'The police station?' said Caitlin, dismayed. 'Why there?'

'That's what I was told. To bring you down to the station.'

Caitlin hesitated in the doorway.

'We should hurry,' said Officer Wheatley.

Caitlin stepped out of the house and pulled the door shut behind her.

'I'll need to confiscate that phone,' the officer said.

Caitlin clutched the cell phone to her heart, as if it were Geordie himself. 'No. I need to keep it.'

'Detective Mathis was very clear about this. That phone

may contain information which is key to your son's whereabouts. You need to hand it over,' said Officer Wheatley.

Caitlin looked at him ruefully.

'You'll get it back,' he assured her.

Caitlin sighed. It wasn't the phone that mattered. It was that letting go of it felt like letting go of Geordie. She knew that it made no sense. She closed her eyes and handed it over.

THE TRIP DOWNTOWN was fast. They traveled with red lights flashing and the siren blaring. Caitlin sat in the back seat, while Officer Wheatley talked on the radio in the front, and his partner drove.

A man walking his dog stared at the squad car as they reached the station, trying to peer in at the criminal who was being brought in. He walked away, disappointed, when Officer Wheatley opened the car door for Caitlin politely.

Escorted by the two officers, Caitlin went up the steps and into the old sandstone police station. They hurried her past the evening's crew of officers on duty and miscreants who looked at her curiously. They arrived at Chief Burns's office and knocked on the door. They were told to enter.

Chief Burns sat behind his desk, and Sam Mathis stood beside him. Noah was seated in a chair in front of the desk. He looked at her as she walked in, his gaze wary but hopeful. A young man in street clothes stood by the American flag in the corner, his arms folded across his chest.

Caitlin spoke directly to her husband. 'Noah,' she cried. 'He called me. Not half an hour ago.'

Chief Burns held up a hand to silence her. 'Where is the phone?' he said.

Officer Wheatley held up a plastic bag with the phone in it.

'Give it to Detective Thurman there.' He pointed to

the young man by the flag. Officer Wheatley handed the detective the phone. Thurman took it and left the room.

'Thank you, officers. Wait outside, please. Close the door.'

Caitlin sensed the negative current in the room. No one offered her a seat. She looked at Noah. He looked away from her.

'What's going on here?' she asked.

'Tell us what happened,' said Chief Burns. Caitlin noted the lack of pleasantries, the chill in his voice.

'My phone rang. I answered it. And I heard Geordie's voice.'

'What did he say?' Sam asked.

'He said, "Hi, Mom," she recounted, and then, almost to her embarrassment, she started to weep. Noah was leaning forward, gripping the arms of his chair as if he was going to stand up, but he remained seated.

Caitlin wiped her eyes and tried to compose herself. 'He asked where his father was. I said he wasn't with me at the moment. I asked him where he was, and if he was all right. He said he couldn't talk. That was it. That was all.'

'Did you look at the number he was calling from?' Sam asked.

'Of course,' said Caitlin. 'I didn't recognize it.'

'Area code?'

'It wasn't local. I tried to call him back. The phone rang and rang.'

'Detective Thurman is our electronics expert. He's going to determine exactly where the last call on your phone originated,' said Sam, who spoke in a kinder tone than the chief.

'Can he do that?' Caitlin asked.

'If there was such a call,' said Chief Burns.

Caitlin looked at the chief, startled. 'Excuse me?' she said.

The chief did not reply.

'Do you think I would lie about this?' She turned and looked at her husband. 'Do you? Noah?'

Noah did not meet her gaze.

'Geordie called me, goddammit. I heard his voice.'

'It could have been a prank,' said Sam, with a hint of apology in his tone. 'People do some really rotten things around a crime like this.'

'No,' she insisted. 'It was Geordie.'

'I sincerely hope so,' said Chief Burns.

'I know so,' Caitlin cried. 'I know my own…boy.'

'I keep asking myself, why would he call you and not his father?' said the chief.

Caitlin stuck out her chin. 'Meaning, because I'm not his "real" parent?'

'Yes, frankly,' said the chief.

'Sometimes his father is in court, or can't be reached. He knows that he can call me if he needs me for any reason. He has my number memorized. For emergencies,' said Caitlin evenly.

Chief Burns sat back in his chair, his hands folded over the belt buckle of his uniform. 'Kind of makes you a hero, doesn't it? Being the one to hear from the victim. The one chosen to receive that call which, by your own admission, gave us virtually no information about his condition or his whereabouts.'

'I asked him those things. We were cut off immediately. As if someone were right there with him, monitoring what he said.'

The chief frowned. 'So, why would the captor allow him to make such a call at all? Just to let you know he was doing OK?'

'I don't know,' Caitlin protested. 'I have no idea how

someone like that would think. I'm just telling you what happened.'

'I learned today,' said Chief Burns, 'that you have already thwarted one police investigation, Mrs Eckhart. Naturally, as a result, I am somewhat skeptical…'

Caitlin looked at him defiantly. 'I'm telling the truth.'

The phone rang on Burns's desk and he picked it up. 'That was quick,' he said to the caller. He listened quietly to what his caller was saying. 'All right. Keep after it.'

Burns hung up the phone. 'That was Detective Thurman. The call was made from a Tracfone purchased in Chicago.'

'Chicago,' Caitlin groaned.

'So we know he is in Chicago?' Noah exclaimed.

'We know the phone was purchased there,' Chief Burns said cautiously. 'We'll contact the Chicago police and put them on high alert. In the meantime, we'll attempt to trace the phone to the store where it was purchased.'

'A Tracfone,' said Noah. 'People buy those things and throw them away.'

'That's correct,' said Burns.

'Is it possible to trace the place where it was purchased?' Noah asked.

'It is possible,' said Burns. 'But with a throwaway phone, that information can be misleading. For example, a person could use a Tracfone to call their own cell phone.' The chief turned back to Caitlin. 'Is that what you did, Mrs Eckhart? Did you buy a phone and call your own number?'

Caitlin's mouth fell open. 'I can't believe… Why would I do such a thing?'

'I'm just asking,' he said. 'Because there's a level at which this doesn't make any sense. The only way the boy could have a Tracfone is if his captor bought it and let him use it. And why would he do that? Why would he want us to know that Geordie is alive? There's been no ransom demand. What else could a call like that serve?'

Caitlin did not want him to see how bitterly painful his words were to her. 'I understand what you're saying. I understand that it sounds bizarre. But the answer to your question is "no." I did not buy a Tracfone and call my own phone. I have never even been in Chicago,' she said evenly.

Chief Burns regarded her coolly. 'An associate, perhaps...'

She reached out and put a hand on Noah's shoulder. He flinched, as if he had been burned. He looked up at her.

She met his agitated gaze. 'I don't care what they think. But I do care if you believe me. Listen to me, Noah. No matter how angry you might be at me, you know I wouldn't lie about this. You know that. And I'm telling you. He's alive. Geordie is alive.'

Tears rushed to his eyes and he blinked them back, looking both skeptical and wildly hopeful.

Chief Burns cleared his throat. 'Sam, escort Mrs Eckhart out of my office. Tell Officer Wheatley to drive her back to her house.'

Caitlin let go of Noah's shoulder and let herself be led out into the waiting area. Sam Mathis spoke to Officer Wheatley, who approached her.

'I'll take you home now,' he said.

'Thank you,' said Caitlin. She went out to the patrol car and got back inside. All the way back to her parents' house she kept thinking about Geordie's voice on the phone, and the look in Noah's eyes at the station.

He is alive, she thought. *You have an advantage over the others because you know that it's true. Hold on to that.*

When they arrived back at the house, Caitlin thanked him for the ride. She heard him pulling out. It wasn't until she was lying in bed, huddled under the covers still in her clothes, that she remembered. They had kept her phone. She had no phone. If Geordie tried to call again... Despite her exhaustion, she tossed and turned, sleepless until dawn.

THIRTEEN

CAITLIN AWOKE AFTER an hour's sleep to a gray day and the sound of someone knocking on the front door. She forced herself to get out of the bed and pull on some clothes. Then she shuffled down the hallway to the front door. When she opened it, she immediately noticed the tow truck in the driveway.

'Mrs Eckhart,' said the officer standing in front of her. 'We've come to impound the truck. Can you sign this please?'

Bleary-eyed, Caitlin signed the form on the clipboard, and then closed the door to avoid watching the men in the tow truck begin their work. They would haul it away and analyze it, and maybe, as a result, she would face being arrested. It was a sickening thought, but no worse than the thought that Geordie was still missing, or the memory of Noah recoiling from her. They would be going through this whole dreary, empty day of waiting separately. No comfort. No love. *Stop,* she thought. *Remember this: Geordie is still alive.* Nothing else mattered. As of last night, anyway, Geordie was still alive.

With that thought for consolation she went into the kitchen, where she rummaged in the cupboards. There was no coffee, and even if there had been, she knew her queasy stomach wouldn't be able to tolerate it black. She opened a box of cereal, a year past it's sell-by date, plunged her hand into the box and pulled out a handful. She tried to chew and swallow it dry. The cereal tasted like faded wallpaper.

I can't do this, she thought. *I can't subsist on expired food and hide in this house.* She reminded herself that there were things she needed to do. *Go and get your phone back,* she thought. *Go and bite the bullet. Go and explain to Emily's family the truth about what happened to their sister and their daughter. They deserve to know, and you have to be the one to tell them. Take this day in hand, before you end up hiding under the covers, paralyzed by your own misery.* She threw the box of cereal into the garbage and turned out the light in the kitchen.

AT THE POLICE station they made her wait for almost an hour, but she emerged from the station with her phone back in her bag. It felt like a victory, however minor. She stood on the station house steps and tried to decide what to do next. Her stomach was gnawing at her, and she suddenly realized that she could not go any farther until she fed herself. She descended the steps and turned in the direction of Jordan's Bakery.

Haley was behind the counter when she walked in, and her face lit up at the sight of Caitlin. Caitlin sat down at the one of the little round marble-topped tables and settled herself while Haley dispatched the customer she was waiting on.

'Is this a visit, or are you here to eat?' Haley called out to her friend.

'Both,' said Caitlin.

'What can I get you?'

'Coffee and a roll,' said Caitlin.

'Done,' said Haley. She busied herself behind the counter, and then emerged carrying a steaming mug and a plate with a golden brioche on it. Haley was wearing her kitchen apron which was spotted with jam and chocolate. She set the plate down on Caitlin's table, and then slipped into the seat beside her. She squeezed Caitlin's hand.

'Is there any news?'

Caitlin fussed with her coffee, realizing how difficult it was going to be to begin to reveal the connection between her brother and Emily's death. The words still stuck in her throat. Luckily, there was news, and she was glad to be able to tell it to someone who would believe her. 'Last night, Geordie called me,' she said.

'Oh, my God!' Haley cried. 'Oh, my God. Did you tell the police? Do you know where he was calling from?'

Caitlin held up a hand to stem the flow of questions. 'Yes, I told the police right away. It was the briefest of calls. He couldn't tell me anything. And then the call ended. But it was Geordie.'

'Thank God,' said Haley. 'Oh, I've got to call Dan. He'll be over the moon.'

'Don't call anybody just yet,' Caitlin said. 'I'm not sure how the police want to handle this. Apparently it was a throwaway phone.' She decided not to mention that the phone was purchased in Chicago. She wasn't sure what the police considered public knowledge and what was confidential.

'Oh, no,' said Haley. 'Damn.'

Caitlin broke off some of the brioche and ate it, and washed it down with Haley's vanilla-scented coffee. 'He's alive, Haley. That's what I have to hold on to.'

'You're right. That's what's important. Someone should really tell the Bergens. They're desperate for news.'

'Noah may have already called them,' said Caitlin.

'Where is Noah?'

Caitlin pressed her lips together, trying to force a smile. 'I'm not sure. We've had a…parting of the ways.'

Haley gaped at her in disbelief. 'The two of you…? I don't believe it.'

Caitlin nodded. 'We're under a lot of stress.'

'It's hard not to fight, I'm sure.'

Caitlin left it at that. 'I've moved back into my parents' house for the time being. It's still on the market so it was empty…'

'That must be depressing,' Haley observed.

'Oh, that doesn't begin to describe it,' said Caitlin.

'I'll bet,' said Haley.

'So, I think I'm going to drive out and see the Eckharts myself. I…need to talk to them, anyway.'

Haley seemed to find this perfectly natural. 'I want to send them some apple cake. Westy loves my apple cake. Will you bring it out there to them?'

'With pleasure,' said Caitlin.

Haley nodded and got up. 'I'll be right back with it,' she said.

That's what I have to do next, Caitlin thought. *Just get it over with.* Whether or not there was a criminal case against her, Caitlin thought, she couldn't escape her moral responsibility. She had known the circumstances of Emily's death all this time. It was up to her to tell Emily's parents and her brother the truth, and ask for their forgiveness. Telling Dan would require a trip to Philly. She would start with Westy and Paula. They would be the worst, after Noah. Maybe even worse than Noah, she thought. Now that she had learned, because of Geordie, how it felt to be a mother, she understood that there could be no greater loss than the loss of a child. She shuddered with the dread of what she had to say to Emily's parents. But she couldn't avoid it any longer.

Haley came back to the table with a white box tied with

twine. 'Yoo hoo,' she said. 'You look like you're miles away.'

'I am,' Caitlin admitted with a sigh.

Haley handed her the box. 'Apple cake for Westy,' she said.

'I'll deliver,' said Caitlin, getting up from her chair. She walked over to the cash register and took out her wallet.

Haley waved her off. 'No, no, put that away. You're family.'

Kind as they were meant to be, the words sounded almost ominous to Caitlin's ears. Sooner or later, she would have to tell Haley the truth as well.

THE HOUSE WHERE the Bergens lived sat on a low rise and their property sloped down to the shores of a marshy lake. At the edge of the lake was Westy's workshop, surrounded by a railing that boasted several telescopes pointed out over the water. An aluminum canoe and its paddles sat upside down on the shore. The yard was beautifully landscaped with gardens and trees and was studded with elaborate birdhouses on poles which Westy had made in that workshop. As she drove onto their property Caitlin was struck by the peaceful charm of the setting. The Bergens' house was probably built in the Colonial era, and had been carefully restored. Paula had a greenhouse out beside the main house, and everything about the place, thanks to Westy, was carefully tended and perfectly maintained.

As she pulled into the driveway, she was surprised to see Travis in the front yard, desultorily raking the leaves into piles which seemed to scatter as soon as he collected them. Caitlin got out of the car and lifted the box of apple cake off the front seat.

'Hi, Travis,' she said. 'Don't you have school?'

'Half day,' said Travis.

'Nice of you to help out with the leaves,' she said.

'She's paying me five bucks.'

'Mrs Bergen?'

'Yeah,' he said.

She's being robbed, Caitlin thought, as Travis dragged the rake through a pile of leaves he had already collected. 'I brought an apple cake,' she said. 'Maybe you could have some.'

Travis shrugged, but Caitlin could see that the burly kid was definitely interested.

Paula came to the front door and opened it. She was stylishly dressed and her hair was highlighted and cut in a fashionable coif, but there were huge dark circles under her eyes that gave evidence of how worried she was. 'Caitlin. Come in. I'm sorry. This place is a wreck. I don't get anything done all day. All I do is worry. I've been trying to work from home just in case we hear something. I can't go to the office. I just can't manage it.'

'Me neither,' said Caitlin.

Caitlin followed Paula into the house. Paula's idea of a 'wreck' was a mystery to Caitlin. The place looked pristine. The ceilings of the old house were low and there was a hearth in the living room which took up most of one wall. There were flowering plants on every windowsill, and prints and watercolors of birds decorated the walls. On the mantle were family photos. Emily, Noah and Geordie when Geordie was born. Dan and Haley's wedding. Westy and Paula on an anniversary. To look at all those smiling faces, you would never know what disaster had ensued. 'You have such a lovely house,' she said.

'Thank you, dear. Come in the kitchen. I'm making Westy his tea.'

'Haley sent this apple cake.'

'Sweet of her. But who can eat?'

'Travis seemed interested,' said Caitlin.

'Travis,' Paula said with a sigh. 'Naomi asked us to pick him up. She's out at recycling and couldn't get downtown. I don't know how she can go to work with Geordie missing. Who can concentrate?'

Caitlin nodded. 'It's impossible.'

'Naomi said I could take him straight home since Martha was there, but I thought it would do him good to rake some leaves and get a little fresh air. Not to mention the five dollars which he was most interested in earning. It's never too early to instill the work ethic in these kids.'

'She was never able to instill it in me,' Westy teased. 'She's still trying.' He wore a plaid shirt and sneakers.

Paula shook her head and rolled her eyes as she took the kettle off the stove. 'You're always working.'

Caitlin was listening to what was being said and answering, but her mind was distracted. She was trying to compose what she was going to say and wondering how in the world she was going to bring herself to say it.

Westy was seated at the kitchen table in front of a well-worn cup that said #1 Grandpa. He had the pale, doughy look of an old man and an air of befuddlement, in contrast to his wife who seemed to vibrate with energy. 'Any news of our boy?' he asked forlornly.

Caitlin looked from Westy to Paula. 'Didn't Noah call you?'

Paula shook her head. 'No. Has something happened?'

Caitlin hesitated. 'I don't know if I'm supposed to say…'

Paula pounced. 'What? What happened?'

'I don't see any reason why I shouldn't tell you. I got a phone call from Geordie last night.'

Paula let out a cry and clapped her hand over her mouth. Westy jumped up from the chair where he was sitting, almost knocking over his mug. He caught it before it slid off the table. 'My God. Is he all right? Where is he?'

'He wasn't able to tell me anything,' said Caitlin apologetically. 'We were cut off almost immediately. But it was him. The police think maybe it was a hoax, but it wasn't. It was Geordie.'

Paula turned to her husband and he held out his arms to her. They embraced for a minute. 'Thank God,' Paula whispered. 'I've hardly dared to hope…'

'Seems odd to me,' said Westy. 'Why would the kidnapper let him call in the first place?'

'The police wondered the same thing,' said Caitlin.

'Did they trace the number?' Westy asked.

Caitlin explained about the Tracfone. Paula nodded, familiar with the current technology. Westy looked somewhat confused by her explanation.

'I got the impression,' said Caitlin, 'that they should be able to pinpoint where the phone was purchased. And maybe that can lead them to Geordie.'

'Good,' said Westy, nodding. 'That's something, anyway.'

'Thank you, Caitlin. This gives us hope,' said Paula. She went over to the sink, wet a rag, and began to quickly wipe up the table where Westy had spilled his tea.

Caitlin frowned. She rubbed the damp palms of her hands on her pants and took a deep breath. 'That's not the only reason I'm here,' she said.

Paula, who had returned to the sink and was refilling the tea kettle, looked up vaguely at Caitlin.

'There's something I need to tell you both. Could I sit down?' she asked, pointing to the chair on her side of the table.

'Yes, of course,' said Paula. 'I'm making some more tea. Would you like a cup? Or something cold?'

Caitlin pulled out the chair. 'No, nothing,' she said, taking a seat. Her legs were trembling, and she did not think she could make this confession standing up.

Paula and Westy glanced at one another, and then back at Caitlin.

Caitlin covered her eyes with the palms of her hands, and then folded her hands in her lap. Paula and Westy's fluffy gray house cat sidled up to Caitlin and rubbed his fur on her pants leg. Caitlin looked down at the cat, wishing she could change her mind. *Say it was nothing. Get up and leave.* But Noah was bound to tell them sooner or later. She was surprised he had not told them already. *Just spit it out,* she thought.

'I want to say, first, that you two have been more than kind to me since Noah and I…got together. You never made me feel like you resented me or anything.'

'Well, Emily would have wanted Noah and Geordie to have someone,' said Westy. 'We knew that.'

'Thank you,' Caitlin whispered. 'That's what makes this all so difficult. Your kindness. Your understanding.'

'Makes what so difficult?' Paula asked, frowning.

Caitlin took a deep breath. She realized that this was a before and after moment. After this moment, Emily's parents would never look at her the same way. Would never treat her with that same kind acceptance. But she had no choice. She had to go forward. She sighed. 'Do you remember…Noah and I met that day that you all planted the garden in Emily's memory at the hospital.'

'Is that when you two met?' Paula asked, frowning. 'I was never clear on that.'

'Yes,' said Caitlin. 'We met that day. I came to that planting of the garden for one reason.'

They were both watching her, but they did not speak.

'I came that day intending to tell you something. But I…lost my nerve.'

Paula's eyes were suddenly filled with apprehension.

'Tell us what?' Westy asked.

'This is so difficult,' Caitlin said.

They stared at her, waiting.

'You see, I knew what happened…to Emily. I knew about Emily's accident.'

'Everyone knew,' said Paula. 'It was all over the news.'

'That's not what I mean,' said Caitlin.

'What do you mean?' Westy asked impatiently.

Caitlin took a deep breath. 'The person who hit Emily with his car—truck, actually…was my brother.'

For a moment, the room was silent.

'Your brother,' said Westy.

'My younger brother, James. He was sixteen. Driving without a license. He panicked. And he ran.'

She glanced up at Emily's parents. Their eyes were wide with horror. It was as if they were watching the accident occur all over again.

'He admitted it to me,' said Caitlin. 'He admitted that he killed Emily. Not at first. At first he just said he had an accident. But then, finally, he told me.'

'Where is that kid now?' Westy growled, and Caitlin had the distinct impression that the mild-mannered Westy was ready to get up and go after him that minute. At least that would not be necessary.

'Was that your brother that died?' Paula asked, dimly remembering this fact about Caitlin's family.

'Yes. James. He died of a drug overdose a few days after the accident. I don't think he could live with the guilt. And I told him that we were going to the police and he was just going to have to suffer the consequences for what he had done.' She looked at her hands in her lap. She could not bear to look them in the eye. 'I should have told you long ago. I should have told Noah. But…I didn't. And now, it's come out and Noah doesn't want anything to do with me. He's furious with me. As I'm sure you are. But I still wanted to be the one to tell you. Too late, of course. But I am doing what I should have done long ago. I'm going to tell Dan, too. I owe all of you that much.'

'You owe us a lot more than that,' said Westy, glowering.

Paula shook her head, and put a hand on his arm. 'Don't,' she said.

'If I could change it,' Caitlin said, 'believe me, I would.'

'No one can change it,' said Paula. She stood up. 'I… think my husband and I need to be alone. If you wouldn't mind leaving, Caitlin…'

Caitlin stood up stiffly. 'Of course. I'm just…so sorry.'

A door banged and Travis trudged into the room. 'I'm finished with those leaves,' he announced. He glanced at the bakery box still unopened on the counter. 'Is that the cake?' he asked.

'Not now, Travis,' said Caitlin.

'Why not?' he asked.

Paula and Westy did not seem to hear him. They were grasping one another's hands, their backs turned on Caitlin and the boy.

'Why don't I take you home?' said Caitlin. She looked at the older couple. 'If it's all right with the Bergens.'

'That might be best,' said Paula stiffly. 'Under the circumstances.'

Travis looked angrily at the cake box and then down at his sneakers. 'I was supposed to get paid,' he said.

'I'll pay you,' said Caitlin. 'Come on.'

FOURTEEN

WHEN THEY WERE seated in the car, Caitlin took her wallet out of her purse and handed Travis five dollars. 'For the leaves,' she said.

'Your hands are shaking,' he said.

'I'm upset, Travis, OK?' said Caitlin.

Travis shrugged and jammed the five dollars in his pants pocket. Then he leaned against the car door and pressed his face to the window, looking out. 'Let's just go,' he said. 'I hate their stupid leaves.'

Caitlin turned on the engine. 'Don't be so nasty, Travis. It didn't kill you to rake a couple of leaves.'

'A couple!' he protested. Then he sighed and shook his head. 'What do you know about it?'

'I know that the Bergens are very good to you. You could try a little harder to be nice.'

'I won't,' he insisted. 'I hate coming here.'

'Why?' Caitlin asked.

'It's boring.'

'Boring?' said Caitlin doubtfully.

'They're old and they smell.'

Caitlin counted to ten. 'You know, Travis, we all have a lot on our minds these days. Geordie is still missing for one thing. So, just zip it. No one wants to hear how tough it is raking a few leaves.'

Travis muttered something under his breath.

'What?' Caitlin asked.

'Nothing,' he said sullenly.

Caitlin shook her head. She turned on the car radio.

'I don't want to listen to this music. It's stupid,' he said.

'Tough,' said Caitlin, turning up the volume. They rode the rest of the way to Naomi's house with Caitlin listening to a classical music station.

Naomi, Travis and Martha lived in an area of Hartwell in which many residents had been hit hard by the economic downturn. At the corner of Naomi's street was a little store which had once been a deli. The deli sign still hung crookedly from the low eaves but the display windows were boarded up, giving the entrance to the street a look of hopelessness. There were 'For Sale' signs outside of several homes on the street, and there were a couple of empty houses where foreclosure had obviously already taken place.

Travis jumped out the car the minute they pulled in the driveway. Caitlin wanted to just leave, but she knew that would be irresponsible. Naomi's Volvo was not in the driveway. She needed to make sure that Martha was there so that Travis would not be in the house alone. She couldn't take a chance.

She followed Travis to the door. Naomi's house was about the size of her parents' house, covered in asbestos shingles on which the paint had faded. Many of the shingles were cracked or broken, so the house looked neglected. The yard was untended, and the windows were grimy, as if they hadn't been washed in years. Travis barreled into the house, letting the screen door slam in Caitlin's face. She could hear Champ inside, barking deliriously at the sight of his master. Caitlin had half a mind to chase after Travis and demand an apology. Instead, she let him go. She came into the living room, which was dark. She could hear the television blaring in another room.

'Martha? Naomi?' she called out.

Just then she heard Martha calling out, 'Travis, is that you? What in the world are you doing?'

Travis mumbled something and then there was sound of breaking glass and then a door slammed. 'Travis!' Martha cried. Caitlin followed the commotion.

Martha was standing in the kitchen door looking in the general direction of the refrigerator. 'Travis,' she demanded, but Travis was not in the room. On the floor was a broken bottle, the contents of which were spreading across the dingy tiles. Caitlin did not want to alarm Noah's mother by coming up on her from behind.

'Martha, it's Caitlin,' she said, announcing herself. 'I just brought Travis home from the Bergens. Paula picked him up from school.'

'I know. She called me,' said Martha.

'Don't move, Martha,' said Caitlin. 'You'll cut yourself. There's glass everywhere on the floor.'

'Travis,' Martha said, shaking her head. 'Where did he get to? He dropped that bottle and just left it there.'

'He must have gone out back. Let me look,' said Caitlin. She tiptoed around the mess and looked out the window of the back door. Travis was sitting on a low, crumbling stone wall, jamming cookies into his mouth. He fed an occasional cookie to Champ, who waited, panting, at his feet. Caitlin opened the door. 'Travis, you left a mess in here.'

'No, I didn't,' he said. 'Grandma did it. She's always dropping things.'

'Travis…' Caitlin knew he was lying, but she was not about to get into an argument with him. 'You can stay outside, but don't leave that yard. You hear me?'

Travis glared at her but did not reply.

Caitlin closed the door. 'He's sitting out there eating cookies with Champ,' said Caitlin.

Martha shook her head. 'He's always eating junk. Then he complains because the other kids call him fat.'

'Let me clean this up,' said Caitlin.

'There's a dustpan and a mop in the pantry,' said Martha. 'I'm sorry about this. I must have startled him when I hollered at him and the bottle slipped.'

Caitlin didn't think that was any excuse for Travis to leave the broken bottle on the floor and flee outside with his snack, but she figured it was not her place to scold him. If his grandmother wasn't going to do it… She went into the pantry and found the mop. She wet it in the sink and started to mop up the glass and sticky liquid on the floor.

'What did he break?' Martha asked.

'I think it's Kool-Aid or punch or something,' said Caitlin. 'It's purple.'

Martha groped around for the back of a kitchen chair and then pulled it out and sat down. 'I'm sorry. I'm no help, Caitlin,' she said.

'That's all right,' said Caitlin. 'No problem.'

'He's just such a handful, that boy,' said Martha. 'He leaves a mess wherever he goes.'

'Boys are like that,' said Caitlin, non-committal.

'Oh, you're just being nice. He's a terror these days. You know, he was such a sweet boy when he was little. Just like Geordie. Have you had any news? I'm so worried. I don't sleep.'

Caitlin squeezed the mop and rinsed it again. 'Actually, there is news. Geordie called me last night.'

'No! What do you mean? On the phone?'

'Yes. On my cell phone. Just for a minute. It was over before I even realized what was happening. But it was Geordie.'

'Oh, my goodness. That's wonderful,' said Martha. 'That means whoever took him didn't…hurt him.'

'He didn't exactly say that, but he sounded OK.'

'That's the best news,' said Martha, her face alight. 'This is part of the problem with Travis. He doesn't say so, but I know he's worried about Geordie, too.'

Caitlin had her doubts, but she didn't express them directly. 'You think that's why he behaves the way he does?' She had mopped up the liquid and now she retrieved the dust pan and began to gather up the glass. 'Because of Geordie?'

Martha waved a hand dismissively. 'Well, not just because of Geordie. He's been like this for a long time. And my daughter is overprotective of him, which doesn't help matters.'

'Overprotective?' Caitlin said doubtfully. Overindulgent, more like it, she thought. Naomi never seemed to notice or correct Travis's bad behavior.

'Like, after Rod died,' said Martha, 'she kept him away from the other kids. If she caught them playing cops or cowboys or soldiers—the way boys do—Naomi would just freak out. Guns were what killed her husband, and she wasn't having it with Travis. So he ended up spending a lot of time alone.

'Of course I started losing my eyesight around the same time, so I wasn't much help to him or Naomi.'

Caitlin had never really had such a personal discussion with Martha before. She was not about to interrupt the flow by explaining her rift with Noah. It would wait. Naomi and Martha would hear about it soon enough. 'That's frustrating, I'm sure,' said Caitlin.

'It truly is,' said Martha. 'And then Emily's passing. Actually, I think that was the last straw for Travis. He seemed to get much worse after Emily died. And now Geordie disappearing like this.'

'It's a heavy load,' Caitlin agreed quietly.

'It's hard enough for us grown-ups with Geordie being gone, and not knowing where he is, or what's become of him. But if Geordie doesn't come home…'

'Don't say that!' Caitlin exclaimed. 'He will.'

'You're right. I'm sorry. I have to stay positive. Especially for Travis.' Her voice faded away and she pressed her lips together. 'They're more than cousins to one another. They're like brothers.'

Brothers? Caitlin thought. She always had the feeling that Travis detested Geordie and was jealous of him at the same time. But she couldn't blame Martha for wanting to cast the relationship between her two grandsons in the best possible light. And who knows, Caitlin thought, perhaps, deep down inside, Travis really was worried about Geordie. It had to be scary for him to have Geordie disappear like that. Despite his hefty appearance and his hostile attitude, he was still a child.

Caitlin put the chunks and shards of glass into a heavy plastic bag before depositing it into the prominently displayed recycling can. 'Nothing's going to happen to Geordie. You mark my words. Geordie is coming back to us,' said Caitlin. 'He has to.'

Martha nodded. 'I pray that you're right, dear,' she said. 'I pray that you're right.'

FIFTEEN

CAITLIN STOOD AT the front door of the house she had shared with Noah and Geordie for two years. She hesitated. She assumed that she was probably legally entitled to open the door and walk in but, finally, she decided to knock. She did not have long to wait.

Noah opened the door. He was pale and unshaven and his clothes were rumpled. The circles under his eyes looked like smudges of charcoal. He looked at her balefully, but he did not speak.

'Noah,' she said, when it became clear that she would have to speak first. 'Is there any news? Did they figure out where the phone was purchased?'

His eyes were glassy. He shook his head.

'I was hoping,' she said.

Noah sighed. 'Apparently the detectives in Chicago are trying to narrow it down. But there are a lot of convenience stores in a city that size.'

'Still, it's something,' she said hopefully.

He studied her face for a moment. Then he said, 'Do you want to come in?'

'Just for a minute,' she said.

He stood aside and she walked into the house. The living room was a mess and the house smelled stale. On the couch was a pillow and a balled-up blanket. There were empty coffee cups and a couple of food containers on the coffee table. He noticed her puzzled gaze. 'I guess I've set up camp in here,' he said. 'I don't sleep much, anyway. Have a seat.' He pointed to a chair.

Caitlin sat down on the edge of the seat cushion. Noah flopped back down on the couch. He ran a hand through his wavy, unwashed hair. 'So?' he asked.

Caitlin took a deep breath. She had not come to make small talk. She knew him well enough to know that he would not tolerate it. 'I came over to…ask if there was any news, of course. But also, I need to get Dan's address from you.'

'Emily's brother, Dan?' he asked.

Caitlin nodded. 'I've already been to the Bergens. By the way, thank you for not telling them about my brother. I wanted to tell them myself.'

'Sure. I wouldn't want to spoil your fun,' he said.

Caitlin's temper flared and she frowned, but she did not rise to the bait.

'Sorry,' he said immediately.

Caitlin nodded.

'How did they take it?'

'Not well. As you can imagine,' she said. 'Now I need to go and talk to Dan.'

'They've probably already called him,' said Noah.

'Nonetheless,' said Caitlin, 'I owe him that much.'

Noah rubbed his face with both hands. 'OK. I'll get it for you,' he said.

She waited while he disappeared into the kitchen. While he was gone she looked around the living room. So, this was where he was sleeping. She thought about their bedroom, where she had known the most happiness and comfort of her life wrapped in Noah's arms, Geordie asleep in the room next door. She couldn't help feeling a little bit… satisfied that he did not want to sleep in there now that she was gone. Instead, he slept here, under the watchful eyes of all his loved ones.

Around the living room there were lots of framed pictures, including one from last summer at the beach. The beach was Geordie's absolute favorite place in the world. Any beach on any ocean. She would tease him and say that he was part fish. He could spend all day in the sun and the sea. On this particular beach day, they had asked someone from a neighboring blanket to take a picture of the three of them. They were all three tanned and laughing, their wet hair plastered to their heads after a swim. It hurt her heart to look at that picture, but at the same time she felt a little bit grateful that Noah had not removed it, or hidden it away.

She picked up the frame and stared at Geordie's little face, his skinny torso, his gap-toothed smile. *I would give anything to have you back,* she thought. She knew it was not an exaggeration. Anything. Anything she had, and gladly.

She heard Noah coming back and set the photo back down on the table. She didn't want him to see her looking at it. He might think she was being manipulative.

There was no use pretending that she didn't care what he thought. She did.

Noah came through the living room and held out a piece of paper. 'Here you go,' he said.

Caitlin stood up and accepted it from him without touching his fingertips.

Noah cleared his throat.

'Noah, I wish…' She started to speak and then she thought better of it. 'I hope you can get some rest.'

'Yeah, it's a nice idea,' he said.

BY THE TIME she arrived in Philadelphia, all the schools were out and children were laughing, shrieking, and running down the leafy streets of Society Hill. Many of the tow-headed children were accompanied by casually dressed young African, Hispanic or Middle European women. As they ambled down the well-appointed blocks of Colonial-era brick homes, they spoke to one another in foreign tongues or heavily accented English while the children gamboled around them in their khaki and plaid school uniforms.

Caitlin drove slowly. She did not really know her way around the neighborhood and she was wary of the exuberant children who were darting out into the streets, chasing one another. Also, she had only visited Dan's house once, and that was at night. To find the house, she needed to search along Spruce Street by the brass numbers above the doors. She finally located Dan's house number and idled in front of the building for a moment. It was red brick like its neighbors, with black shutters and window-boxes filled with winter pansies, the epitome of Philadelphia tradition and elegance.

All right, she thought. *This is it.* She trolled the block for a parking space. In the middle of the next block she stopped to consider her chances of fitting her car into an economy-sized space. But she was not in the habit of parallel parking, and finally decided that she was unlikely to be able to wedge her car into it. She drove around the block again and then, to her surprise and relief, she found a space near the corner, almost across from his door, which she could easily pull into. Once parked, she sat there for a few minutes, gazing across the street at his elegant house.

No one seeing that house could doubt Dan's success, and in the arena of sports, which made his career doubly enviable to most men. He had excelled in athletics and in Spanish and, during journalism school, decided to explore the reasons why professional baseball had so many Hispanic superstars for his thesis. This had entailed landing a grant for a summer-long research trip to Puerto Rico, where he stayed with a local family and surfed in his spare time—a coup which Noah never failed to describe with admiration as every guy's dream. But Dan's thesis, which focused on one young Sandlot player, ultimately resulted in that young man, Ricardo Ortiz, landing a contract with the Padres, where he had a stellar career. Ortiz was now a batting coach for the Cubs, and Dan was still regarded in sports circles as something of a guru.

She realized that he might not be home. His schedule, between the radio station and his web sports blog, was famously erratic and revolved around the schedules of various Philadelphia teams. But she was willing to wait. She was here now, and it had taken all her will to get here. She intended to get it over with. Perhaps, like his parents, Dan wouldn't want to discuss it, but at least she would get it said. She needed to admit her guilt for concealing James's crime, and hope for some eventual understanding.

Caitlin took a deep breath, got out of her car and started down the block towards Dan's house. Just as she did so, another car rolled past her, and the driver jockeyed the car into the space in the next block which Caitlin had dismissed as too small. She recognized the car right away. *Well,* she thought, *no more hesitating. Time to face the music.* While Dan maneuvered into the tiny space, Caitlin approached his car from behind on the sidewalk.

He turned off the lights, got out of the car and locked the doors.

'Dan,' said Caitlin.

Dan jumped and looked up at her. He was a large, handsome man with the frame of a pro-athlete himself. Normally, Dan greeted Caitlin with a twinkle in his eye and the utmost affability. But today, at the sight of her, a thundercloud seemed to roll over his rugged features.

'What do you want?' he demanded.

He already knows, she thought. 'Dan, there's something I need to talk to you about,' she said.

Dan slung an expensive-looking backpack over his right shoulder. 'I don't think we have anything to say to each other,' he said.

Caitlin nodded. 'You've talked to your parents.'

'They called me at work,' he said.

Caitlin looked down at her feet. 'I thought they might,' she said. 'But I came anyway. Look, I just wanted to tell you in person how sorry I am.'

'Sorry won't bring my sister back,' he said coldly.

'I understand how you feel,' she said. 'I really do. All I can say is that my brother was a kid with…a lot of problems.'

Dan jabbed a finger at her. 'No. Your brother was a criminal. Try and understand the distinction.'

Caitlin gasped, a little taken aback by the ferocity of his reaction. 'Dan, he took his own life. I think that proves that he suffered from a lot of guilt about what happened to Emily.'

Dan shook his head. 'You know what, Caitlin? You're just kidding yourself. Everybody's got an excuse. I'm tired of excuses.'

'He was a kid. Sixteen. Yes, he did something terrible but…'

'I don't want to hear it. I am up to here with all of it,' Dan cried, slashing his hand across his neck. 'Boo hoo. He had his reasons. Just…beat it. Get away from me. I don't want to talk to you. I don't want to see you. Just go.'

Before he had even finished speaking, he stepped out into the street. There was a screech of brakes as an oncoming car tried to avoid hitting him. Dan did not even look up. He strode across the street toward his house.

Caitlin stood beside his car, too stunned to react. She knew Dan as the most friendly, even-tempered of people. She had expected him to be…upset. She had not anticipated his rage. For a moment she thought about his marriage to Haley, and wondered if that anger was the reason it had come undone. Well, she reminded herself, he was entitled to his anger. She was the one in the wrong. If he felt that strongly she could not blame him.

Caitlin collapsed against Dan's car, resting for a moment against the shiny hood. She glanced through the windshield and smiled at the pair of miniature boxing gloves which dangled from the rear-view mirror. She thought about Geordie, and how much he liked those gloves. Whenever Uncle Dan came to visit, Geordie loved to climb into the front seat of Dan's car. The gloves were just the right size for Bandit's paws. Using Bandit as his surrogate, Geordie would ping the gloves so that they twirled, feinting against the air.

Dan had not even asked about Geordie, Caitlin thought. He had not even mentioned Geordie to her. Maybe, like everyone else, he thought her status as a stepmother disqualified her from feeling love and fear. *Let him think what he wants,* she thought. Geordie knew. Geordie could have called anyone, and he called her. She looked in again at those miniature boxing gloves, wishing she could see him, eyes alight behind his glasses, using Bandit to set those gloves in motion.

Suddenly, she frowned. Past the gloves and the dashboard, past the steering wheel and the gear shift between the seats, she saw something that did not belong in Dan's car. She squeezed her eyes shut and then opened them again. *No,* she thought. *You are thinking so hard about Geordie that you are imagining things.* The interior of the car was dark. It had to be a trick of the light. She looked again. Harder. Wedged between the passenger seat and the console, she saw a black button nose. A furry, masked face. One ear hanging down that needed sewing. Bandit.

SIXTEEN

HER HEART HAMMERING, Caitlin flattened her face and hands against the windshield. The inside of the car was dark and she could not be sure. She banged the palms of her hands against the glass as if she was trying to rouse the little dog from his inanimate status to that of an actual barking pup. She was no Gepetto, she thought. The button eyes did not register her alarm.

Caitlin covered her face with her hands and tried to think. How could it be Bandit? How could Bandit be in Dan Bergen's car? She tried to think back. Had Geordie taken Bandit to school in his backpack the day he disappeared? He wasn't supposed to take him to school, but he could have hidden the toy in his pack. He had been known to do it. The last time she could remember seeing Bandit was…the day of the party. She had asked Geordie to put Bandit in her room, so she could sew that dangling ear back on. He had run off to do that, and…that was all she could remember. She didn't remember seeing, or not seeing, the toy on her bureau after that. In all the hub-bub she had forgotten all about it. She knew that she had not sewn the ear back on. And then, Geordie had disappeared. Any thought of Bandit had been obliterated by Geordie's absence.

Stop, she thought. *It might not even be Bandit. You can't really see what's in there.* For a moment she was tempted to march over to Dan's house, bang on the door and demand to know why he had Geordie's toy dog in his car. And then she remembered why she had come here. She had come to confess her own guilty secret. Dan would not react kindly to any demand from her. He would probably call the police to come and arrest her.

And even if it was Bandit, what did she think it meant? That Dan had taken Geordie? Dan was a fond uncle who could see Geordie any time he wanted. Why would Dan ever put them through this kind of suffering? To what end? Besides, Dan had just come home from being at work all day. He had come home alone. Even a bachelor would know better than to leave a six-year-old alone. And if Geordie was alone, wouldn't he find the phone and call them? He had called once. What would stop him? No, she thought. No. She told herself that she was just getting crazy from all the anxiety and the waiting and the fear. But then Caitlin turned back to the windshield, flattened herself against it, and stared into the car again. She had to know. That was all there was to it. She had to find out. She tried the door handles on the car, but without much hope. It was the city. People didn't leave their cars unlocked.

She stepped away from the car, leaned against the front steps of the nearest house and tried to think. In the old days you heard of people using coat hangers to unlock a car door, but this was a late model Lexus. It was not going to open with the help of a bent hanger. Plus, if a cop saw her trying to do that, he would probably arrest her first and ask questions later.

Cops, she thought. She could ask a cop to help her. Claim that it was her car and she had locked her purse inside. Somehow, she couldn't picture it. A Philly cop agreeably popping the lock on a late model car, just on her say so. No. It would never work.

She pushed away from the steps and returned to the parked car, rattling the handle in frustration. Behind her, she heard a door open. A young man in a spandex running shorts and top came down the steps and began to stretch his legs, using the railing of the stairs to pull against his weight. He glanced over at Caitlin.

'Locked out?' he asked pleasantly.

Caitlin nodded.

The young man grimaced. 'That sucks,' he said amiably.

Caitlin sighed. 'Yeah. I locked the keys inside.'

'Do you have AAA?' he asked.

Caitlin looked at him in surprise. 'Yes, as a matter of fact.'

'Call them,' he said. 'They'll come and open it for you.'

Caitlin hesitated. 'Oh, I don't think so. It's…not even my car.'

'It's not?' the young man asked.

Caitlin hesitated. 'It's my brother-in-law's car. I borrowed it.'

'Oh. I don't think they care about that. As long as you're a member.' He bent down and touched his toes several times. Then he leaned back, reaching behind him. Finally, he straightened up and shook out his legs, one at a time.

'Really?' she said.

'I'm not sure. But you can try.'

She reached in her bag for her phone. 'I think I will. Thanks.'

'Good luck with it,' he said, waving. He took off at a loping jog across the street and down the sun-dappled street, veering out around a young Hispanic woman walking in the opposite direction, holding the hand of a boy in a Phillies baseball cap.

Caitlin called information, got connected and prayed that she could sound calm and reasonable as she explained her problem. The guy she reached at a local garage was indifferent. He asked for her name, her membership information and her location. He told her his man would be over in fifteen minutes.

HE ARRIVED IN less than ten. He double parked his tow truck and hopped out of the cab, a burly bald guy with a beard. Caitlin did not have to try too hard to appear confused and helpless. The guy gave her a clipboard with some paperwork to sign and asked to see her license. He didn't even ask her if it was her car. The traffic on Spruce Street was having difficulty going around him, and motorists were honking and complaining loudly as they passed by. Caitlin could tell that he wanted to get out of there. He took out a simple tool and popped the lock.

'Oh, thank you,' said Caitlin. 'You're a lifesaver.' She had put her own keys in her pocket before he arrived. She leaned into the front seat of the car and made a search of the floor, lifting the floor mats. He watched both her and the traffic which was going out around him. Then she leaned over the console and felt around the back of the passenger seat. As she did so, she pulled the toy out from between the passenger seat and the console and put it under her own arm. Exclaiming with relief, she came up with her keys.

'Thank God,' she said, emerging from the car. She dangled the keys for a moment in his face. 'And I got my daughter's pup,' she said, indicating the toy under her arm. 'I guess she left him in here. She's gonna be glad to see you,' she said, addressing Bandit. 'Thank you so much,' she said to the man from the service station. She slipped him a twenty. 'You really saved my butt.'

'No problem,' he said. He jumped back into the cab of

his truck, checked the traffic moving toward them and then found his moment to pull away from the curb.

Caitlin closed all the car doors and stood back, aiming her keys at the car as if to lock the doors. Of course, since she was wielding keys from her own car, Dan's car remained unlocked. Anyone could come along and steal it. Caitlin didn't really care. She clutched Bandit and walked down the block toward her own vehicle, her heart pounding in her ears.

When she got to her car, she opened the doors and slipped into the driver's seat, though she made no move to turn on the engine. She held the stuffed animal to her face and inhaled its familiar scent. Geordie.

Now what? she thought. Her options, when she thought about them, were not great. Part of her wanted to call the police and insist that they storm Dan's house to look for Geordie, but she knew that as a plan that was almost laughable. She had nothing to offer the cops as a reason except for a stuffed animal which she had obtained by illegally entering Dan's car. And it was not as if Geordie had never been in his uncle's car with Bandit. It was those miniature boxing gloves hanging from the mirror which had made her look more closely into the car in the first place. For all she knew, Geordie might have gotten into the car at some point during his birthday party. Dan wouldn't have locked the car in their driveway. Geordie might have climbed in, Bandit under his arm, to play with the dangling gloves, then rejoined the party excitement, leaving the pup in Dan's car. Now that she thought about it, that explanation made a lot more sense than the notion that Dan might have been the one who abducted Geordie.

She took her phone out of her pocketbook and thought about calling Noah. Asking him if he remembered the last time he had seen Bandit in the house. But her heart sank at the thought of Noah's reaction to her question. He would insist on an explanation, be furious at the thought that she had gone to Dan to apologize, and now was trying to implicate him somehow in Geordie's disappearance. *No, you can't call Noah,* she thought.

She held Bandit close and stared at the well-kept house across the street. She tried to imagine the worst about Dan, but it was impossible. As an uncle he was…dutiful. That was the word. He never forgot a birthday or a holiday, and he was fond of Geordie, almost in spite of the fact that Geordie was a kid. She remembered Haley saying that he didn't like kids and wasn't interested in having any of his own. It had been a sore point between them in their marriage. Caitlin tried to picture Dan as some kind of monster with a secret, grasping side, but it was an image that would not come into focus, no matter how she tried.

No. All that was left for her was to go home. Forget about it and go home. Geordie had left Bandit in Dan's car during the party. That was the only possibility that made sense. *Go home,* she thought.

She looked across the street again. She couldn't go home. Whether it made sense or not, she knew she couldn't leave. Not without going over to Dan's house and asking him to explain. If there was even the ghost of a chance that Geordie was in there, she had to pursue it. She hesitated for a moment, wondering what Dan might think of her, and what he might say to Noah about her. Then she shook her head.

She didn't care what Dan thought of her. Or Noah. Or anybody else. In the long run it didn't matter. Nothing else mattered. All that mattered was Geordie.

She got out of the car, still clutching Bandit, locked the

doors and, looking out for the oncoming traffic, walked across the street to Dan's house. Squeezing her hands into fists, she hesitated for a moment, and then she knocked on the door.

SEVENTEEN

DAN, WEARING READING glasses and holding a bottle of beer, looked at her in disbelief. 'Are you still here? What do you want?' he said.

'I want to come in,' said Caitlin.

'I'm busy,' said Dan. 'I'm working.'

'I don't care,' she said. 'I need to talk to you.'

'Caitlin, we have nothing else to say to one another. I've said everything I'm going to about this. You betrayed all of us. I hear that Noah kicked you out. I wasn't sorry to hear it.'

'This is about Geordie,' she said.

Dan blanched. 'What about him?'

'First, let me in,' she said.

Dan looked away from her, as if considering her request. Finally, he opened the door a little more. 'All right. Come in.'

Caitlin followed him into the vestibule and then into the living room. It was a living room with a masculine look. All the furniture was chrome, glass and leather, but the sleekness of the decor was counterbalanced by the piles of magazines and newspapers, along with a clutter of unwashed plates and coffee mugs on various surfaces. A general air of disarray pervaded the place.

Caitlin looked around for a place to sit. Dan shook his head.

'Whoa. I didn't tell you to make yourself comfortable,' he said. 'What about Geordie?'

Caitlin pulled Bandit out of her satchel and held him up by the neck. 'This was in your car,' she said.

Dan's eyes widened. 'What the... What are you...?'

'This is Geordie's favorite toy. I found it wedged between the console and the passenger seat in your car.'

'Well, how did you get it? What the hell were you doing in my car? Did you... If you fucked with my car...'

She noticed that there were beads of sweat along his hairline. It was warm in the house, but not stifling. She thought he looked pale as well. Of course, it could be from anxiety about his expensive car. 'Never mind how I got it. I want to know what it was doing in there.'

'I don't know,' he cried. 'How do I know? Maybe... I don't know.'

A calm feeling had come over her at the sight of his anxiety. 'Is Geordie with you?' she said.

'With me?' He slammed the beer bottle down on the glass-topped computer desk. 'You crazy bitch. What are you... Get out of my house.'

'Just answer me,' she said. 'Is he here?'

'What are you accusing me of...?' he demanded.

'I want to know how Bandit got into your car.'

'I don't have to explain anything to you.'

'Yes, you do. I'm Geordie's...mother.'

'Oh, that's gall,' he said. 'Listen, lady. My sister was Geordie's mother. That is, until your brother ran her over in his car.'

Caitlin closed her eyes for a moment and sighed. 'Dan,' she said, 'you can't make me feel any worse than I already do about Emily's death. That's why I came here today. To try to explain to you... But then I saw Bandit in your car. Now, you have something to explain to me.'

'Let me make sure I understand this,' said Dan. 'Somehow you broke into my car. And now you're accusing me…'

'Stop,' Caitlin pleaded. 'Stop with the righteous anger. Just tell the truth. Don't you care about Geordie?'

Dan stared at her. 'Of course I do.'

'Is he here? Is he here in your house?' she asked.

'No,' he said. 'Certainly not.'

'Can I see for myself…?' she asked.

'You know, I'm beginning to think the stress is getting to you. Are you…all right?'

Caitlin brandished the raggedy pup. 'This stuffed animal was in your car. How is that possible?'

Dan shook his head. 'Look, I don't know, Caitlin. Maybe…on his birthday. That was the last time I saw Geordie. Maybe he was playing in my car. He loves my car. He likes those boxing gloves I have.'

Caitlin's shoulders slumped.

'Maybe he climbed in to play around…and he left it there. I'm sorry. I can't think of any other way…'

'Why didn't you notice it?' she demanded.

Dan looked around at the mess in his living room with a sigh. 'I don't know. I don't sit in the passenger seat. Besides, with me, everything is not in its place,' he admitted.

'Can I look for myself…?' she asked.

'What?' he asked.

'In your house. Can I look?'

Dan shook his head. 'No. Now I've had enough. You cannot roam through my house.'

'Why not?' she demanded.

'Because I want you gone. This is completely nuts. Why would I take Geordie? How could you even think…'

Caitlin slipped past him and started up the staircase, screaming. 'Geordie, are you here? Answer me. It's Mom.'

The house was silent. She climbed a few more steps

and looked up at the second-floor landing. 'Geordie, don't be afraid. Answer me,' she cried. There was no response.

'Geordie!'

'You can scream till you're blue in the face,' said Dan in a steely tone, opening the front door again. 'Nobody's going to answer.'

Caitlin sighed and descended the stairs. Without looking at Dan, she walked out onto the front step. She could feel his gaze on her. She looked back at Dan. He was studying her with an expression she could not define in his eyes.

'What?' she demanded.

Dan shook his head. 'You really do love that kid,' he said.

Caitlin's chin trembled, and tears rose to her eyes. 'Don't sound so shocked.'

'You never know,' he said.

'You'd know if you paid attention,' she said angrily.

Dan pointed a finger at her. 'Watch it, Caitlin. You're lucky I didn't call the police on you. If there's any damage to my car...'

'I used to like you,' she said, shaking her head. 'I used to think you were a good guy.'

'Chill out,' he said. Then he closed the door in her face.

CAITLIN CALLED HALEY before she left the city and Haley met her at a bistro in Hartwell. They each had a hamburger and a glass of wine, and then mounted the steps in the Jordan Bakery building to the apartment on the second floor. Haley had wisely bought the building at a favorable price when she decided to open. Noah had helped her to negotiate the deal. Now, she lived on the second and third floors of the building, and her business hummed along at the street level, not subject to arbitrary raises in rent.

'Call me a bad person,' said Haley, unlocking her apartment door and ushering Caitlin inside. 'I…just don't see it. I mean, you weren't the one at the wheel. If that had been the case…'

'But, it wasn't,' said Caitlin.

'Exactly,' said Haley. 'So, you were in a terrible position. I mean, surely they can see that. I feel sure that Noah will come around.'

'I hope you're right,' said Caitlin. She accepted a second glass of wine which Haley poured from the selection of bottles on her kitchen counter. Haley poured herself a glass as well, and led the way to her comfortable sitting room which looked out over Main Street. The gaslights on the street were illuminated and their glow shifted with the rustling trees. Most of the stores on Main Street were closed except for a couple of pubs and restaurants, so there was a peaceful atmosphere in the apartment.

'Tell me more about your visit to Dan,' said Haley. 'Was the new girlfriend in her Jimmy Choos there?'

Caitlin shook her head. She had deliberately not said very much to Haley about her visit with Dan. On reflection, she was a little a bit ashamed that she had virtually accused Dan of having a part in Geordie's disappearance. From this distance, it seemed insane. And she knew that Haley would not take kindly to that suggestion.

'No, he was…definitely by himself,' said Caitlin. 'Why? Do you think this one is a keeper for Dan?'

Haley swirled her wine in her glass and frowned. 'No. Not really. Dan likes to avoid…entangling alliances, shall we say.'

'He married you, didn't he?'

Haley shrugged. 'We were high school sweethearts. When you're young like that, it's easy to…make the wrong choice.'

'Are you kidding?' said Caitlin. 'You were a prize. He was a fool to ever let you go.'

Haley chuckled. 'Oh, thanks, but...I think we both realized it was a mistake.'

'Really?' said Caitlin. She had always assumed, from Haley's lingering fondness for Dan, that he was the one who had chosen to quit the marriage.

'Well, he was adamant about not wanting kids. And, call me a cockeyed optimist, but that is still something I want to do in my life.'

'You will,' said Caitlin.

'I hope so.'

They were both quiet for a moment. Caitlin's mind returned to Bandit, stuffed in the front seat of Dan's car. 'Why didn't he want kids?' Caitlin asked.

'The usual male...ego,' said Haley. 'He wanted to do exactly what he's doing. He lives for sports. He comes and goes as he pleases. He lives a pretty...idyllic life for a man. There's really no room for kids in it. Or a wife.'

'I suppose not,' said Caitlin.

Haley raised her face and looked out the window. The gaslight from the street illuminated her soft profile. 'It's not only that. Sometimes it was just...hard to get close to him. He's very...detached. Most of the women in his life are...temporary. In fact, the night of Geordie's party, when he got so sick, he sent Jimmy Choos back to Philly on the bus.'

'You're kidding,' said Caitlin. 'He was really sick? I thought he was faking it that night so he could leave the party.'

'Oh, no, he felt wretched,' said Haley. 'He spent the night here. In the guest room. He showed up at my door and he was in such a bad way that I couldn't turn him away. I thought of taking him to the emergency room at one point. His head was killing him and he threw up until he had the dry heaves. The next day he was just pale and limp. I tried to get him to stay and rest for the day, but he had work so he headed back.'

In spite of herself, Caitlin felt a surge of anxiety at this discovery. 'So he was here in Hartwell that day. The day that Geordie was taken…'

Haley frowned. 'Well, not really. He went back to Philly as soon as he could get out of bed.'

Caitlin hesitated. 'Was he wearing an Eagles cap?' she asked, thinking of the account of the teacher's aide at Geordie's school.

'What?' Haley asked.

'Was he?'

'He may have been. I don't remember. Why would you ask me that?'

'No reason,' Caitlin said, although she had a sick feeling in the pit of her stomach. 'I'm just desperate. God, I hate the thought of going back to my parents' house. Every miserable thing that ever happened there is weighing on me the moment I walk in the door. And without Noah to turn to, I just tie myself up in knots thinking about Geordie. About what has happened to him. Where he could be…'

'You can stay here, in the guest room,' said Haley.

'You are a really good friend, you know it?' Caitlin said. 'Nobody else even wants to speak to me.'

'Noah's gonna get over this. You wait and see. He really loves you.'

'He loved Emily,' said Caitlin.

Haley nodded. 'Yes, he did.'

Caitlin wished she hadn't mentioned it. She knew it was true, but she felt as if now that Noah had thrown her out, he was waiting for Geordie's return with Emily's ghost for company. After all, Noah probably still felt closest to her. Emily was Geordie's mother. Emily, whom Caitlin's brother had left to die in the street. 'Why did it have to be Emily?' Caitlin said aloud.

Haley met her gaze sadly. 'I know,' she said.

EIGHTEEN

SAM MATHIS SAT at the kitchen table while Caitlin put on the coffee pot and took out a bag of muffins which Haley had given her before she left her house last night. She offered one to Sam.

Sam held up a hand and shook his head. 'I've eaten,' he said.

'Do you mind…?' she asked, pointing to her coffee mug.

Sam shook his head again and Caitlin poured herself some coffee and sat down with a muffin in front of her on a napkin. She began to pick at it.

'Well,' she said. 'Judging from the look on your face, this isn't good news. I know it's not about Geordie. You would have told me already.'

'True,' he said. 'We located the man that the cable TV guy saw on the street. They live in the neighborhood. His kid was sick and he came to take him home.'

Caitlin sighed.

'I'm sorry,' said Sam.

She could see the discouragement in Sam Mathis's eyes. 'I know you're doing all you can,' she said.

'That's kind of you,' he said.

'Believe me, if I thought cursing you out would bring him back,' she said grimly, 'I'd call you every name in the book.'

Sam acknowledged the truth of this with a brief smile.

Caitlin hesitated. 'I went to see Geordie's Uncle Dan yesterday in Philly. I went to apologize about Emily. But while I was there, I found Geordie's favorite toy, a stuffed dog named Bandit, in his car.'

Sam immediately straightened up. 'You're sure it was Geordie's toy?'

'Positive,' she said.

'Did you ask him about it?'

Caitlin sighed. 'I did more than that. I…entered his car and took it.'

'How did you do that?' Sam asked.

'I'd rather not say,' she said, avoiding his gaze. 'The car was not damaged, I'll say that much. Anyway, I confronted Dan with Bandit. He seemed more angry that I'd gotten into his car than anything else.'

'How did he explain having the toy?'

'Well, at first he just seemed baffled. In the end, he came to the same conclusion I did. Geordie was probably fooling around in his car at the birthday party and left Bandit there. I know that's the last time I can remember seeing him—Bandit. On Geordie's birthday.'

'Is that what you think happened?' Sam asked.

'Probably,' she admitted.

'Was it possible that Geordie had the stuffed animal with him when he was taken? In his backpack maybe?'

'We forbid him to bring Bandit to school with him. Bandit was like a…security blanket for him. And it got him that kind of negative attention. The bullies love things like that. So he knew better than to take it with him. Although I know he didn't always obey us about that,' Caitlin said.

'But to your best recollection, the last time you saw the toy was the day of the party?'

Caitlin nodded.

'We questioned Geordie's uncle, of course. I couldn't

find any reason to pursue it. Do you know of anything we might have missed? Was there reason to suspect Dan Bergen? Has he ever behaved…inappropriately toward his nephew? Anything that set off alarm bells?'

'No. Truthfully, no. I think I just went a little crazy when I saw Bandit. I insisted on coming into his house. When he tried to get me leave I started screaming for Geordie. As loud as I could. But there was nothing.'

'Well, I think I had better pay him another visit, all the same. Just to be cautious,' said Sam. 'I'll go see him today.'

'Dan's gonna be furious with me,' said Caitlin. 'I'm already his least favorite person in the world.'

'Because of Emily's…accident,' said Sam.

Caitlin nodded. 'But go ahead. I don't care what he thinks. He's always going to hate me. They all will. Because of Emily.'

Sam nodded. 'Actually, Emily's accident is what I came here about.'

Caitlin looked at him warily. 'Let's have it.'

'Your father's truck,' said Sam.

She waited, but didn't ask.

'They've gone over it very carefully. There are traces of blood, but it was too deteriorated to give us DNA. All that time out in the elements…'

'It wasn't in the elements,' Caitlin protested. 'It's been in the garage all these years.'

'The garage is hardly a controlled environment. We found evidence of squirrels, raccoons, birds. A lot of rust.'

'So what are you saying?' Caitlin asked.

'Well, we cross-checked your father's truck against the forensic evidence we found on Emily's body…'

'And…' Caitlin urged him on.

'We know that the vehicle which hit her had a very

similar paint job. We're trying to see if it can be matched exactly.'

Caitlin shook her head. 'What do you mean, "the vehicle which hit her?" I told you who hit her. It was my brother.'

Sam shrugged. 'I have no reason to doubt that what you said about your brother was…well, the truth as you perceived it…. I mean, there would be no reason for you to tell such a tale. It only reflected badly on you and was very destructive to your marriage. Obviously.'

Caitlin stared at him, waiting.

'There's something odd about that truck,' he said.

Caitlin shook her head, as if she wasn't able to make out his words.

'Maybe I will have some coffee,' he said. 'Half a cup.'

Caitlin wanted to shake him and refuse him even a sip of coffee before he explained himself, but she forced herself to remain calm. She got up, poured him the coffee and even offered cream and sugar. Then she set the mug in front of him and sat back down at the table.

'The truck…' she said.

Sam blew on the coffee and then took a sip. He frowned, as if he were trying to figure something out while he was speaking. 'I noticed this when you first showed me the truck in the garage. The guys at the lab noticed the same thing. The damage to the truck is in the center of the front bumper. I mean, it is caved in from the impact of hitting someone, or something.'

'Wait a minute, wait a minute,' said Caitlin, waving a hand as if to flag him down. 'Something? You act like there is some doubt about who was hit by that truck. I'm telling you, there is no doubt. When I heard about the hit-and-run on the news and confronted James, he admitted it. He described the woman. It was Emily. Hell, he was haunted by the thought of her eyes. Trust me. He didn't take his own life because he hit a deer.'

'I suppose not,' said Sam.

'And he was able to tell me the exact location of the accident. I'm not wrong about this, Detective.'

'I understand,' said Sam. 'I do. But the evidence contradicts that story. Emily left Geordie asleep in his car seat and came down the drive to pick up her mail. She was hit as she was standing by her mailbox at the side of the road. We know this for a fact. The mailbox was still hanging open. The mail was scattered everywhere. That means that whoever hit her veered over to the side of the road, either because they were impaired at the time or they lost control of their vehicle. Judging from where the body came to rest, they had to have collided with her with the right-hand side of their bumper. That's where the impact was. That's what should be damaged on your father's truck if that was the vehicle that hit Emily. Not the middle. The right-hand side. The passenger side.'

Caitlin put her elbows on the table and covered her mouth with her hands. Was it possible that she had been wrong? Had she hounded her brother to death for something he hadn't done? She thought about it for a moment and then dismissed it. No. He admitted it to her. She didn't put words in his mouth. He had hit a woman. Then he had driven away and left her to die in the road. It didn't matter what Sam Mathis said about the truck. That was the truth.

'In any case,' said Sam, standing up from the table, 'this is good news for you. As of right now, there will be no charges filed against you. The evidence doesn't support your version of the crime.'

Caitlin frowned at him. 'You're lying!'

'You're welcome,' he said.

AFTER HE LEFT, she sat at the table for a long time, thinking about what Sam had said. Finally, she forced herself to get up and go down the hall to James's room. She had never cleaned it out after he died. She didn't have the heart. She always thought of the messy, cave-like room as his lair. A dark hole in the house that she avoided at all costs. She sat down on the edge of his bed and looked around at the rubble of his belongings on the floor, and his Gothic fantasy posters on the walls. Every one of them depicted razor-wielding creatures in black, dripping blood.

Her job involved dealing with young people, but the young people whom she saw at the college seemed to be surrounded by light. Many had grown up in poverty, but they were earnest and hopeful and hard-working. They were envisioning a bright future and her job was to help that become a reality.

James had never been that way. His whole world had been dark, as long as Caitlin could remember. She used to feel so sorry for her parents, trying their best to cope with a child whom they could not understand. 'Why is he like this?' her father had asked her once in exasperation. 'You've taken all these courses on psychology. Why does he do the things he does?'

Caitlin claimed to have no idea. But she knew that her mother's pregnancy with James had been unplanned and unwelcome. They had never intended to raise a teenager in their late fifties. She also knew that they would never have said as much to James. Never. In the end, they loved James, just as they had always loved her. But that sense that he was unwanted may have crept into James's psyche. *There are so many ways,* she thought, *that those feelings could be communicated.*

Oh, James, she thought. *I couldn't bear to find out now that you had admitted a crime you didn't commit.* She began to look, in a desultory fashion, through his belongings. His school papers were still there in folders. Unlike her, he had never been the brightest student, and the teachers hectoring comments, the underlined red Ds and Fs on the papers, were a reminder of what a torture school had become for him. She opened the drawer in his bedside table and there, on a pile of opened letters, was a school photo of Karla. Love you, she wrote across it, with a heart-shaped kiss. Caitlin picked up the letters and looked. They were all from Karla, sent from the rehab center where she had been confined. Caitlin riffled through a few of the pages. The content was stupefyingly banal, like most people's letters, Caitlin reminded herself. But to James, obviously, they had been important. He had kept them, and her picture right there beside him.

And, Caitlin thought, he had told Karla about the accident. She recalled now that something in Karla's recounting of it had struck her as odd, but she couldn't remember what. Too much else was happening that day. She wondered if she could call Karla now and ask her about it again. Maybe that would be useful. She felt ghoulish, rummaging in the pile of clothing on the floor, but she had not taken Karla's information when she was here. At that time she was hoping to never have to set eyes on her again. But now…James's phone was still in the pocket of his jeans. Caitlin pulled it out. The battery was dead. She would have to recharge the phone to find Karla's number. She put it into the charger on his bureau and, to her relief, the phone immediately blinked that it was charging.

'Caitlin?'

She jumped and cried out. She heard footsteps coming through the house. She put a hand to her thudding heart in relief as Noah appeared in the doorway to James's room.

He looked at her face and grimaced. 'Sorry,' he said. 'I didn't mean to scare you.'

Caitlin was not going to deny that she was scared. She also was not going to let Noah look around James's room. James was still her brother. She felt some primitive urge to protect his privacy.

She left the room, pulling the door shut behind her.

'I probably shouldn't have just come over here,' said Noah.

'It's all right,' said Caitlin. 'Anything…?' They stood awkwardly, facing each other in the narrow hallway.

Noah ran a hand through his shaggy, unwashed hair. His face had become positively gaunt in the last week. 'Sam Mathis told me that Bandit was in Dan's car. That you found him there. He was heading off to talk to him again.'

'That's true,' said Caitlin. 'I went there to apologize… about Emily.'

'I know,' said Noah. 'I'm just…having trouble with this. I mean, I know Dan would never… It's…unthinkable. But Bandit…?'

He looked at her so helplessly that her heart ached at the sight of his face. She knew that he was picturing Geordie, Bandit tucked protectively under his arm, no matter how many times kids made fun of him for it.

'Come here,' she said. She thought of taking his hand but then she didn't. She gestured for him to follow her. She went down the hall to the guest room and turned on the bedside lamp. Then she stepped back and indicated the stuffed animal on the pillow.

Noah walked over to the bed and lifted Bandit off the pillow. He frowned at her. 'How did you get him out of Dan's car?'

Caitlin hesitated, and then told him about her call to Triple A.

'You're a born outlaw,' he said.

Caitlin didn't know if he meant it as an insult. She didn't think so. 'I sewed his ear back on last night,' she pointed out.

Noah nodded, wiping his eyes. 'He was about to lose it.'

'I couldn't let that happen,' said Caitlin. 'I promised Geordie. I wanted it to be done for when he comes home.'

Noah sighed and shook his head. 'It's like the earth has swallowed him up. He's just vanished.'

He looked across at her, his capable, discerning glance now veiled in tears and fearful as a child. And he was turning to her for encouragement. She felt suddenly calm. 'He's gonna come home. We have to just keep on believing that.'

Noah hesitated. 'I was wrong to accuse you,' he said. 'I know you would never do anything to hurt him.'

Caitlin felt as if he had lifted a weight off of her chest. 'No. Never,' she said.

NINETEEN

'MAYBE YOU SHOULD take Bandit home,' she said. 'We want him right there and waiting when the time comes...' She offered him the stuffed animal, even though it pained her to do so. Noah was surrounded by Geordie's belongings, with all their attendant comfort and pain. She had only Bandit.

'No, you keep him. For the time being.'

'It's so hard to go through this alone,' she blurted out.

Noah nodded absently, as if he did not understand what she was saying, and got into his car. She watched him pull out of the driveway, and the rest of the day seemed to crash on top of her. She thought about calling the college and telling them she would come back to work, just so she wouldn't have to face the long, empty hours, but then she thought better of it. She couldn't imagine putting on her work clothes, answering people's questions and listening to their problems while her heart was crying out, 'My child is missing.' She was not ready for that.

Searching her mind for a task other than housework, she thought of James's phone. Maybe it was charged enough by now. She went back down to his room, found and pressed the buttons to reveal the last calls he made. Sure enough, the number for the reformatory was there. But not Karla's home number. She tried scrolling back all the way on his phone, but the saved numbers were only for fifty calls.

Caitlin tried to think. What was Karla's last name anyway? She checked the return address on her letters, but it was just initials. Caitlin could picture Karla's house. She had driven James over there when she was home on a visit, before her parents moved to South Jersey. Karla's family lived in a dilapidated ranch house on a weedy patch of woods outside of Coatesville. She could find the place with no problem but she couldn't, for the life of her, remember their name.

Caitlin looked at the clock. It was a two-hour drive. She wouldn't get back here till dark. *So what?* she thought miserably. *You have no one waiting for you. Nowhere to be. And Karla might know something important.*

She hesitated for a moment, and then made up her mind. She put Bandit back on her pillow. 'I'll be back,' she whispered, as if the pup were alive.

THE TOWN OF COATESVILLE had once been known at the Pittsburgh of the East when Lukens Steel was headquartered there. Along with the American steel industry, Coatesville had fallen on hard times. Valiant efforts were being made by preservationists to revive shuttered businesses and boarded-up buildings, but the town had an air of fatigue, as if it were all too much to ask.

Caitlin's father had worked his whole life in Coatesville in the Public Works department. When his time for retirement came, despite a lifetime spent in this town, he seemed to have no desire to stay. He and Caitlin's mother were solitary types, not joiners, and though Caitlin had a strong sense of the area where she grew up, she did not feel connected to the people there. Her parents kept to themselves and neither one had much family to speak of. A million memories assailed her as she drove through the environs of the town, but she tried not to get lost in nostalgia. She was here for a purpose.

It took her several tries to find the road which led to Karla's house. She finally found it and wended her way through scruffy woods until she came to a house she recognized.

It was a graceless ranch house, low to the ground and covered in moldy, beige vinyl siding, with a few tiny windows. There were plastic barrels along the side of the house and a clothesline hung with clothes in the front yard. A blue and orange plastic slide and picnic table rested on an incline not far from the drying clothes. A couple of plastic pots of dead mums sat on the cement slab in front of the door.

There were children playing in the woods. Caitlin could hear their shouts as she got out of the car. Karla's car, the one she had driven to their house, was parked in the dirt driveway. Caitlin exhaled with relief. It would have been a long trip to make only to learn that Karla had decamped for another place.

She walked up to the door and knocked. There were net curtains over the window but she could hear movement inside. The door opened and Karla looked out at her in surprise. She was barefoot, wearing a baggy black T-shirt over pink leggings, and still had a cross hanging prominently around her neck. Her hair was a lifeless fluff.

'Caitlin,' she exclaimed. 'I can't believe it. What brings you here?'

'I came to see you, Karla,' she said.

'Awesome. Hold on a minute. I'm watching the kids while my mom's on her shift. I have to holler at them.'

'OK,' said Caitlin.

Karla stepped out onto the cement and screeched in the voice of a fishmonger, 'Cliffie, Brianna, Ardella. Answer me.'

The shrieking in the woods stopped for a moment, and then an angry boy's voice called out, 'What?'

'I can't see you. Come back in the yard where I can see you.'

A boy's defiant voice yelled, 'Why da we haf to?'

'Mom told me to watch you,' Karla cried out. 'Now come back in the yard.'

There was a rustling of leaves and then a pint-sized, skinny kid with baggy clothes and a swagger appeared in the clearing. Two little girls in pink and purple jackets gamboled along behind him. He gestured at his narrow chest with his thumbs. 'Here I am. Ya see me?' he defied her.

Karla nodded. 'Stay where I can see ya,' she said.

'Who's that?' the boy asked, nodding in Caitlin's direction.

'This is James's sister. Remember James?' Karla asked.

'Your druggie boyfriend?' Cliffie sneered.

'Don't mind him,' Karla said to Caitlin. 'Stay put,' she shot back at the boy as she opened the door to the house. 'Come on in.'

The inside of the house defied Caitlin's expectations somewhat. Everything was tidy and, though worn, looked comfortable. She glanced in the living room. The grayish brown sectional sofa almost disappeared against the fake paneling on the walls, and it faced an enormous flat-screen TV. There were knitted throws on the arms of every piece of the sectional. The walls were hung with religious images. On the Formica kitchen table was an open Bible as well as some school books.

'Caught me studying,' said Karla apologetically. 'Can I get you anything? A soda?'

'Yeah, a soda would be great,' said Caitlin. She sat down at the table. 'What are you working on?'

'Well, my Bible study, of course. Plus, I have to take the GED exam next week.' Karla opened the small refrigerator, pulled out a can of Wink and opened it, pouring it into a plastic cup. She handed it to Caitlin.

Caitlin nodded. 'Thanks. Are you ready for that?'

Karla frowned. 'I think so. They tell you what to study.'

'That's a good thing to be doing,' said Caitlin.

'After that I'm going to try to go to college,' Karla confided.

'Really?' said Caitlin.

Karla looked around the tidy house and then leaned toward Caitlin. 'I don't want to end up here,' she said. 'Or in jail.'

'That's great,' Caitlin said. 'You've got plans for yourself.'

Karla shrugged and smiled. 'I've seen a lot of really bad stuff in my life. So, I'm trying.'

'Good for you,' said Caitlin. She felt that she had been too harsh on this girl in her thoughts about her. Sometimes people did change.

'So what did you want to ask me?' Karla asked.

Caitlin hesitated. 'I have to admit. I was thinking about James's accident.'

'I figured it was about that,' said Karla, and there was a little note of let down in her voice. 'What did you want to know?'

'Well, I have so many questions. The way you described it the other day. I thought I knew what happened, but now I'm wondering… What did he tell you about that day? Can you remember?'

'Oh, yeah. I wouldn't forget that. He said the woman used him to kill herself.'

Caitlin recoiled at the bald statement. 'What?'

Karla nodded sharply. 'That's what he said. He said she

ran right out in front of his car. He didn't have a chance to stop.'

Emily? Caitlin thought. She remembered what Sam said about the location of the damage to her father's truck. 'Are you sure about that?'

'Positive,' said Karla. 'I have the letter he sent me about it.'

Caitlin felt as if an electric charge had surged through her. 'You do?'

'Yeah. Do you want me to go get it?'

'Would you do that?'

'Sure,' she said. She got up from her chair and took a moment to peer out the kitchen window. Then she opened the door and screeched again. 'Cliffie.'

'We're right here,' the boy replied in a surly tone.

'Good,' she said and slammed the door. She turned to Caitlin. 'I'll be right back.' She disappeared down the dark hallway past the living room. Caitlin didn't know what to think. James had never said a word to her about anyone running in front of him. Was that true? Or was he lying to Karla?

Karla returned with the letter, still in its envelope. She handed it to Caitlin. It was addressed, in James's small handwriting, to Karla Dawson at Hopelight House.

Caitlin reached into the envelope and hesitated, looking up at Karla. 'May I?'

'Sure. That's why I got it for you.'

Caitlin pulled it out and scanned it, realizing as she did that she was looking at James's suicide note. *My sister will never believe me,* he had written. *She gave up on me just like my parents. I did take a couple of pills that day, but I wasn't high when I hit that woman. Driving along, minding my own business and suddenly she flew out from the driveway and right in front of my truck. She looked right*

at me. I'll never forget her eyes. Like something in a hor-
ror movie. I can't close my own eyes without seeing her.
The sound when the truck hit her was the most sickening
thing I can ever remember. I can't stop hearing it or see-
ing her face. I knew right away that it was all over for me.
I had killed a person with the car and I had no license. No
one would ever believe that she used me like that to off
herself. Why would anybody do that? I just kept driving.

I wish I could be with you. I'm all alone. Something bad
is gonna happen. I love you and I'm sorry. James.

Caitlin read it twice and then looked up at Karla in be-
wilderment.

'By the time I got it he was already gone,' said Karla
matter-of-factly. 'You can only get "snail mail" there. Part
of the punishment is no computer access. And then, when
it comes, they always hold your mail up in that place.'

Caitlin slowly replaced the letter in the envelope.

'Does that letter tell you what you wanted to know?'
Karla asked.

Caitlin nodded. 'In a way.' She held up the envelope.
'I know this is very private and I hate to ask this of you,
but could I keep this for a while? I'll get it back to you.'

'You can take it,' said Karla. 'James was a part of my
other life. I'm not going back there.'

'That's wise,' said Caitlin. She slipped the letter into her
pocketbook. 'I can't tell you how much I appreciate this.'

'Glad to help. You know, I always looked up to you. The
way you went away to school and all. Once I got straight I
thought about you sometimes, and how I'd like to be like
you. Only a Christian version of you.'

Caitlin did not take offense. 'Actually, I've been doing
a lot of praying lately.'

'Your boy is still missing?'

Caitlin nodded.

'I'm praying for him too,' said Karla. Then she got up and looked out the window again, catching the eye of the children outside and pointing at them.

Caitlin stood up. 'I'd better be getting back. It's a long drive.' She reached into her pocketbook and pulled out a business card. 'When you get ready to think about college, get in touch with me. I'm in charge of diversity recruitment at this college. Maybe I can help.'

'That would be awesome. Thanks,' said Karla, beaming. Then she frowned. 'Is it a Christian school?'

'Christians go there,' said Caitlin.

'I'll think about it,' Karla said.

TWENTY

DESPITE THE FACT that she had grown up in Coatesville, Caitlin had no desire to linger once she left Karla's house. As she drove back toward the highway through the familiar streets, she was not remembering her life in this place. All she was feeling was a distinct unease, being so far away from Hartwell, from the place where Geordie had disappeared. It was more of an instinct than a rational thought. She wanted to be where Geordie could find her if he came back. Even living in her parents' house made her feel too far away from him. He wouldn't know to look for her there. He would expect to see her at the home they had shared. Not that he could look for her, Caitlin reminded herself. He was just a little boy. But the thought that he might return, and that she might not be there waiting for him when he did, filled her with a panic that made it hard to breathe.

She stopped for gas just before she got on the highway and called Noah while the gas was pumping. His phone went to voice mail. She hesitated, then left a message. 'Noah,' she said. 'Any news about Geordie? Anything? I am in Coatesville, but I am on my way back…home,' she said. 'Has Sam Mathis called? Did he go to see Dan? I'll… call you later,' she said.

She knew that Noah probably didn't want her to call him but she didn't care. She had to call and ask. It was the only way to keep the anxiety from overwhelming her. 'Is your little boy still missing?' Karla had asked. Yes, she thought. Yes, he was her little boy and, yes, no matter how she wished it weren't so, he was still missing.

The tank of her car filled, Caitlin got onto the highway and drove too fast toward Hartwell. She kept glancing at her phone, waiting for Noah to return her call, but he did not. Whatever disgust he might have felt about her seemed to be lessening. She realized that he might be too exhausted and depleted over Geordie to sustain his anger towards her. That didn't mean that he would want her back. She could not force him to forgive her. She wondered what he would think if he learned what James had said about Emily.

Karla's account, and James's letter, seemed to dovetail with what Sam Mathis had discovered about the truck. If Emily had run out in front of the truck she would have been hit squarely in the center of the front bumper and grill. But that didn't make any sense. Caitlin remembered all too well the news accounts of the hit-and-run. At the time she had pored over the details, virtually memorizing them. Emily had left Geordie asleep in the car seat.

Even if she were suicidal, Emily would not have left her sleeping toddler alone, fastened in a car seat with no one to mind him and no means of escape. No suicide could be that impulsive. Caitlin had been Geordie's mother for two years, and she understood how impossible that would be. A mother was still a mother, no matter what. As far as Caitlin was concerned, that ruled out the possibility of suicide. So, why did Emily run out in front of the truck? What could have possessed her to do something so dangerous? Caitlin wondered.

She felt as if there was no one she could ask. She could not even breathe Emily's name to Noah or her parents. But the evidence of the truck supported James's version. And then another thought occurred to her that made her feel almost faint at the wheel. Sam Mathis had said that it was almost unbelievable, all the terrible things that had happened to Noah. Was it, in fact, an unbelievable coincidence? Could it be that it was not a coincidence at all? Did Emily's death have something to do with the disappearance of Geordie, all these years later? Was there someone trying to destroy Noah and his family? If you had an enemy that vicious, that determined, wouldn't you know it?

The drive, which had seemed interminable going up, flew by on the way home as Caitlin puzzled over these confusing possibilities. Before she knew it, she was exiting the highway and winding south through the wooded countryside. On the outskirts of Hartwell, Caitlin passed several signs indicating the proximity of the County Recycling Center. She thought of Naomi and her free bookstore. If anyone might remember what was going on in Noah's life in those days, it was Naomi.

On an impulse, Caitlin turned at the sign for the recycling center, passed through the open chain-link gates, and wended her way down the curving, bumpy dirt road to where the recyclables were collected. There was a manned booth at the entrance. Just beyond the booth was a clearing ringed by enormous Dumpsters marked with signs for aluminum, paper and leaves. Next to one of the Dumpsters was a mound of discarded appliances, air conditioners and even some furniture. Next to that was a small, neat gray trailer. Caitlin pulled up to the booth and the man within, a hefty guy in filthy canvas coveralls, mild eyes, and frizzy hair beneath a knitted cap.

'You have a sticker?' he asked.

Caitlin shook her head.

'Can't drop stuff off without a sticker,' he said.

'Oh, I'm not dropping off. I just wanted to visit the free bookstore.'

The man pointed to an old Airstream trailer. As he did

so, Caitlin recognized Naomi's ancient Volvo parked in front of it. 'Right in there,' he said. 'Closing soon.'

'I'll be quick,' said Caitlin. She pulled up beside the Volvo and parked her car. As she got out of her car, Champ suddenly leaped in the back seat of the Volvo and began hurling himself at the smudged up back window, barking at her. Startled, Caitlin jumped back. 'Easy there, Champ,' she said as she climbed the steps to the trailer and opened the door.

The smell of mildew was almost overwhelming in the stuffy space. The trailer was completely lined with shelves, and every shelf had a neatly hand-lettered sign with the type of book it contained and the alphabetical arrangement of authors. Naomi, dressed in coveralls, was down near the end of the trailer, lifting books one by one from a plastic milk crate, examining their jackets and spines, and putting them into their proper place. Travis was sitting on a folding metal chair near the front hunched over a Game Boy. He looked up and glowered at Caitlin as she came through the door.

'What are you doing here?' he demanded.

'Hi, Travis. I came to talk to your mother.'

Naomi heard the voices from the far end of the trailer and looked up. 'Caitlin,' she said. 'Has something happened?'

Caitlin shook her head. 'No. Not really. I just wanted to talk to you.'

Naomi set the book she was holding back down into the crate and wiped her hands on her coveralls as she walked down between the aisles of books.

'This bookstore is really something,' Caitlin said. 'You have done an amazing job here.'

'She loves books,' Travis said in a tone that was both proud and grumpy at once.

'Guilty,' said Naomi. 'I couldn't bear to see all these books being turned back into mulch. I figured I'd give them another chance at life. Of course, when I started it was just a shelf or two. Now, look.'

Caitlin nodded. 'Do a lot of people use it?'

'Oh, yeah,' said Naomi. 'Weekends I probably give away a hundred or a hundred and fifty books.'

'Wow,' said Caitlin.

'Do you want to have a look?' Naomi asked.

'Not today,' said Caitlin. 'But I'll come back when there's more time.'

'We've got some great stuff,' Naomi said, gazing over the carefully arranged rows of moldy books. 'So, what's up? I talked to Noah this morning. He said there's no news.'

'No. I'm afraid not,' said Caitlin. 'I just wanted to ask you something. About Geordie's mother. About Emily.'

'Emily? What about her?' Naomi asked. 'Oh, and by the way, I know about what your brother did.'

Caitlin was taken aback and her face reddened. 'I'm so sorry about that, Naomi,' she said. 'I should have admitted it from the very beginning. I'm sure you must think the worst of me.'

Naomi shrugged. 'It's a little weird. But I told Noah I would have done the same for him that you did. You were just being loyal to your brother. What good would it do to tell after he was already dead? It couldn't bring Emily back.'

Caitlin was surprised. 'Thanks. That's really generous of you,' she said.

Naomi sighed. 'None of us is perfect.'

'No,' said Caitlin.

'So what did you want to know about Emily?' Naomi asked.

'Oh. Well, ever since this all…came out about my

brother, I've been thinking about that accident. Was she… Around the time of the…accident, was Emily acting differently than usual?'

Naomi frowned. 'Differently, how?'

'Maybe, just… I don't know. Did she seem upset or worried or anything?'

Naomi scratched her curly hair with her ring finger. 'No. She had no worries. She and Noah were good. They had Geordie. That nice house. She didn't have anything to be upset about.'

'Were you and she close?'

'No. I mean, we got along well enough. She was good to us after Rod died. Always willing to help out. For family, you know. It goes to show you don't really know people sometimes. I couldn't stand her in high school. We went to high school together but we were definitely not friends. She was in the popular crowd. Nice clothes. Never had to work,' said Naomi ruefully.

Caitlin nodded. 'What about Noah? Did he have any… enemies? Disgruntled clients? Anybody who might have wanted to hurt him?'

'No. Why do you ask? The police already asked me all this stuff.'

Caitlin hesitated. She decided it might be a good idea to stick to the truth. 'Well, the police say that the damage to my father's truck wasn't consistent with their theory of what happened to Emily.'

Naomi shook her head. 'Meaning?'

'Well, the damage to the truck and my brother's account suggest that Emily ran out in front of the truck instead of being hit by the side of the road.'

'Why would she do that?'

'I don't know,' said Caitlin. 'My brother thought she was trying to commit suicide.'

'Suicide? Emily?' Naomi snorted. 'That's ridiculous. No. She had the world on a string. That's why it was such a shock when she died.' Naomi shook her head. 'I'll never forget Noah calling me. Sobbing. I could barely understand him. Saying she'd been hit by a car and was dead. I couldn't believe my ears. We were all just…stunned.'

'I'm sure,' said Caitlin.

'First we lose Rod in Iraq. That was bad enough. Then, Emily. It was just too much to take in—we felt like our family was cursed. My mother was hysterical. I was, too. Everybody but you, right, Travis? My little man. He never batted an eye when we heard the news about his aunt. He didn't even seem surprised. I kept telling him it was OK to cry but he said he was fine.'

Naomi turned to Travis. 'You remember that? When we heard about Geordie's mom? You were eating supper. I'll never forget it. I told you about it, trying to break it to you gently, and you just looked at me and said, "Can I have some more macaroni?" You remember that?'

'No,' Travis snapped.

Naomi sighed. 'His teacher said he might be traumatized, and I should think about taking him to a counselor or something. But Travis insisted he was fine.'

'Why do you have to talk about this?' Travis demanded. He threw his Game Boy across the room. It bounced off a shelf of cookbooks and fell to the floor.

Naomi did not seem bothered by his show of temper. 'No matter how he acts, I know he felt bad about it. We're not saying it to upset you, Travis,' Naomi explained. Then she turned to Caitlin. 'What are you hoping to find out, anyway?'

'I'm just trying to figure out what happened,' said Caitlin. 'Trying to figure out if Geordie's…disappearance is somehow related to Emily's death.'

Naomi frowned. 'I don't see what one thing has to do with the other.'

'Well, at the moment, neither do I, but...'

'Then just shut up,' Travis murmured.

Shocked by his language, Caitlin looked from the boy to his mother, waiting for Naomi to scold him.

Naomi acted as if she had not heard what the boy said. 'Well, I wish I could help you.' She looked at her watch. ''Bout time for us to leave. You ready, Travis?'

Travis got up from the folding chair without looking at Caitlin, went over and retrieved the Game Boy he had thrown against the books. 'What's for dinner?' he demanded.

'I was thinking Taco Bell,' said Naomi.

'Yay, I love Taco Bell,' said Travis.

'Do you want to join us?' Naomi asked.

'No, she doesn't,' said Travis.

'Thanks anyway,' said Caitlin. She turned and opened the door to the trailer and began to descend the steps. 'Another time, maybe.'

'Come back and browse sometime,' said Naomi cheerfully.

'Thanks,' said Caitlin. She glanced back at Travis but he was bent over the Game Boy again, fiddling with the screen, and she had the distinct feeling that he was avoiding her gaze.

TWENTY-ONE

CAITLIN GLANCED AT her phone, just to be sure, but Noah had not called her back while she was in the free bookstore. There was, however, a call from Sam Mathis. She returned the call immediately.

'Sam, it's Caitlin,' she said.

'Where are you? I need you to bring that toy of Geordie's down the station,' he said.

'Bandit?' Caitlin asked. 'Why?'

'We need to send it to the lab. How far away are you?'

'Not too far. Does this have something to do with your visit to Dan?' she asked.

Sam was silent for a moment. Then he said, 'We'll talk when you get here.'

'Can't you tell me on the phone?' she said. But Sam had already ended the call. Her blood drumming in her ears, Caitlin drove as quickly as she could back up the bumpy road which led to the recycling center and turned out onto the highway, trying to just drive and not think about what it could be. She made a hasty stop at her parents' house, retrieved Bandit from her bedroom, and went directly downtown to the police station.

She parked outside and ran up the sandstone steps. She was trying to gauge what was going on from the expressions of the officers coming and going. Her imagination was running away with her. When the desk sergeant asked whom she wanted to see, she said that Detective Mathis was waiting for her and brushed by his desk, not waiting to be allowed to pass.

The door to Chief Burns's office was closed and it was dark inside. She rushed down the hallway to Sam's office and was relieved to see that the door was wide open. 'Sam, I'm here,' she said as she burst in.

Sam looked up gravely and pointed to the chair in front of this desk.

Caitlin sat down. 'What?' she demanded. 'What is it?'

'Hand that over,' he said, waggling a hand at Bandit.

Reluctantly she offered the toy to the detective, who held out a plastic bag for her to drop it into. Once she had placed Bandit it in the bag he sealed it, wrote on it, and made a call. In a moment, a uniformed patrolman arrived at the door of his office. 'Take this to the lab,' he said. 'Tell Dr Murphy this is the toy I was telling him about.'

The patrolman nodded and took Bandit away. Caitlin watched him disappear and then turned back to Sam. 'What is going on?' she asked.

'I'm not sure yet,' Sam said grimly. 'I need you to tell me every single thing that happened when you were there at Dan's house yesterday.'

'Why?' Caitlin asked.

'Just…go through it with me.'

Caitlin did not equivocate. Starting from the moment she arrived in Society Hill, she described everything that happened, exactly as it happened. She even, after a moment's hesitation, included her call to AAA, and the manner in which she had tricked the fellow who had arrived to aid her in unlocking Dan's car.

Sam listened intently. 'You said that he let you into the house, and that you yelled for Geordie. You're absolutely sure that there was no response? You saw no sign of the boy in Dan's house?'

'Of course I'm sure,' said Caitlin. 'I wouldn't have left if there were any indication… What's going on?'

'I went to see Uncle Dan today,' he said.

Caitlin felt a sudden rush of fear. 'Yes.'

'He wasn't there. There was no one in the house.'

'You went inside?' she asked.

'I couldn't go inside. I went there to question him. I had no warrant. Unlike you, I have to obey the law and respect the rights of citizens.' It wasn't exactly a joke, but Caitlin could tell that he wasn't speaking out of anger. 'No one answered. I banged on the door for a long time.'

Caitlin raised her hands as if to express the fact that she did not understand how this was important.

'So, I went to the station where he works,' said Sam.

'And?'

'He wasn't there either. He hadn't come in today.'

Caitlin felt her hopes deflating. 'So…what was so urgent?'

'While I was at the station, I checked out Uncle Dan's work schedule. On Tuesday, the Phillies were playing the White Sox.'

Caitlin shook her head. 'I don't…'

'The Chicago White Sox,' said Sam. 'It was a home game for Chicago.'

Caitlin's eyes widened. 'Dan…'

'…was there,' said Sam. 'He went to Chicago for the game.'

Caitlin shook her head and stared at him.

'I've scanned his photo and sent it down to the detectives who are helping us in Chicago. They are going back to the stores in the area we know the tracphone was purchased.'

'Oh, my God.'

Sam met her gaze without speaking.

'Then where is Geordie?'

'I don't know. I hope to have an answer on the purchase of the phone very soon.'

'What about the flight? Was Geordie with him on the flight? Did you check on that?'

'First thing. He traveled alone. The minute I get a confirmation on the photo I will put out an APB on Dan and get a warrant to enter his house.'

'But what if Geordie is in there all alone or something? What if he's…' She closed her eyes, unable to allow herself to visualize her child alone, suffering.

'If he's there we'll get him out. I'll make sure to have medical personnel standing by.'

'Does Noah know?' she asked.

'I spoke to him,' said Sam.

'I've been trying to reach him. He's not calling me back. What about the Bergens?'

'I've sent a couple of men out there to see if Dan's parents might know where Dan is. We have to tread carefully with them. They've been through a lot. We weren't able to find their daughter's killer. I don't want to accuse their son until I know something for sure. But I'm beginning to have a bad feeling.'

'Uncle Dan?' Caitlin cried, trying to imagine the unimaginable. 'Why?'

'You said that you never saw him act in an inappropriate way with the boy?'

'Never,' said Caitlin emphatically. 'Never once. He… was fond of Geordie, but he never showed any interest in spending time alone with him or…anything like that. And he could have. Easily. I sometimes thought that Noah wished Dan would make more of an effort to spend time with Geordie. You know, offer to take Geordie and Travis to a game or something, but Dan never took the hint.

I mean, kids are not his thing. Beautiful women are his thing. And, besides, why all of a sudden, out of a clear blue sky…?'

'What about his ex-wife?'

'Haley?' Caitlin shook her head. 'What about her? She knows nothing. I'd swear to it. Although…'

'What?' Sam demanded.

Caitlin felt her blood run cold as she realized that this information might now be crucial. 'She did tell me that Dan was in Hartwell the morning that Geordie was taken. He had fallen ill at the birthday party, and ended up staying over in her apartment. He was too sick to drive home. He wasn't faking. She said he threw up all night. He left that morning.'

'I need that warrant,' Sam growled, almost to himself.

Caitlin's mind was racing. 'If Geordie was with Dan… Dan would never hurt Geordie. I'm sure of that.'

Sam frowned at her. 'I wish I could be so sure,' he said.

Caitlin shook her head. 'Not his nephew,' she said. 'Not a little boy. Maybe it's some kind of awful misunderstanding.'

Sam looked at her with raised eyebrows. 'Yesterday you broke into his car. You were screaming for Geordie in his house.'

Caitlin shook her head miserably. 'I know I did. But I also know that Dan loves Geordie. Geordie is all he has left of his sister.'

'Caitlin, taking that little boy, hiding him from the police, keeping him from his parents—that was a desperate act. There's no turning back once you've committed a crime like that. That's life in prison. And Geordie is both the victim and the sole witness.'

'Don't say that,' she protested. 'No one could be that evil.'

'I don't have to tell you. People do some truly terrible things,' said Sam. He got up and came around the desk. 'I'm going to see if I can speed it along. Will you excuse me?' he said.

Caitlin nodded dumbly. She pulled her phone out of her bag and tried Noah's number again. It went directly to voice mail. *Where are you?* she thought.

She got unsteadily to her feet and walked out of Sam's office. A policeman in the hallway brushed past her and frowned at her, as if to indicate that she was in the way. *You are in the way,* she thought. *Let them do their job. That's all you can do right now.* She thought of Geordie's face, his sweet eyes behind his glasses, his gap-tooth smile. Who could ever hurt him? And then she forced the question from her mind. She had to. She couldn't bear to consider the possibilities.

TWENTY-TWO

THE SHOPS ON Hartwell Avenue were beginning to close up for the day, while the bars and restaurants were turning on their twinkle lights and starting to look more lively. Caitlin walked in the direction of Jordan's Bakery. She felt the need to talk to Haley, to have Haley reassure her that Dan was incapable of hurting a child for any reason. She knew that was what she would hear.

When she reached the bakery window and glanced inside, Caitlin saw Haley sitting at one of the little marble-topped tables, speaking to two men in jackets and ties who were seated at the table with her. One man was writing in a notebook. Caitlin recognized him right away. He was a detective who had been working with Sam all along through this nightmare. She stared in at them through the window.

Haley looked up and then did a double take as she recognized Caitlin through the glass. Caitlin raised a hand in greeting but Haley's normally welcoming smile did not appear. She gave Caitlin a frosty stare and then turned her attention back to the detectives.

Caitlin lowered her hand, turned away and walked back to her own car.

Now what? she thought. She drove first to her parents' house and sat in the car in the driveway for a few minutes. She felt an almost physical revulsion at the prospect of going back in there. She tried Noah again, both his home and cell phone numbers, to no avail. Either he was avoiding her calls or he was not at home.

She felt an urgent desire to see him, to be with him, to talk over what Sam had said about Dan. He had been almost kind at their last meeting. He had even apologized for accusing her in Geordie's disappearance. Surely he would want to discuss this latest news.

She decided to go to the house and wait for him there. When he got home and found her there, the worst he would be able to do was to send her packing. She realized that a rejection like that would not upset her too much. Not after this week in hell. How much could it hurt? Besides, anything was better than entering her parents' house. She backed out of the driveway with a distinct feeling of relief, and began to drive toward the house which had been, until lately, the home she had always imagined for herself.

SHE WAS USED to seeing at least one police car in the driveway, but there was no one parked there when she arrived. No lights were on in the house. She immediately felt that she had done the right thing by coming here. What if Geordie were to come home and find the house like this, cold and unlit? As if no one cared. She would turn on the lights until the place glowed, she thought. She would warm up some rolls in the oven so the house would smell good. Just in case.

She got out of her car and stood beside it for a moment. A twilight mist was settling in the trees, winding through their low branches. Caitlin jammed her hands in her pockets and looked back down toward the highway, hidden by the dense woods. She hesitated, and then walked down the sloping driveway, watching her step as she made her way down the gravel surface. The grade of the driveway was steep enough that she had to use her feet and shins as brakes when she walked along. That was one reason why they had left it as gravel. If it had been paved, any ball which hit the surface would bounce down into the road. At the least the gravel inhibited bouncing and rolling. With a little boy who loved playing catch, you had to think of these things.

Caitlin reached the end of the driveway and looked over at the mailbox. She thought about Emily on that fateful day. The police believed that she had left Geordie in the car and walked down this same grade. She had walked over to the mailbox. Caitlin did that now and pulled open the mailbox door. The box was stuffed, as if Noah had not looked inside it for several days. Caitlin reached in and pulled out the mail inside. Headlights from an oncoming car grazed her in the gloom as the car sped by. She could feel the breeze as it passed. How easy it would be, in the gray twilight, for a driver not to see someone standing here at the mailbox.

On the other hand, she thought, looking around her, it would be impossible to stand at this mailbox without being aware of the proximity of oncoming cars. It would be unnatural not to notice the oncoming headlights, to sense that they were too close, to dive into the bushes and out of harm's way. You would have to be completely distracted not to be alert as you stood at this mailbox.

James said that Emily had run out in front of his car. Caitlin clutched the pile of mail to her chest and tried to imagine it. The grade of the driveway was so steep that if, for some reason, she had been running down the driveway, it would be difficult to break her own momentum. But why would Emily be running down the driveway in the first place? James suggested that she had been trying to deliberately kill herself. Caitlin was sure that Emily would never choose that method, would never leave her baby stranded in his car seat. So why else would she be running? Caitlin stared up the driveway, trying to picture Emily running down that driveway. Moving so fast that she ran right out into the street and in front of a speeding truck.

She would never do that unless… Unless she was running away from something, Caitlin thought. Or someone. Unless she was being chased.

Caitlin shivered at the thought. *No. You're just imagining things,* she thought. *That doesn't explain the mail scattered everywhere.*

Clutching the pile of mail to her chest, she closed the mailbox and walked slowly back up the driveway toward the house. She climbed the steps, pulled out her keys, and went to insert them in the front door. At that moment it occurred to her: what if Noah had changed the locks? He had been angry enough to do it.

The key slid into the lock and turned, and Caitlin felt her heart lighten a little bit. She turned on the porch lights and then went around switching on the lamps. She put the mail down on the kitchen table and, after she had taken her coat off and hung it up, she began to clear up the debris of take-out boxes and coffee cups which Noah had left scattered through the house. She folded up his bedding on the sofa into a neat pile and set it on the far cushion. She emptied the vases of flowers, now dead, and washed them out. She looked in the freezer and found a box of cheese and spinach turnovers. She preheated the oven, set the pastries on a metal cookie sheet and slipped the sheet into the oven. Soon the house smelled of baking piecrust. It was better now, she thought. If Geordie came home, he wouldn't find it looking and smelling like a homeless shelter. It would look like his home, with his mom there checking out the window, watching for him, waiting.

Now, she thought. If only his father would come home.

But Noah did not arrive. She waited as long as she could. Finally, she went into the kitchen and took the cheese and spinach pastries from the oven before they burned. Realizing that she was hungry, she sat down alone at the table, and placed one of the turnovers on a plate in front of her. She sat at the table, staring out the kitchen window, remembering when this had been her favorite time of day.

As THE HOUR grew later she began to feel a little uneasy about still being in the house. What if Noah was out with someone? A woman. It seemed impossible under the circumstances. He seemed to barely be able to pull himself together since Geordie had gone missing, but lately she didn't know what to think anymore. What if he came home with someone, expecting to find the house empty? Several times she thought of leaving, but she decided against it. What if the police found Geordie and brought him home? She would be here waiting. She stayed.

She watched a little bit of television in the den, pulling the throw up over her as she curled up in the chair. She was not aware of being tired, but before she knew it, she had dozed off.

She awoke with a start to the find the television still on, some pitchman droning on about car insurance. Caitlin snapped off the TV and leaned her head back against the chair.

With the television off, the room was perfectly silent. Caitlin could hear every creak in the house as the wind rose outside and started to whip the trees, the branches snapping against the windows. She had loved that sound when Noah and Geordie were here, and a fire crackled in the fireplace. It made her feel snug and safe. Tonight, alone in this house where she no longer belonged, her mind filled with questions and worries, she felt anything but snug and safe. Every gust of wind, every rustling branch made her edgy. *It's nothing,* she reminded herself. *Just a little wind blowing up. Maybe rain coming in.* At the thought of rain, she couldn't help but imagine Geordie, alone and unprotected in the storm, and it was hard to catch her breath from the anxiety.

And then, from somewhere outside the window, Caitlin heard a sound that made her freeze. She told herself she was imagining it. It was the wind playing tricks. But it came again. Faint, almost indistinct. It was human. And barely audible. A moan.

For a moment she sat rigid, unable to move from the chair. *Who's there?* she thought, but she did not say it aloud. Her heart was thudding in her ears. She was terrified to budge and terrified not to. It was coming from outside the window. *Get up,* she thought. *Get out the chair.*

She had to go out and look. There was no choice. What else could she do? Call the police and say there was a noise in the yard? She wasn't even supposed to be in this house and the police knew it. They knew she had been put out. She was trespassing. *Get up,* she told herself.

Her legs refused to obey her brain's command. She did not hear the sound again, and she began to tell herself that it really was her imagination. It had not really happened.

And then she had another terrible thought. Noah had been incommunicado all day. What if he had collapsed or had some kind of accident outside in the yard? What if it was Noah? *Get up and go out there,* she thought. Spurred by the thought that it might be her husband, that he might need her help, she was able to force herself to do it.

She hurried through the first floor of the house, putting on a jacket of Noah's because she was shivering, and trying to think what she might need outside. She slipped her phone into the jacket pocket. Flashlight, she thought. It was so dark out there. She tried to remember where they kept the flashlights in case of a power outage. Her brain refused to cooperate at first. But as she checked several likely places, she suddenly remembered. The laundry room. She went to the laundry room beside the kitchen and found the flashlights on the shelf above the washer. There were two of them, standing on end beside the tool box. She reached for the largest flashlight. Tool box, she thought. She rummaged in the tool box and took out a hammer, the heaviest one. *All right,* she thought, wielding the hammer in one hand and the flashlight in the other. *Now go.*

Front or back door? she wondered. The den was in the front of the house, closer to the front door. But somehow it felt safer to let herself out the back door of the house. She hesitated, took a deep breath and opened the door off the kitchen. She stepped out into the night.

There was a moon that was nearly full, although it was obscured by dark, scudding clouds. Still, between the moon and the lights of the house, she was able to see the shapes of the trees in the backyard and the strange nighttime shadows that danced in the wind. She edged along the back of the house and around the corner.

She could see down to the front yard although the side yard was much darker than the backyard had been. Nothing seemed to be awry. There was an alley of trees to her left and an unruly hedge along the side of the house. She began to make her way slowly between them. She didn't want to turn on the flashlight, but it was too dark to make out if there was anything or anyone concealed by the bushes or the trees.

With shaking hands she snapped on the flashlight, and the beam traveled wildly over the trees and the bushes. There was no sign of anything or anyone. *See?* she told herself. *You're just imagining things.*

But the memory of that faint moan was too vivid to ignore. She edged her way down the side yard, sweeping the flashlight from side to side. She had almost reached the den window. She could see the light from the window in the den shining out, making a pattern on the grass. She was about to put her foot into the light's reflection when, from just behind her, a human voice moaned.

Caitlin jumped, her heart pounding, and whirled around, turning the flashlight like a weapon in the direction of the sound. 'Who's there?' she cried.

The beam of the flashlight bounced and came to rest in the spot where she had heard the sound. At first she could not tell what she was seeing. And then, as her eyes adjusted, she recognized it. At the base of the hedge, propped up by the roots, its face turned into the leaves, was a body. A man lying on the ground.

'Oh, Jesus!' she cried. She wanted to run screaming, but instead she screwed up her courage and stepped closer.

'Noah?' she whispered, fearing what she might see. She pushed away the branches of the hedge and looked down.

His eyes were closed and his face was obscured by dark rivulets, his hair matted with blood. The body looked gray and limp, even in the flashlight's glare. Caitlin wanted nothing more than to look away, to run. Instead, she turned her flashlight full on the face.

She screamed and jumped back.

The flashlight's beam careened crazily over the house as she fumbled in her pocket for her phone. She pressed the familiar number on her speed dial and waited interminably for the ring, feeling like she wanted to pee, to cry, to faint. She gripped the phone with a sweaty, trembling hand. Sam Mathis answered on the second ring.

'Caitlin?' he said.

'Sam. I'm at home. At Noah's. Come right away,' she said. 'With an ambulance. Hurry.'

'An ambulance? Are you all right?'

'Yes, it's not me,' she said. Caitlin looked at the body on the ground. 'It's Dan.'

TWENTY-THREE

POLICE CARS AND an ambulance crowded the driveway, their lights flashing like red lightning in the darkness. Radios crackled and officers with flashlights combed the perimeter of the yard and beyond. Caitlin sat on the front porch steps, shivering, even though a policewoman had gone inside, fetched a blanket and draped it around her.

She saw the EMTs moving a body on a stretcher and sliding it into the bay of the ambulance. She heard the heavy doors of the bay slam, and the siren's scream pierced the night as the ambulance started down the driveway.

Sam came over to the steps and sat down beside her.

'Will he live?' she asked.

Sam shrugged. 'Don't know. The EMTs were working on him.'

Caitlin nodded and pulled the blanket more closely around her. 'What happened to him?'

'I don't know that either. It looks like someone or something hit him hard enough to crack his skull.'

Caitlin winced.

'You heard nothing?' Sam asked, incredulous. 'No struggle? No yelling?'

'I heard nothing until I heard the moan that I told you about. It was very faint—I couldn't have heard it from anywhere else in the house but the den. And even then, it wasn't until I turned the TV off.'

'How long were you in the house?'

'I got here hours ago. It was not yet dark. Maybe five o'clock.'

'He'd been lying there for hours. In addition to his injuries he's suffering from hypothermia. His clothes were soaked through with dampness from the ground. As well as blood.'

'I never saw him. I didn't know…'

Sam nodded and peered at Caitlin. 'What were you doing here?' Sam asked. 'I thought you were living at your folks' house.'

'I am. I…I don't know. I was waiting for Noah to come home. I wanted to get the house ready for Geordie. I know it sounds crazy, but I thought we might be getting closer to finding him. Besides, I didn't want to go back to my parents' house. It's awful being there.'

A car pulled into the driveway and stopped. Sam frowned as he looked at it. 'That's not one of my men,' he said.

Caitlin peered at the car and then gasped in recognition as the driver emerged and started to walk toward them. 'It's Noah,' she said.

Noah walked up to the steps and into the arc of light on the lawn thrown off by the porch lights. 'What's going on?' he demanded, panic and hope in his voice. 'Is it Geordie?'

Caitlin jumped up, shedding the blanket, and ran down the steps to him. 'What happened to you?' Caitlin demanded.

'I'm all right,' he said. 'It's nothing. Why are the police here? Is Geordie here?'

'No,' said Sam, shaking his head. 'We don't know anything more about Geordie. What happened to your face?'

Noah put his fingertips self-consciously to the bruises and cuts on his face. 'Nothing. Nothing important.'

'I'll be the judge of that,' said Sam, standing up.

'I got into a little…altercation. If you must know.'

'With who?' Sam asked.

'My brother-in-law, Dan.'

'Noah,' Caitlin blurted out. 'Don't! Don't admit to anything.'

'Why?' Noah said. 'What do you mean? We had a… fist-fight. Did he call the cops? What a wuss. Is that why you're here?'

'Dan is badly hurt,' said Caitlin. 'That's who the ambulance was here for. I found Dan lying half-dead by the side of the house.'

'That's enough,' Sam barked at her. 'Don't say another word.'

'Dan?' Noah exclaimed. 'You found him here?'

'Right where you left him,' said Sam grimly. 'He may not live through the night.'

'Are you kidding?' Noah demanded. 'I didn't hurt Dan. I wanted to hurt him, but I didn't.' He touched his own bruised face again. 'I actually got the worst of it. He knocked me out.'

'When did he show up here?' Sam asked.

'He didn't show up here. I saw him at the cemetery,' said Noah.

'The cemetery?'

'After you told me your suspicions about Dan,' said Noah, 'I called him. I wanted answers. He told me he was already on his way here, and to meet him at Emily's grave. So I went out there. When I got to the cemetery Dan was already there, putting flowers on Emily's grave. That really pissed me off.'

'I should never have told you about Dan,' Sam said angrily. 'I didn't know you'd go vigilante on me.'

'I didn't,' Noah insisted.

'Don't say any more,' Caitlin urged him.

'Caitlin, no, I have nothing to hide. Look, it's my son who's missing and I wanted answers. But no matter what I asked, he wouldn't tell me anything. He kept saying that he couldn't tell me anything and that he'd tell me in good time. Good time? Every waking moment I am agonizing about Geordie. We argued, and I guess I lost my temper. I threw a punch at him. Then he decked me.'

'And where have you been since this run-in with your brother-in-law?' asked Sam.

'Well, as I said, he knocked me out. When I came to, I found that he had taken my phone and messed my car up somehow. I couldn't get it to start. I had to start walking back. It's kind of…isolated out there by the cemetery. No one would stop for me or pick me up. I guess I look pretty bad,' he admitted.

'And yet, you still seem to be driving your car,' said Sam acidly.

'Some guy on a motorcycle stopped and asked me if I needed help. I told him about the car and the guy said he might be able to help me. I got on the back of his bike and we went back to the cemetery. The guy started looking at the car. I mean, he knew a lot about cars, I guess, but it took him a number of tries to figure out what the problem was and fix it. I wanted to borrow his phone and call a service station, but he was determined to help me whether I liked it or not. I didn't want to be rude to the guy when he was trying to help. So I just hung around there, waiting, while he checked out one thing after another. It turned out it wasn't anything major. I just don't know a lot about cars,' Noah admitted.

'That's true, he doesn't,' said Caitlin.

'I need to speak to this man to corroborate your story,' said Sam.

'It's not a story,' Noah insisted.

'All the same, I need to speak to him.'

Noah shook his head. 'That's gonna be difficult. He was just passing through on his way to some biker fundraiser in Washington. The Veterans Memorial Fundraiser—that was it.'

'Can you describe this guy? Do you know his name?'

'His name was Jim. I don't know his last name. He was older—probably a Vietnam vet. He had a gray beard and ponytail and a big gut.'

'Sounds like every biker you see on the road these days,' said Sam. 'Where was he coming from?'

'Oh…let me think. Providence, I think. He was coming down the back roads 'cause he hates riding on the GSP or the Turnpike.'

Sam sighed. 'You're going to have to come down to the station until we can check this story out. Will you come voluntarily, or do I have to place you under arrest?'

'Arrest?' Caitlin cried.

'I'll cooperate with you in any way I can,' said Noah. 'But I'm telling you, there's no time. Dan Bergen knows where my son is.'

'Well, thanks to someone taking the law into their own hands, he may never be able to tell us anything,' said Sam grimly.

Noah turned to Caitlin. 'Call David Alvarez,' he said, naming one of the partners in his firm, 'and have him meet me down at the police station. Will you do that?'

'Of course,' she said.

'Don't worry,' said Noah. 'We'll get this straightened out.'

Caitlin nodded as Sam took Noah by the arm and led him away.

DAVID ALVAREZ WAS a stocky, gray-haired man with piercing black eyes. Tie askew and briefcase in hand, he was already at the police station when Caitlin arrived. He assured Caitlin that everything would be all right, and then accompanied Noah into the interrogation room, along with Sam and another detective.

Caitlin sat outside, waiting. She called Naomi to tell her what had happened, and Naomi announced that she was on her way before Caitlin could get the story out. Caitlin went to a vending machine, bought herself a Coke and sat back down to wait. In a few minutes, Caitlin heard a commotion at the front door of the station house. Naomi, Martha and Travis arrived. Travis, dressed in his pajamas, slippers and a jacket, had Champ with him on a leash, and the desk sergeant was refusing to admit the boy with his dog.

Martha, normally quiet and seemingly pliant, was shaking with indignation. 'I want to talk to Chief Burns,' she insisted. 'Right now.'

'Take it easy, Mom,' Naomi said, trying to soothe her.

'I intend to give him a piece of my mind,' Martha insisted.

'That's all well and good, ma'am,' said the desk sergeant. 'But that dog is not allowed in here. Now you take him out of here right now.'

'Come on, Ma,' said Naomi. 'We'll have to go.'

'I'm not budging,' Martha insisted, gazing off into the middle distance. She was balanced against Naomi's arm and her small, pudgy frame was trembling. 'My son lost his wife and this police department did nothing. Then my grandson disappeared. Still nothing. Now they are trying to blame this…insanity on Noah!'

'Ma, take it easy,' said Naomi. 'We don't want to make it worse.'

Caitlin felt suddenly very sorry for Naomi, who looked as if she couldn't tolerate any more stress. Champ had begun to yip, which wasn't helping matters.

'Naomi,' Caitlin said, 'I can go outside with Travis and Champ while you two meet with the chief. We'll go down to the 7-Eleven and get a Slurpee or something.'

'They won't let him in there, either,' said Naomi in exasperation. 'Travis, I told you to leave the dog at home.'

Travis stuck his lip out and looked away.

'Don't worry,' said Caitlin. 'I'll figure something out. I won't go far. I want to be here when Noah gets done with this.'

Naomi glanced at her mother, who was fuming and clearly did not intend to budge. 'Really? That would be great,' said Naomi.

'Come on, Travis,' said Caitlin. 'Bring Champ with you.'

Travis looked to his mother. 'Do I have to?'

'Yes,' said Naomi. 'It's your own fault for bringing that dog everywhere.'

Travis frowned and did as he was told while the desk sergeant called Chief Burns to see if he could make time to see Martha Eckhart and her daughter.

Caitlin stepped outside onto the front steps with Travis and the dog.

'It's freezing out here,' said Travis.

'It has gotten cold,' said Caitlin. She glanced at her watch. 'Tell you what. Why don't we get in my car and wait? I'm parked right over there.'

Travis sighed but he clearly didn't want to wait outside in the windy September night. He followed Caitlin to her car. Caitlin opened the passenger door, but Travis balked. 'I want to sit in the back with Champ.'

'That's fine,' said Caitlin. She opened the back door and Champ leapt into the car. Travis climbed in behind him, and Caitlin closed the door. Then she went around the car to the driver's seat.

'I'm hungry,' Travis complained.

'Did you have dinner?' Caitlin asked.

'Ages ago,' said Travis. 'Let's go to McDonald's.'

Caitlin was about to protest that Travis probably didn't need a second dinner when she realized that they could get something at the drive-thru window without taking the dog inside. She thought about the nearest McDonald's. It wasn't far. It would give her a chance to engage him while he was eating his second meal of the night. 'All right,' she said.

'Cool,' said Travis.

They drove in silence to the fast-food restaurant. Champ was a model pup, quiet throughout the journey. Caitlin pulled up to the speaker where one placed an order.

'What do you want?' she asked.

'Three cheeseburgers, a large fries and a chocolate shake,' Travis said promptly.

'You don't need all that,' said Caitlin. She spoke into the speaker. 'A burger, small fries and a small Coke,' she said.

'I need a burger for Champ,' Travis protested.

Caitlin doubted that Champ would see a bite but, after a moment's hesitation, she amended the order.

'Pull up to the window,' a disembodied voice replied.

She paid for and picked up the order and then pulled into a parking space just beyond the drive-thru window. She handed the bag back to Travis. There was rustling of paper in the back seat as Travis dove into it.

'How come you didn't get any?' he asked through a mouthful of food.

'I'm not hungry,' said Caitlin. 'I'm too worried about your uncle.'

'What did Uncle Noah do?' Travis asked.

'The police think he hurt Geordie's Uncle Dan,' said Caitlin.

'Did he?' Travis asked through a mouthful of food.

'I…don't think so,' she said. Then she hesitated. 'You know Uncle Dan, right?'

'He's the one with the nice car. He goes to all the games,' said Travis.

'That's the one,' said Caitlin.

'Geordie's always bragging that his uncle Dan is going to take him to the games but he never does. I told Geordie nobody wants a little first-grade baby around at those big games.'

Caitlin glanced into the rear-view mirror. To her mild surprise she saw that Travis was dutifully sharing a hamburger with Champ. 'How's Champ liking that burger?' she said.

Travis looked up, his expression furtive and guilty, and caught her gaze in the mirror. 'I told you he would eat it,' Travis said defensively.

'I know, I know. It's fine.'

'Why are you looking at us like that?'

'I'm not. I just wanted to ask you something.'

'What?' Travis asked suspiciously.

'Travis, did Geordie ever say anything about his uncle Dan to you?' she asked.

'No,' said Travis.

'Are you sure? Think about it, Travis. Sometimes adults ask kids to do stuff with them that they…shouldn't. Things they're ashamed of. Things their parents don't know about. Stuff they need to keep secret.'

Travis stopped chewing and was silent for a moment. Then he balled up the paper bag and punched it, making it pop.

Caitlin turned around in the seat and looked at him gravely. He was frowning at Champ, raking his fingers through the dog's furry coat. 'Do you know about anything like that?'

Travis glared at her. 'No.'

'Travis, if you know something, no matter how bad it is, you have to tell me now. This is a matter of life and death. There can't be any more secrets now. Do you understand me?'

Travis glared at her. 'I'm not telling anything. You can't make me.'

'You do know something. What do you know?' Caitlin demanded.

'Take me back. I want to go back,' he insisted.

'Travis, you can't go back. Not if you know something. You had better tell me right now. I'm not playing games with you, Travis.'

'NO,' he cried. 'Leave me alone.'

Part of her wanted to take him and shake the truth out of him, but she knew it was wrong to threaten him. 'OK,' said Caitlin. 'OK. Take it easy.'

Travis grabbed Champ and hugged him around the neck. Champ made a little pleading whine in Travis's ferocious embrace.

'OK, calm down now. We're gonna go back.'

'Right now!' he screamed.

Caitlin had to resist the urge to slap him. She felt sure that he knew something about Geordie and he wouldn't say it, even though Geordie's life might depend on it. But she couldn't force him to tell, no matter how angry she felt. She needed to calm down herself. She took a deep breath. 'Here, Travis, give me that bag and I'll throw it in the trash can over there,' Caitlin said. 'Just take it easy. There's nothing to worry about, OK?'

Travis hesitated, and then handed the bag over the seat. Caitlin took it from him. 'I'll just throw this away and then I'll take you right back to your mom. OK?'

Travis did not reply, but watched her with suspicion in his eyes.

She opened the door on her side and got out, feeling like she needed a moment to think. Obviously there was a secret, and Travis knew it. What did he know? And what did it have to do with Dan and Geordie? Was it possible that Dan had somehow been meeting secretly with Geordie? No, she thought. How could it be? She always knew where Geordie was—she made sure of that. Or she thought she knew.

She felt sick to her stomach at the idea that Geordie might have been a victim of some terrible, adult design, and she hadn't known it. She had to find a way to learn whatever secret it was that Travis was hiding. When she thought about it, he had reacted strangely this afternoon too, when she asked about Emily. It was as if he was furious with her for bringing up Emily's death. Well, he was probably too upset to tell her anything now. Maybe she could appeal to Naomi to try and get him to part with whatever it was he knew.

She put the bag into the trash can, turned and walked back to the car. She opened the door and slid back into the driver's seat. 'I'm sorry if I upset you, Travis,' she said. 'I didn't mean to. I'm just upset myself, and this is a hard time for everybody.' She turned around to look at him. There was no one in the back seat. Travis and Champ were gone.

TWENTY-FOUR

'OH, MY GOD. TRAVIS!' she cried, jumping out of the car and scanning the well-lit parking lot. He was nowhere in sight. 'Travis!'

She ran out to the street and looked up and down, but neither the boy nor the dog was visible in the darkness. Where could he have gone? Could someone have snatched him and put him in their car? Caitlin felt like she couldn't catch her breath.

She ran back to the drive-thru window. The clerk, a bored-looking teenage girl wearing a visor, seemed vaguely startled to see her standing there.

'Did you see a little boy get out of that car over there? With a dog?' she cried.

'You can't walk up to this window,' said the girl. 'You have to be in your car.'

'I'm asking you a question. This is important,' Caitlin demanded.

'I didn't see anything,' the girl said irritably.

Caitlin ran around to the front of the restaurant, which sat on a corner, darted across the parking lot and looked down the other street. 'Travis!' she called out. But there was no answer.

Is he hiding from me? she thought. Her hands were shaking, and her heart was hammering. *Stop,* she thought. *Get a grip. Maybe he wanted ice cream or something and went back into the restaurant. It will take one minute to look. If he's not there,* she thought, *I'll have to call the police.*

She ran down to the doors nearest the service counter and jerked them open. She burst into the restaurant with panic written on her face. As she rushed up to the counter, she came face-to-face with Geordie's photo on a 'Missing' poster which was taped to the back of the register. Caitlin stopped and stared, momentarily poleaxed by the unexpected sight of her missing child's face.

A mild-looking, middle-aged man in a striped shirt approached her. He was wearing a name tag which identified him as the manager. 'Are you all right, ma'am?' he asked.

'I can't find…him. A little boy—about ten—and his dog. We were eating out in the car. And I went to throw away the trash. He's gone. Have you seen a boy and a little dog?'

The manager looked at his crew behind the counter, who all shook their heads.

'I'm afraid not,' he said. 'How long ago…?'

'Just a few minutes ago. No more than a few minutes.'

'I'm sorry,' he said.

'I've seen him,' said an older man wearing a golfer's cap, in a loud, cranky voice. He had a sour expression and was shaking his head. He started to sit down with the old woman who was waiting for him when he caught sight of the manager.

'Damned unsanitary if you ask me. A dog in the men's room?'

Caitlin let out a cry and doubled over in relief. 'Oh, thank God. Oh, thank you.' She began to run to the door of the men's room.

'Hey, wait a minute,' said the manager. 'You can't…'

She didn't give him time to finish. She pushed open the men's room and door and burst inside. There was no one standing at the urinals, for which she was grateful. She bent down and instantly saw furry haunches and a pair of sheepskin slippers beneath pajamas in one of the stalls.

'Travis!' she cried.

The manager followed her inside.

Before he could protest, she pointed to the stall. 'They're in there,' she said.

Champ let out an accommodating bark.

'Son, you need to come out of there,' said the manager. 'There's no dogs allowed in here.'

'No,' said Travis.

'Your mom here is awfully worried,' he said. 'Now come on out, right now.'

'She's not my mom,' Travis cried in a voice full of indignation.

Caitlin's face burned as the manager frowned at her. 'It's true. I'm his aunt.'

'Why did you say you were his mother?' the manager asked suspiciously.

'I…didn't.'

'You know we've had a kidnapping recently in this town. I'm not going to send this child off with just anybody,' he scolded her.

'You're right. I should have explained. I'm sorry,' said Caitlin.

'This lady says she's your aunt? Is that right?' he called out to Travis.

'Don't make me go with her,' Travis protested.

'Travis, stop it,' Caitlin said.

The manager reached in his pocket and pulled out his phone. 'Nobody's going to make you go anywhere, son.' He began to punch in some numbers.

'What are you doing?' Caitlin asked.

'Could you please exit the men's room, ma'am. I'm

going to have the police come get this boy and they can sort it out.'

'What about Travis?' Caitlin demanded.

'He'll be fine in there for the time being until the police get here. I'll stay right here with him.'

CAITLIN HAD NO choice but to accept his decision. She went and sat at a two-person Formica table by the front window. She pressed Naomi's number and waited for her sister-in-law to answer.

As soon as Naomi heard her voice she cried, 'What is going on, Caitlin? An officer just told me that Travis is locked in a bathroom at the McDonald's?'

'I take it you're still at the police station,' said Caitlin.

'We were just leaving,' said Naomi. 'Noah's going to have stay here tonight.'

'Oh, no,' said Caitlin.

'I asked you about Travis,' Naomi said impatiently.

'He's fine. He's all right,' said Caitlin. 'He and Champ are in the bathroom and they won't come out until you get here.'

'You were supposed to be minding him. Thanks a lot, Caitlin,' said Naomi sarcastically. 'I need this right now.'

Naomi hung up before Caitlin could apologize and as Caitlin saw a squad car, lights flashing, pulling into the fast-food emporium's parking lot.

Caitlin put her elbows on the table and rested her face in her hands. The police came in, knocked on the bathroom door and then pushed it in. While they were in the bathroom, presumably trying to reason with Travis, Naomi's old Volvo made a right-hand turn into the parking lot and pulled up haphazardly to park. Leaving Martha inside, Naomi hopped out and came into the restaurant. She looked around and immediately spotted Caitlin.

'Where is he?' she demanded.

'Still in the men's room,' said Caitlin.

Naomi looked at the men's room door. They could both hear voices coming from inside and the sound of Champ barking. 'Oh, for heaven's sake,' said Naomi. 'Why did you let him come in here with that dog anyway? The whole point was to keep the dog outside…'

'I didn't let him come in with the dog. We were in the car. Travis took Champ and sneaked in here while I was tossing out the garbage.'

'What were you thinking? You can't let them out of your sight,' Naomi cried. 'Didn't you learn anything from what happened to Geordie?'

Caitlin felt Naomi's words like a lash but she was not about to enter into this discussion. 'Look, why is Noah staying in jail? What about David Alvarez? Couldn't he do anything?'

'Call him yourself,' said Naomi irritably.

'Mom!'

Naomi turned to see Travis emerging from the bathroom, flanked by the police and the manager. Champ was in the lead, straining at his leash. 'Travis, what on earth were you doing in there with Champ?' Naomi demanded.

Travis stopped short when he saw Caitlin. 'Hiding from her,' he said.

'Why?' Naomi cried in exasperation.

'So she can't hurt me. Don't make me talk to her. Please.'

Naomi frowned at Caitlin. 'What did you say to him to upset him like this?'

Caitlin shook her head. 'Nothing, I swear. I asked him if he knew anything about Geordie…'

'What could Travis know?' demanded Naomi. 'He's just a little boy. Come on, Travis. You're going with me.' She turned to the police and the manager. With as much dignity as she could muster, she apologized for wasting their time.

'Oh, that's all right. From now on, though, no dogs in a restaurant, son,' one of the officers said cheerfully to Travis. Then he looked more closely at Naomi. 'Aren't you Rod Pelletier's wife?'

'Yes,' said Naomi, exhaling with relief at being recognized. 'Thank you so much for this.'

'No problem. Better get him home,' said the cop. 'He's up kind of late.'

Naomi ushered Travis out the door without a backward glance at Caitlin.

Caitlin remained seated at the little Formica table until her knees stopped shaking. Then, followed by the snickers and whispers of the teenaged employees, she got up and went back out to her car.

Still sitting in the parking lot, Caitlin called Noah's partner. David Alvarez answered, sounding tired. 'He has been arrested, yes,' said David. 'Attempted murder. They found Dan's blood in his car.'

'This is insane,' said Caitlin. 'Of course there's blood in the car. They had a fight. But Noah wouldn't try to kill him. Or anybody. It's just not his nature.'

'Well, presumably he believed that Dan kidnapped his son. That could drive anyone to violence. Look, Caitlin, so far the police have been unable to locate the guy whom Noah claimed helped him get his car running. His alibi, if you will. I'm hoping that the police will locate this witness before the arraignment tomorrow. It's set for eleven o'clock. Then we can get this cleared up before Noah has to enter a plea. Try not to worry. Get some sleep. I'll take good care of him.'

Caitlin thanked the attorney and ended the call. The exhaustion of the day was catching up to her, but she couldn't quit just yet. She wouldn't sleep anyway for wondering. She knew she would not be welcome, but she was going anyway. There was nowhere that she felt welcome anymore. She started the car, eased out of the parking lot and headed for the hospital.

TWENTY-FIVE

CAITLIN KNEW HER way around the hospital. She had been here often enough with her parents during their final illnesses. Even though the parking lot was nearly empty, visiting hours long over, she knew that intensive care never really shut down. She knew which door to go into, and she knew enough to look as if she were confident of where she was going. Even though visits to the patients in the ICU were limited and brief, there were always worried friends and relatives camped in the waiting room outside.

Caitlin greeted the hospital personnel she passed with a brittle smile and continued on her way. The waiting room for the ICU was nearly empty at this late hour. There was a heavyset couple asleep on one another's shoulders in one corner. Sick child, Caitlin thought. She glanced around and met the frigid gaze of Haley, who was thumbing through a magazine in a chair near the door. Beside Haley, on a little Naugahyde settee was Paula Bergen, fast asleep, covered by a coat.

'What are you doing here?' Haley demanded in a low voice.

'How's Dan?' Caitlin asked.

'Alive. No thanks to your husband,' said Haley.

'Is he conscious?'

'Caitlin, what do you want?'

Caitlin shook her head. 'Haley, there's no way that Noah did this. I found Dan. I saw the shape that he was in. Noah isn't capable of hurting someone like that.'

'Oh, really? Well, there's no way that Dan took Geordie. But you and Noah seem to be convinced of this all the same,' said Haley in disgust.

'The police are the ones who found out about the cell phone…'

Haley raised a hand to silence her. 'Caitlin, I don't want to discuss it.'

Caitlin glanced over at Paula, who looked spent and exhausted, even in sleep. 'Is Westy in there with him now?' she asked.

'No, he went out to get us some coffee. But you'd better leave before he gets back. He's not going to be happy to see you.'

'OK, OK, I'm going,' said Caitlin. She backed out of the waiting room and started down the hall. She passed a nurse coming out of the ICU. She hesitated, trying to formulate a plausible story, and then accosted the woman. 'Excuse me,' she said quietly.

The nurse smiled.

'How's my brother doing? I just got here from the airport, and I haven't seen him yet.'

'Your brother is…?' The nurse frowned.

'Dan Bergen.'

The nurse nodded. 'About the same. Did you want to see him for a minute?'

'Could I?' said Caitlin.

'Sure,' said the nurse. 'But there's a five-minute limit.'

Caitlin nodded. 'I'd appreciate it.'

'This way,' said the nurse. She led Caitlin down the hall to the ICU. In contrast to the dark, quiet halls of the rest of the hospital at night, the ICU was brightly lit and almost noisy with the sounds of machines. She followed the nurse to a curtained alcove where Dan lay in a hospital bed, tethered to a variety of beeping pumps, lines and monitors.

'Five minutes,' the nurse repeated.

Caitlin nodded. She walked up beside the bars on Dan's bed and looked down on him. The rivulets of blood were gone from his face but his skin was pale and waxy as a corpse. His eyes looked to be half-open. Caitlin put her hand over his and pressed on it, hoping to rouse him. She looked around and then put her mouth close to his ear. He smelled terrible—as if putrefaction was already setting in.

'Dan,' she said in a low voice. 'It's Caitlin. Where is Geordie? Please, tell me.'

She saw his eyelids flutter but he remained silent, breathing phlegmatically.

'Did you leave him alone somewhere? I'm scared to death,' she said, more to herself than to Dan. 'Tell me where I can find Geordie. Squeeze my hand if you can hear me.'

Dan lay unresponsive on the bed. His hand remained limp in her own. Caitlin's heart sank. Then, she noticed that his lips, which were cracking from dryness, seemed to be moving. 'What is it?' she asked. 'What are you saying?'

Dan's eyes remained half-closed. The tip of his tongue came out and touched his top lip. She saw his lips tremble and put her ear close to them.

'S...el...da...' he whispered.

'Soldier?' Caitlin asked urgently.

'What the hell are you doing in here?'

Caitlin jumped and looked up. Westy was standing at the foot of the bed, glaring at her. His pale eyes, red-rimmed with exhaustion, seemed to be smoking like dry ice. 'Get away from my son's bed. What kind of a hospital is this? See, I told you it wasn't my daughter,' he said, without turning his gaze from Caitlin, to the nurse who had offered Caitlin a chance to see Dan. 'My daughter is dead.'

'I'm terribly sorry,' said the nurse. 'Miss, you have to get out of here. Right now, or I'll call security.'

'I'm sorry. I'm leaving,' said Caitlin.

A gargling sound erupted from the man on the bed. All three of them looked in Dan's direction.

'Get her out of here,' Westy commanded. Then he went to Dan's side and took up one of Dan's limp hands in his own. 'What is it, son?' he asked in a pleading voice. 'What are you trying to say?'

Caitlin wanted desperately to stay, to wait, to see if there was something useful in the words Dan was trying to utter. But she knew that was not going to happen. The nurse was glaring at her, worried, no doubt, that her kindness-induced lapse in protocol might cost her her job.

'I'm sorry,' said Caitlin as she rushed from the ICU. 'My son is missing. I thought he might know something.'

'Go,' said the nurse. Caitlin went.

CAITLIN STUMBLED OUT to her car and turned on the engine, even though she knew she was not fit to drive. She tried to watch the road but her head was filled with images of Dan, lying in that hospital bed, trying to tell her something about Geordie. About where he was? Or was that what he was saying? She couldn't honestly tell. She had no idea if he even knew what she was asking him.

But what if he left Geordie alone in that house of his? What if he was a prisoner in there, in the dark? Restrained somehow. Afraid. No one answering when he called out. She needed to get to him. She had to get to Philly. She had to reach her son somehow. Caitlin felt a squeezing pain in her chest, and her breath was so shallow that she thought she might be having a heart attack. She thought about turning around and heading back to the emergency room, but instead she kept driving, trying to catch her breath.

After a few minutes she could go no farther. She pulled over to the side of the road and opened the car door to try and get some air.

It didn't work. With every moment, it was becoming harder and harder to breathe. She should have gone back to the hospital, she thought. She was going to die out here by the side of the road of a heart attack and Geordie would have no one to help him. All of a sudden her phone rang, and her already laboring heart leapt up in her chest. She answered the phone in a thin, shaky voice.

'Caitlin?'

Caitlin recognized Sam's voice. 'Yes, what?' she breathed into the phone.

'What's the matter?' Sam asked.

'Can't breathe,' she said. 'I think it's my heart.'

'It's probably an anxiety attack,' said Sam. 'You need to make yourself relax. Close your eyes. Put your head back and try to think of something soothing. Palm trees.'

Caitlin could not think of palm trees. All she could think of was Geordie. 'Why are you calling at this hour?' she asked. She glanced at the digital clock on the dashboard. It was after midnight.

'I knew you would want to hear this,' he said. 'Are you sure you're OK to talk? I mean, it's probably not your heart but those panic attacks can still be dangerous.'

'Hear what?' she cried in a strangled voice.

'The Chicago police located the store where Dan bought the phone. The clerk made a positive ID of his photo. Caitlin, are you there?'

Caitlin was trying to draw in breaths, and her whole body was shuddering. 'Yes,' she managed to squeak out.

'I just talked to the police in Philly. They are on their way to Dan's house even as we speak. They will swarm that place top to bottom. If Geordie is there, they will find him. Even if he's not, they will confiscate his computer, check all his communications. The answer is bound to be there. Also, we have confirmed Dan's DNA on the stuffed animal...'

'Bandit,' she whispered.

'It's only a matter of time now. Don't worry. The Philly police have the manpower. They will find Geordie. I'll call you the minute we know anything.'

Caitlin could feel the tightness in her chest beginning to ease as tears rose to her eyes. The police were probably already there, bursting in. They would find Geordie in no time. They had to.

'OK?' said Sam.

'What about Noah?' she asked.

'Well, Noah's going to have to stay put for the moment. We're checking out his alibi. Even if Dan was the one who took Geordie, that didn't give Noah the right to beat him nearly to death. Are you sure you're OK?'

'I'm OK,' she said.

'I'll talk to you soon,' said Sam.

Caitlin nodded. She could feel the breath entering her lungs in a steady stream. She ended the call and drove the rest of the way to Noah's house. She let herself in and turned on the lights. She roamed through the house, finally went into Geordie's room and sat down on the rug beside his bed.

Her mind was still racing, but her heart had settled back into a normal rhythm. She tried to think about all that had happened today but her thoughts kept returning to the same question. Why would Noah have beaten Dan up that way? Why would he have done that before he knew where Geordie could be found? Why would he ever do that?

Stop. Back up, she thought suddenly. *Was this really a question?* she thought. *Make up your mind. Either you believe Noah or you don't. Which is it?* She forced herself to stop riding her racing thoughts and tried to think clearly. If Noah believed that Dan had Geordie, would he try to kill him?

The only thing that mattered to either one of them was to find their boy. Not punishment. Not retribution. Just Geordie. Just Geordie, safely home.

She felt a sudden sense of peace envelop her like a silky veil as she realized that this was undoubtedly the truth. Somebody tried to kill Dan. But it couldn't have been Noah. Geordie was missing and Dan might know his whereabouts. So Noah could not be guilty. He would never have tried to kill their link to Geordie. Never.

The relief of that realization was so profound that it seemed to take every last remnant of energy out of her. The exhaustion of the day finally overwhelmed her, and forced her to sleep.

TWENTY-SIX

IT WAS THE fact that the phone had not rung which entered her dreams and woke her. The moment she opened her eyes, she broke out in a cold sweat. She fumbled for her phone but there was no message. No word from Sam. That meant only one thing: the Philly police had not found Geordie. She called Sam immediately. He answered on the first ring. Caitlin could hear the roar of engines in the background. 'Sam. Have you heard anything from the Philly police?'

'I've been in frequent contact with the lieutenant in charge. They broke in and searched the place top to bottom. Geordie is not there, and it doesn't appear that he has ever been there.'

'Oh, my God,' said Caitlin desperately. 'Where is he?'

'They confiscated Dan's computer. His hard drive is being examined by their digital forensics team. They're questioning all Dan's colleagues and his friends. By the way, I spoke to the hospital. They're moving Dan out of the ICU. He's still unresponsive but he's stable now. They're putting him in a private room.'

'Sam, I know that it wasn't Noah that tried to kill him. It was someone else.'

'Well, of course, you want to give Noah the benefit of the doubt…'

'No, listen to me. I thought it through. If it was one of your kids, and only one person knew where they were being held, would you kill that person? Would you take the chance of silencing them forever? Would vengeance be more important than finding your child?' she demanded.

Sam was silent for a minute.

'I'm right. Admit it,' said Caitlin.

'Yes. You have a point. And I already have an officer assigned to guard his room in the hospital. Just in case.'

Caitlin could barely hear his voice through the roaring in the background. 'Sam, can you still hear me? What's that racket?'

'I'm at the Biker's War Memorial convention in Washington. I'm trying to find the elusive Jim. I was actually on my way here when I spoke to you last night,' he said.

'Wow. That's kind of beyond the call of duty, isn't it?' she asked.

'Probably,' Sam admitted. 'But, nonetheless…'

'Thank you, Sam. I mean it.'

'You just have to try and be patient, Caitlin. We've blanketed the media with a plea for whoever it was who helped Noah with his car to come forward. And I am trudging around among this bunch of graying Hells Angels in their orthopedic shoes to see if I can find that fellow. If I can locate him, we can confirm Noah's story. Until then we have to hold him.'

'It wasn't Noah,' she insisted.

'Later, Caitlin,' he said and ended the call.

Caitlin splashed water on her face, ate some yogurt standing by the open door of the refrigerator and brushed her teeth. She didn't bother to change her clothes. She walked out the back door of the house and went around to where she had found Dan left for dead in the bushes the night before, and stared down at the broken branches, the flattened brown grass. Why had someone tried to kill him? Would they try again? Caitlin took out her phone and pressed a number. She stood in the yard, looking at the looming storm clouds, and waited.

Haley answered the phone on the second ring.

'Haley, it's Caitlin. Don't hang up.'

'What do you want, Caitlin?' Haley asked.

'Where are you?' Caitlin asked. 'Are you at the hospital?'

'What business is that of yours?' Haley demanded.

'I have a reason for asking,' said Caitlin.

'Yes, I'm at the hospital.'

'How is Dan doing? Is he conscious?'

'In and out,' said Haley.

'I heard they moved him to a private room.'

'Yes. He's somewhat improved.'

'Haley, listen to me. Dan's life is still in danger,' said Caitlin.

'Oh, is Noah out of jail?' Haley asked.

'This is serious, Haley.'

'There's a police officer posted outside his room, if it makes you feel any better,' said Haley sarcastically.

'I know that. But I'm worried that it's not enough. That it's not going to protect him,' said Caitlin. 'You need to get inside his room and stay there. Sit by his bedside. Don't let anyone visit him unless you are there.'

Haley was quiet for a moment. 'Why are you saying this?' she asked.

'My reasons are selfish. I believe that Dan is the only one who can lead us to Geordie. Please,' said Caitlin, 'will you just do as I ask? Stay with him. Refuse to move, no matter what anybody says.'

'I was going to do it anyway,' said Haley.

'Thank you,' said Caitlin. 'I have to go.'

Now that she felt certain that Noah had not been the one to try to kill Dan, she needed to think about what had happened yesterday in a different way. Noah had gone to meet Dan at the cemetery. Could Dan possibly have brought Geordie with him? Kept him out of sight somehow? All of sudden, Caitlin was struck with a thought that was both horrible and electrifying. Was Geordie still here, right here in Hartwell? Was he now the prisoner of the person who had tried to kill Dan?

She felt her chest begin to tighten again. *Think palm trees,* she thought. This was no time for fainting. She had to be strong.

Retrace everything, she thought. *Start with the cemetery.*

As SHE DROVE through the quiet, empty lanes which divided the graves, she thought about Dan's car. Where was it now? If Dan had brought Geordie here with him, could Dan have left Geordie in the car when he got out to meet Noah? She knew Geordie well enough to know that he would not just have sat still. He would have acted up. Unless he was restrained or sedated somehow. The thought of Geordie drugged was repulsive to her, and she had to banish it from her mind.

She knew where Emily's grave was. They had taken Geordie there on several occasions. Caitlin parked and got out of her car. Now that she was here, she wondered what it was that she thought she might find here. The police had already scoured this area. Was she seeking some sign of Geordie having been here? Maybe it was that. She walked down the rows of graves until she came to the simple stone between two small conifers with Emily's name on it. Beloved wife and mother, it said. Beneath that were dates of her birth and death.

On the occasions when she had come here with Noah and Geordie, she had always felt overwhelmed by guilt, knowing that her own brother was responsible for Emily's death. Furtively, she would watch Noah and Geordie, torturing herself by imagining what they would think of her if they knew her secret. Whenever they came here, Noah was always silent, distant, as he threw out the lifeless flowers, rinsed out the liner and put fresh blooms in the permanent vase. Geordie often left a little plastic car or animal figure on the grave. Caitlin knew how much Geordie hated to part with any of his toys. But he always left some token for his mother which he would pat tenderly before he got up and scampered away among the headstones. The last time they were here, he left a Kung Fu Panda which he had received as a party favor. The panda was still peeking out from the bed of begonias planted in front of Emily's headstone.

The flowers in the vase were fresh. They must have been the ones that Dan had brought. She remembered Noah saying that it angered him to see Dan putting flowers on Emily's grave. Fleetingly, Caitlin wished she had brought a flower to leave on the grave. She had never really spent a moment alone at this monument. She closed her eyes, bowed her head and thought about the woman buried there. In her mind, Emily existed only in photographs. Bright-eyed, smiling, silent.

Something terrible has happened to your little boy, she thought. *To our little boy. If you have the power to intercede, to point us in the right direction, do it. Please.* She reached out and touched the top of the stone. *Amen,* she thought. Then she turned away. She didn't believe in spirits that remained among the living after death, but if they did... She walked back to her car and sat down in the driver's seat, looking back at the grave. She tried to think about Dan. He was Emily's brother. Uncle to Emily's son. He had come to her grave and brought fresh flowers to adorn it. Why would he do that if he had kidnapped Emily's child? Maybe if he'd come here to spit on her grave, that would be in keeping with his actions. But, to bring flowers? It did not make sense. All of Dan's actions seemed…contradictory.

Caitlin's thoughts traveled back to last night at the fast-food restaurant. It was her questions about Dan which had upset Travis and caused him to take Champ and try to hide from her.

Travis knew something, she thought. She was increasingly convinced of that. But he would not talk to her now. And Naomi would not let her anywhere near her son. Not after last night. He was probably in school anyway, she thought. And then she reminded herself that no—it was Saturday. Travis had Boy Scouts on Saturday. That was why they had decided to have Geordie's party on a Sunday—so that Travis could come. Hard to fathom, she thought, that Geordie's birthday was only a week ago.

She looked at the dashboard clock. Travis would probably be at Scouts right now. She knew where the Scouts met. Like everyone else in the family, Caitlin had been called upon to give him a ride to and fro from time to time. They had a lodge near the reservoir where they met for campfires and hikes in the woods. She had met one of the Scoutmasters, a guy named Bernie, one time when Geordie was with her. Geordie was awed by his glimpse of the group and couldn't wait until he was old enough to join. Travis, on the other hand, always seemed reluctant to attend. The Scouts were entirely too energetic for Travis, who preferred his video games. Naomi insisted that he go because one of the Scout leaders had been in Iraq with Rod and took a special interest in Travis.

Maybe if she ambushed Travis at Scouts and was able to assure him that he had nothing to fear by talking, he would reveal whatever it was that he knew. She was taking a chance that Travis would scream bloody murder at the sight of her and tell her nothing. But she had to try.

She looked back at the gravestone between the fir trees. 'Be with Geordie,' she said aloud into the somber silence. 'Keep our boy safe until we can find him.' Then Caitlin turned on the ignition and headed out of the cemetery.

CAITLIN PASSED THE road to the reservoir where the Scout camp was located twice before she recognized it and turned in. The dirt road was narrow and rutted, and she was forced to drive slowly and take the bumps carefully. A late-model Mercedes coming from the direction of the lodge hit the ruts in the road with determined abandon. Caitlin was barely able to get out of the way before the Mercedes lurched by, the woman at the wheel talking animatedly on her cell phone. Caitlin continued on down the road, pulling over to the side to allow a giant yellow Hummer to get by. She couldn't even see the driver of that car, they were so high off the ground.

Finally, she spotted the lodge in the distance, a rudimentary, oversized log cabin at the edge of the reservoir. There were boys shrieking and chasing each other around the picnic tables.

A Subaru Forester was idling up ahead at the end of the road, and Caitlin glimpsed the couple in the front seat exchange a quick kiss. Then the car door opened on the passenger side and a stocky, dark-haired man wearing a buffalo plaid shirt and heavy work boots and an Eagles cap emerged. Caitlin frowned at the sight of him. He looked so familiar. He leaned down and spoke to the driver through the passenger-side window. Then he straightened up, tapped on the hood and started to walk in the direction of the lodge. Several of the Boy Scouts caught sight of him and swarmed in his direction, seemingly thrilled to see him arrive. The man high-fived the rambunctious boys who trailed beside him like a school of pilot fish as he made his way to the lodge. The Scoutmaster, whom Caitlin recognized as Bernie, hailed the newcomer, who was obviously another of the Scout leaders.

The Forester made a K-turn and started back up the road. As the car approached, Caitlin noticed the fire department license plate, and suddenly she remembered why that car looked so familiar. She had ridden in that same car during the search in the marshes for Geordie. What was that guy's name? Jerry. A nice guy, she thought. A fireman, a Scoutmaster, a guy who would search for a missing child in his free time. This had to be the guy Naomi had mentioned. The one who was in Iraq with Rod Pelletier.

The Forester was almost even with her car now, and Caitlin stopped to let it pass. As the car passed by her, she gazed in at the driver.

For a moment, she thought her eyes were deceiving her. The driver, intent on negotiating the rutted road, paid no attention to Caitlin's car. Caitlin was free to stare, and stare she did. No wonder Jerry had gotten out of the car so far from the lodge, she thought. He wouldn't have wanted to be caught kissing the driver of the Forester, because the driver of the Forester was another man. And not just any man. Caitlin recognized him right away. It was Geordie's teacher, Alan Needleman.

TWENTY-SEVEN

THE SOUND OF a horn honking behind her jolted Caitlin, and she resumed driving down the road toward the lodge. The woman in the car behind her stopped far short of the lodge and let out a pair of boys who looked to be about Travis's age. *Travis,* she thought. She had come to talk to Travis, but instead she was processing the shock of the realization she had just made. She had heard the rumors that Alan Needleman lived with a man. She may have even heard it was a fireman. But now all the connections locked together and seemed jarring.

She parked her car near the lodge, got out and approached the porch. The assembled boys were joking with Jerry and the other Scoutmaster, Bernie, who was several years older than the stocky young fireman. Caitlin did not see Travis anywhere among them. She stood at the foot of the wooden steps, not sure what it was she wanted to ask any longer.

'Can we help you, ma'am?' the Scoutmaster named Bernie asked politely.

'I want to talk to Jerry,' Caitlin said.

Jerry removed his cap and stuffed it in his back pocket. He looked at her and frowned while the boys erupted into choruses of 'Woo-Woo.'

'All right, knock it off,' Jerry said to the boys. He came down the steps and looked at Caitlin with a puzzled expression on his face. She could see that he was trying to place her.

Caitlin helped him out. 'You gave me a ride to the search the other day. The search for Geordie,' she said.

Jerry nodded and then looked more puzzled than ever. 'I'm sorry, I remember you but I forget your name.'

'I told you my name was Kate,' she said.

Jerry grimaced and nodded. 'What can I do for you, Kate?' he asked.

'Actually, my name is Caitlin,' she said. 'Caitlin Eckhart. I'm… Geordie Eckhart is my boy.'

Jerry was taken aback at first. Then his eyes were filled with sympathy. 'You never mentioned it,' he said. 'I'm so sorry.'

Caitlin looked at him with narrowed eyes. 'If I had, would you have mentioned our connection?' she asked.

Jerry frowned. 'What connection?'

The boys on the porch were all leaning over the railings, trying to listen. Caitlin was tempted to blurt it out in front of them, but she stopped herself. 'Why don't we talk over there,' she said, pointing to the picnic table.

Jerry frowned and then shrugged. 'OK. I'll be right back, guys.'

He followed Caitlin, dried leaves crunching under his boots, over to the picnic table. Caitlin turned on him before he could sit down.

'Alan Needleman is my son's teacher,' she said bluntly.

Jerry did not flinch. He didn't smile either. 'Yes. I know that.' He gazed at her steadily. 'He's been terribly upset about Geordie's disappearance.'

'Well, it seems like quite a coincidence.'

'Does it?' he asked, shifting his weight into a more aggressive stance.

'Frankly, yes,' she said.

'Did you see us together just now? Was that you in the car behind us?'

'Yes, it was,' she said.

'I'm sorry you have a problem with that,' he said coldly.

Caitlin was undaunted. 'I don't have a problem with your…relationship. I have a problem with secrets,' she said. 'I have a problem with hiding your identity.'

'It's called a "private life" for a reason,' said Jerry.

'Oh, no,' Caitlin said angrily. 'My child is missing. I don't give a damn about your privacy. My child is gone. Whoever took him is living a lie. Pretending to be…something they're not.'

'I'm sure that's true. But it's got nothing to do with me.'

'Really?' Caitlin asked. 'I know for a fact that my nephew, Travis, is afraid of somebody or something. He never wants to come to Scouts. Is that because of you?'

Jerry gave a mirthless laugh. 'Travis does tend to be… reluctant. I think it's because we insist that he get off his butt.'

'This isn't funny,' she said.

'All right. Do you want to talk about Travis? The kid has problems. No doubt. He's…angry. I try not to be too hard on him. He's suffered a huge loss. I know. I was in Iraq with his Dad,' said Jerry.

Caitlin nodded. 'I wondered about that.' She thought about Naomi, suggesting Alan Needleman might be to blame for Geordie's disappearance. She must have no idea that this Scoutmaster, whom she had encouraged Travis to emulate, was Alan Needleman's partner. 'Does Naomi know…?'

'That I'm gay? What do you think?'

'I think she doesn't,' said Caitlin. 'I know she doesn't. For one thing, you could never be a Scoutmaster if they knew you were gay.'

'They?'

'The Boy Scouts.'

'That's true. I don't deny it. It's a homophobic orga-
nization.'

'So, why are you here?'

Jerry folded his arms across his chest and glanced back
at the boys who were goofing around at the lodge. 'Look,
Mrs Eckhart. My son is in this troop.'

Caitlin was taken aback. 'Your son?'

'Yes. I encouraged him to join the Scouts because I always loved being a Scout when I was a kid. I loved the
camping and the outdoor activities. I thought it would be
good for my son, too. The troop needed another leader
and I volunteered.'

'Oh,' she said. 'I…didn't realize…'

'Between my divorce and my ex-wife's anger toward
me, he's had to put up with a lot already. He doesn't say
it, but I know he'd rather all these kids in his Scout troop
didn't know about his Dad and Mr Needleman. I can't tell
you what to do, but my son didn't do anything to deserve
that hassle,' he said.

'No, of course not,' she said. Caitlin realized, sheepishly
and too late, that she was being as bigoted in her thinking
as the Boy Scout hierarchy.

Jerry's tone had an edge. 'These boys are in no danger
from me,' he said. 'The kids at school are in no danger
from Alan. We're just trying to help out, set a good example and live our lives.'

'You're right. I shouldn't have suggested…' she said.

'What are you doing here anyway?' Jerry asked.

Caitlin sighed. 'I came to talk to Travis,' she said. 'Is
he here?'

Jerry frowned and looked at the gaggle of boys on the
porch. 'I don't see him. Let me check.'

Jerry walked back through the leaves in the direction
of the lodge. 'Hey Bernie,' he called out. He gestured for

the other Scoutmaster to come down the stairs and join him. As Bernie arrived where they were standing, Jerry asked, 'Is Travis Pelletier here today?'

Bernie shook his head. 'His mother called. It seems he lost his dog and he was too upset to come today.'

'This is Mrs Eckhart,' Jerry said to his fellow Scoutmaster. 'Her boy is the one who disappeared from the elementary school.'

Bernie looked at her sadly. 'Oh, sure. We've met before. That's so terrible.'

'Thank you. You say that Travis lost his dog?' Caitlin asked. 'When?'

'I don't know,' said Bernie.

Caitlin instantly felt uneasy. Travis never let that dog out of his sight. The two of them seemed glued together. That dog would not just run away. 'I have to go,' said Caitlin abruptly. She turned and started back to her car. Then she stopped and spoke again to Jerry, who was heading back to the troop. 'I'm sorry about this. About what I said to you. I was unfair,' she said.

'I'm used to it,' Jerry said.

Caitlin thought about the police, initially seeing her as a suspect in Geordie's disappearance just because she was his stepmother, rather than his birth mother. She thought about Noah, accusing her of being complicit in Geordie's disappearance, because she had kept that secret about her brother. She had been pained and outraged by those assumptions. And yet, though she knew better, she had succumbed to the exact same sort of thinking. Of course she was frightened for Geordie. But that was no excuse. She had been critical of Naomi for jumping to conclusions. And then she did it herself. It was instructive, she thought, to realize how quickly one's convictions could vanish in the face of fear.

'I never thought of myself that way,' she said.

'What way?'

'Biased,' she said.

Jerry's expression softened. 'Well, don't be too hard on yourself. I wouldn't trust anyone either,' he said, 'if I was in your shoes.'

ON THE WAY to Naomi's house, Caitlin wondered how in the world she was going to convince Travis to talk to her. Even if Naomi was at the free bookstore today, she was pretty sure that Martha had been warned to keep Caitlin away from Travis. She thought about what she had heard at the Boy Scout camp. Champ had disappeared. She couldn't imagine how that could have happened. Dogs were faithful creatures and she had rarely seen an owner and pup more attached than Champ and Travis. She parked in a side street just across from Naomi's house. She could see the house and she noticed that Naomi's Volvo was gone from the driveway. That made things easier. *Now,* she thought, *what to say?* Finally, she had an idea.

She crossed the street, walked up to the front door and knocked. Martha hollered out that she was coming, and Caitlin waited as Martha made her way to the front door and opened it. She squinted out at the figure on the step. 'Yes.'

'Martha, it's me. It's Caitlin.'

'Caitlin,' she exclaimed. 'Have they let Noah go yet?'

'Not yet,' said Caitlin. 'They're still looking for the biker who stopped to help Noah with his car. Detective Mathis went down to Washington to see if he could get a line on the guy.'

'I'm so disgusted with that police department,' Martha said. 'They couldn't find their nose on their face. What about Geordie? Anything?'

'Nothing,' said Caitlin.

'Lord,' said Martha with a sigh.

'Look, Martha, I had a little misunderstanding last night with Travis. I'm really sorry about that…'

Martha shook her head. 'He deserved to get in trouble. He knows not to take a dog into a restaurant,' she said.

'Well, I just came to apologize. And then I heard about Champ running away. What happened? Did he get out the back door or something?'

'I don't know,' said Martha. 'I didn't even know he was gone until Travis mentioned it.'

Mentioned it? Caitlin thought. She would have expected Travis to be nearly hysterical to find his dog gone. Then again, she remembered his mother saying that he was the only one who didn't react when Emily died. 'Well, I wanted to offer to help him look for Champ. Do you think he'd like some help? We can cover a lot more territory in the car than he could on foot.'

'That's nice, dear. I'll tell him you came by,' Martha said. Caitlin noticed that she was not invited into the house.

'Is he out looking for Champ now?'

Martha frowned and looked back into the dark house. 'No. The last time I checked on him he said he was playing a video game.'

'Really?' Caitlin said, taken aback.

'I told him to get busy making some posters with Champ's picture. He can go hang 'em up around the neighborhood. If it was my dog I'd be out there looking high and low. But he's addicted to those games.'

'I could take him around in the car to hang the posters up,' Caitlin offered.

'Never mind. He's better off walking. It would do that boy good. I will tell him you were here though,' Martha said firmly, closing the door with a little wave.

Caitlin walked back across the street to her car and sat down in the driver's seat. She had been surprised to hear that Champ had run away in the first place. Champ and Travis seemed to be almost inseparable. But the thought that Travis wasn't even out looking for his beloved dog made no sense at all. She would have sworn that Travis loved that dog more than anything. Obviously, she had been mistaken.

Caitlin sat staring at the little house across the way. Whatever Travis knew, she was not going to get close to it. Clearly, she wasn't welcome in that house. She knew she should turn on the engine and leave but she felt completely tapped out. Where was there to go? She called David Alvarez to ask about Noah, but got his voice mail. She could check with the hospital again to see if Dan was conscious and able to speak, but even as she thought it she knew they would never tell her that over the phone. She wouldn't be allowed anywhere near the patient, and Haley had made it clear that she was no longer a fan of Caitlin's.

Geordie, she thought. *I've done you no good at all. I've alienated everyone and I am no closer to finding you now than I ever was.*

As she sat slumped in the driver's seat, feeling defeated and trying to think of what to do next, she saw the front door of Naomi's house open. Instantly, she was alert. Travis stepped out onto the front steps with a small backpack slung over his shoulder. He looked around furtively and then stepped off into the yard. He walked out to the sidewalk, reached into the backpack and pulled out a flyer. He thumb-tacked the flyer to the nearest telephone pole. Then he started to lumber down toward the end of the street. Caitlin watched him, wondering how she could approach him without him running away from her, calling for help.

He was a puzzling child, she thought. He did not look

distraught. He looked almost—pleased with himself. She watched him as he walked down the block. When he got to the end of the street, instead of turning right or left, he looked all around him once again. Obviously, he did not recognize Caitlin's parked car around the corner from his house, or the driver crouched there, peering over the wheel.

Once he seemed certain that he was not being watched, Travis sneaked behind the boarded-up deli at the corner. Caitlin had to crane her neck to see him. He was crouched down by the boarded-up back door. Then, suddenly, backpack and all, he disappeared from view.

TWENTY-EIGHT

CAITLIN GOT OUT of her car and hurried across the street and down the block. Her heart was beating out of proportion to the exertion. Suddenly, that boarded-up deli was presenting her with a thought too staggering to take in.

Was it possible? Was Geordie there, inside that store? Was this the secret that Travis was hiding? Had Dan somehow enlisted Travis's help? Could Travis be that cruel and evil a child? He hadn't seemed to care that his dog ran away. He had asked for more macaroni upon learning that his Aunt Emily was killed in an accident. Maybe he was some sort of incipient psychopath who was helping Dan for some promised reward. She had read that there were children like that. As awful as it seemed, everything inside of Caitlin was praying that this was the answer—that Geordie was in that abandoned store and still alive. If she could only find him, if it was not too late, she knew she could summon help and protect him until that help arrived.

She moved as quietly as possible, not wanting Travis to be alerted to her presence. She went around to the back of the store and nearly knocked over an empty garbage can in her haste, but managed to right it before it fell over with a clatter. She took a deep breath to try and calm her pounding heart.

The plywood panel on the back door was awry, but she knew it would be impossible to push it in and get into the building without making any noise. She wanted to take

Travis by surprise and, if he had a hostage, to make sure that no harm came to that hostage. A boy who would help to hold his cousin prisoner was capable of anything. She could not think of any way to get that door open without a racket, so she had to rely on the element of surprise. If she pushed through that panel quickly enough, Travis would not have time to react.

Caitlin looked around the alley behind the store for something she could use to bust the panel if it resisted. She had little to choose from. The trash from the deli had long ago been carried away. There were still empty cardboard boxes and plastic milk crates, but they would not be much help. There was an old broom, left outside in the alley, probably since the store had closed. She wondered if she might be able to use the broomstick as a makeshift crowbar to pry off the plywood.

Caitlin examined the door. There was a panel on the upper half of the door, too. Perhaps she could loosen it, reach in and unlock the door. She decided to try it. She pressed against the corner nearest the doorknob, but the panel was tightly nailed into place. She pressed again, harder, but it did not budge. Travis had already loosened the lower panel. She would have to use that.

Crouching down, Caitlin placed her palm against the lower panel and felt it give. Somehow Travis had fit himself through that opening. She doubted that she would be able to enter through that same space, even though he was a stocky child and she was relatively slim. She needed to push the plywood out of the frame. Visualizing her son on the other side of that door, she wedged the broom handle in between the plywood and the door frame and began to jimmy it. The light, pressed wood splintered but did not break. She kept up the pressure, gently but firmly forcing the plywood free of the frame. She wondered how far she needed to push it before she could ease herself inside. All of a sudden there was a resounding crack and the panel gave way. The plywood broke off in a jagged lengthwise piece and clattered to the floor, leaving a large, dark gap in the door. She crawled through the newly opened lower panel and into the storeroom of the deli onto a filthy linoleum floor. *So much for the element of surprise,* she thought. Now she had to move quickly.

She dragged herself all the way inside and scrambled to her feet in the dark room lined with almost empty shelves, and illuminated by gray light through a single dirty window at the far end.

The place was absolutely silent. It was as if the building was empty. She began to cross the room to the door which led to the deli itself. Her arms were extended so that she did not bump into something and knock it on top of herself. She got to the door, reached out and pulled it open.

In front of her was a counter and an empty cold case. She walked around the counter and into the vacant store, blinking as her eyes tried to adjust to the dark. At the front of the store, beneath each boarded up window, was a shelf on which yellowing shopper's guides and free newspapers were still scattered. Facing the counter were several tables and chairs decorated with plastic flowers in little jelly jars, salt, pepper and napkin holders. She stepped farther into the room. 'Geordie?' she whispered.

There was no answer but she heard something. She stopped and listened. Labored breathing and a muffled, high-pitched whine was coming from one of the tables by the wall. Wishing she had a flashlight, she bent over to look.

Under one of the tables Travis sat huddled, his pudgy face pale with fright. Crushed to his chest was Champ,

Travis's hand muzzling him, his leash attached to his collar and tied, at the other end, to the radiator along the wall.

Caitlin stared. 'Travis,' she said. 'What in the world…'

Travis stared back at her, wide-eyed.

'What are you doing under there? Is Geordie here?' Caitlin demanded.

Travis looked completely perplexed by her question. 'Geordie?' he said. 'Geordie got kidnapped.'

Caitlin had known, before she had even asked, that her wild conjectures were just that—hope against hope. Geordie was not here. She gazed around the legs of the table. There was a bowl of water on the floor and a bowl of dog food as well. And a little pallet made out of dish towels and newspapers. 'Is this some kind of secret clubhouse?' she asked.

'None of your business,' said Travis.

'What is Champ doing here?' Caitlin demanded. 'I thought he ran away. Travis, come out from under that table and answer me.'

Travis shook his head and squeezed Champ more tightly.

Caitlin crouched down and looked closer and, to her surprise, saw tears rolling down Travis's face. Instantly, she felt guilty for having alarmed him. For having discovered his hiding place. 'Travis, what's the matter?'

Travis wiped his face with his hand, leaving filthy streaks on his cheeks. 'Now where will I hide him?' he wailed.

Caitlin hesitated for a moment, and then she got all the way down on the filthy floor on her hands and knees. Slowly, she crawled under the table, joining Travis and his dog. Travis gripped Champ and pulled away from her when she tried to touch his shoulder. Caitlin watched him closely. Finally, she said, 'Why do you need to hide him?'

Travis shook his head angrily.

'Travis? Did your Mom say you couldn't keep him?'

'NO, stupidhead,' Travis shouted.

Caitlin was a little more familiar with this Travis, the defiant one. But as soon as he had yelled at her he seemed to deflate like a punctured balloon. Caitlin chose her next question carefully.

'Who are you hiding him from?' Caitlin asked as gently as possible.

Travis shook his head.

'Did someone say they'd steal him from you?'

'Not steal him,' said Travis.

'Did someone say they were going to hurt Champ?' Caitlin asked.

Travis was silent, sniffling.

'Was it a kid? Was it another kid who threatened to hurt him?'

Travis shook his head.

'Was it a grown-up?' Caitlin asked.

'Now that you know where he is, you'll tell everyone,' Travis said angrily.

'I'm not going to tell anyone,' said Caitlin.

'Yes, you will. And then…'

'Then what?' Caitlin asked.

'You know what,' Travis cried. 'They'll kill him.'

Caitlin drew in a sharp breath, shocked in spite of herself. 'Kill Champ? Who said that?' she cried indignantly.

Travis did not reply.

Caitlin slowly reached out her hand past Travis and patted the fur on Champ's head. 'You listen to me, Travis,' Caitlin said. 'And listen good. Nobody is going to hurt this dog. Do you hear me? Nobody. I promise you. No matter what.'

Travis looked up at Caitlin with wary eyes. He wiped

away tears with the back of his hand. Caitlin felt ashamed for how she had misjudged his motives. She gazed back at him somberly. 'No matter what. Do you understand me? Do you believe me?'

Travis shrugged.

'No person who had any decency would say a thing like that,' said Caitlin. 'Anyone who would say that is a very, very bad person. Do you understand?'

This time Travis's response was unequivocal. 'I know,' he said.

Caitlin continued to pet the dog with gentle, smooth strokes. 'Why did this very bad person threaten to kill Champ?' she asked carefully.

'For telling the secret!' Travis cried. 'It's your fault. I never told anybody. But then you said that I had to tell every secret so we could find Geordie. And I knew if I told the secret...'

Caitlin's pulse began to race but she kept her voice calm. 'I understand,' said Caitlin. 'You were afraid of what would happen to Champ.'

Travis nodded. 'That's why I hid him in here. I thought if he was hidden somewhere then I could tell the secret and still keep Champ safe.'

Caitlin's heart was pounding. She tried to keep her voice calm. 'Travis, is your secret about Geordie?' she asked quietly. 'Do you know where he is?'

Travis looked perplexed and shook his head. 'No. No. I don't know nothing about Geordie.'

Caitlin could feel her own disappointment filling the room. Her boy was not here. Travis's secret wasn't about Geordie. She was no closer than she had been before to having him back in her arms. She wanted to cry out in frustration.

'It's about me,' Travis said. 'And the bad stuff...that

happened. You said I had to tell it. And about Aunt Emily. All of it.'

Caitlin stared at him. 'Aunt Emily? What are you talking about, Travis?'

'You won't get mad at me?'

'No,' she said.

Travis looked at her with narrowed eyes. 'You promise nothing will happen to Champ.'

'Promise,' said Caitlin, trying to keep her voice from shaking. 'Now, tell me.'

TWENTY-NINE

CAITLIN DROVE OVER the low rise and looked down at the peaceful surface of the lake. There were a couple of boats near the far shore, manned by fishermen patiently trying to catch dinner. Up the slope she could see Paula and Westy's house, the afternoon sun glinting off the windows, flowers still blooming among the autumn leaves like a photo from a calendar, captioned, Can this really be in New Jersey?

Oh, yeah, Caitlin thought. She drove down toward Westy's workshop and parked her car in a cul-de-sac so it would be out of sight. Then she got out and walked up to the tidy, free-standing building. The telescopes on the porch were pointing out over the water at crazy angles. Caitlin let herself inside.

The interior was nothing fancy but it was neat and organized. The square building had a woodstove for heat. The woodstove was not fired up today, so the gloomy interior was chilly. The rows of windows were built high up under the eaves. There were two worktables and an old cupboard filled with jars of hardware—nails, screws and washers—and rows of tools. Two birdhouses in the process of being completed sat on a wide table. Along one wall was a Danish-style sofa from the fifties and a couple of plastic chairs. There were charts on the walls with pictures of birds and their identifying characteristics. There was a birding map of the region, its endless marshes and waterways notable for which birds were likely to be seen there.

Caitlin looked around the tidy workshop with a feeling a revulsion. She almost wished she had a can of spray paint so she could deface these walls. So that the defiled appearance of the place would match its history.

The door of the workshop opened, and Caitlin turned around. Westy Bergen walked in and stared at her.

'Surprised?' she asked.

Westy pulled himself up in a dignified manner. 'Well, yes. I don't usually find people in my workshop unless I invite them,' he said.

'I did the inviting today,' she said.

'I'm sorry?' he said, looking puzzled.

'Don't bother,' she said. 'Just…don't bother. We both know why you're here.'

'I don't know what you're talking about, Caitlin,' he said. 'I came down here to get my slicker. I left it in the closet over there and those storm clouds look like…'

Caitlin shook her head. 'I knew you'd come when I left you that message. You had to find out how much I knew about what really happened to Emily.'

Westy looked indignant. 'As I recall,' he said frostily, 'my daughter was killed. By your brother. Now, if you'll excuse me…'

'Travis told me everything,' she said.

Westy's face paled and he seemed to sag for a moment. 'I don't know what you mean,' he said, but his tone was uncertain.

'I have to admit, you did a bang-up job of scaring him into silence—threatening to kill his dog—but he finally broke down and told me everything.'

Westy pretended to ignore her. He walked over to a narrow closet and opened it, rummaging around intently. 'I have no idea what you're talking about,' said Westy.

Caitlin watched him, consumed with disgust and hatred. 'Yes, you do. Travis told me what really happened on the day that Emily died. Surely you haven't forgotten that day?'

Westy turned to her with all the dignity he could muster. 'Frankly,' said Westy calmly, 'it's amazing to me that you would breathe a word about Emily's death. It was your brother who killed her.'

'It was my brother who hit her,' said Caitlin. 'That's true. And he paid the ultimate price for it. But you were the one to blame.'

Westy's eyes flashed. 'I was to blame. That's amusing. If it wasn't so sick.'

Caitlin shook her head. 'I know what happened now. I know how it happened. Emily brought her baby over here, probably to surprise her parents. No one was at the house. Of course not. You made sure Paula would be at work. But Emily came looking for you in the workshop. She walked in on you and Travis. She saw her father molesting an six-year-old child,' Caitlin said, her voice filled with loathing.

Westy's gaze was steady. 'You're out of your mind. That's disgusting.'

'Travis remembers Emily screaming at him to pull up his pants and rushing him out of here. She was crying hysterically when she put him in the car. Travis felt guilty. He thought it was his fault.'

Westy raised his chin defiantly. 'Quite an imagination on that child.'

'Travis didn't make this up,' said Caitlin. 'He wouldn't know how.'

'The only thing more preposterous than this story is that you would repeat it,' said Westy. 'Get out of here. Get off my property.'

Caitlin shook her head. 'No. I knew the truth the minute I heard it. This was your doing. You followed them back to Emily's house. You and Emily were arguing in the driveway. Travis saw it all. He saw her running down the driveway, probably trying to escape from you and your pitiful excuses. He heard the crash.

'You know, my brother said that she tried to commit suicide in front of his truck. He probably wasn't too far wrong. She must have felt like dying, finding that out about her father.'

'Stop trying to get your worthless brother off the hook. My daughter did not try to kill herself,' Westy insisted.

'No,' said Catilin. 'She was running away from you. You chased after her, and she ran out into the road and right in front of an oncoming truck.'

Westy shook his head. 'Travis is a disturbed child to make up a story like that. And the fact that you believe him... That is really troubling. Everybody knows that Emily was out at her mailbox, picking up the mail when your brother came around the bend like a bat out of hell and hit her,' Westy said.

'Yes,' said Caitlin. 'I was thinking about that, on my way over here. That mail scattered everywhere. It took me a while to figure that out.'

Westy was staring at her contemptuously. 'Figure what out?'

'Once my brother fled the scene, instead of calling for help, you took the precaution of removing the mail from the mailbox and scattering it all around the spot where Emily's body was lying. Staging the accident. And then you told Travis, before you put him in your car and dropped him off at home, that if he ever said anything about the events of that afternoon, you would kill his dog. Kill Champ.'

'Ridiculous,' Westy scoffed, but there was an undercurrent of uncertainty in his voice.

'Ridiculous?' Caitlin cried. 'Monstrous is more like it.

That kid hasn't had a day when he wasn't afraid in these last four years.'

'Travis,' Westy scoffed. 'Who would believe that greedy little brute? He was always happy enough to take my money and the gifts. When I picked him up from school he was always ready to come with me.'

Caitlin felt like she going to be sick to her stomach. 'You paid him? A fatherless six-year-old boy? You offered him gifts? How long did this go on? How many times did you assault him?'

'Assault.' Westy shook his head. 'This is what I get for my kindness to that kid? You call it assault?'

Caitlin stared at him, trying to imagine how twisted a person would have to be to call a child's rape 'kindness.' 'I think the police will call it assault,' she said. 'I'm quite sure of that.'

Westy's eyes were cold. 'Travis is a liar. As for you, you would do anything to try to blame someone else for what your brother did. I suggest you keep this ridiculous story to yourself.'

Caitlin shook her head. 'Or else what? Do you think you can scare me with your threats? I'm not a child. I'm not afraid of you. And in case you have ideas about silencing me or Travis before I even came over here I called the police. And I made sure that Travis and Champ were somewhere safe. You are not going to get away with this. I should have let the police come for you, but I just couldn't resist seeing your face when you realized that you were caught in your lies.'

Caitlin heard her phone ring in her jacket pocket. 'That will be Detective Mathis now,' she said. She reached down into her pocket and pulled out her phone. Before she could even register the name on the ID, Westy knocked the phone from her hands, and it skittered across the room.

She chased after it. As she bent to pick it up, she looked up and saw him looming over her, a hammer in his hand.

'You should not have come here,' he said.

THE DOOR TO Sam Mathis's office opened and a heavyset, gray-haired man in torn jeans, a leather vest and a bandana headband came out. 'Is that it?' he said.

'That's it,' said the detective.

'Do I need to come back?' the man asked.

'Nope. I appreciate your taking the time to come here. As for you,' said Sam, turning to Noah, who was sitting between his attorney, David Alvarez, and a uniformed officer, 'you're a lucky guy. This man just gave you an airtight alibi.'

Noah stood up and reached out to shake the man's hand. 'Thanks, Jim. That's the second time you saved my butt. I can't tell you how much I appreciate it.'

Jim shrugged. 'Glad to help you out.'

'It doesn't seem fair that your good deed screwed up the convention for you. Are you headed back there?' Noah asked.

Jim shook his head. 'I don't think so. No, I think Detective Mathis here saved me from making a big mistake.'

'Oh?' Noah asked.

'I ran into my ex-wife there. She was getting the "Linda loves Jim" tattoo removed from her shoulder blade. We got to talking and before you know it she was telling the guy removing the tattoo that she'd changed her mind. I may have dodged a bullet.'

The other men nodded knowingly.

Jim waved and headed for the door. David Alvarez turned to Sam. 'My client is free to go then?'

Sam nodded. 'We need to get back to finding his little boy.'

'Thanks for the effort you put into this,' said David. He shook hands with Sam, and then with Noah, and promised to be in touch. Then he picked up his briefcase and walked out.

Noah sighed. 'How is Dan doing anyway? Has he regained consciousness? You need to question him about Geordie as soon as he comes around.'

'I'm aware,' said Sam, holding his phone to his ear and frowning as he listened to his voice mail. He punched a number into his phone and waited. Then he looked at Noah. 'Caitlin left me a voice mail saying it was important but she's not answering.' He led the way to the chief clerk's desk where he signed a release for Noah's belongings. He handed the manila envelope to Noah.

'I'll find out what it was,' said Noah, emptying out the envelope on a nearby desktop. He put his watch back on, put his wallet in his pocket and stuck his phone in his jacket pocket. 'Are you on your way to see Dan?'

'That's my next stop,' said Sam.

'Mind if I come along?' said Noah.

'No. I don't want you at that hospital. Dan's family has been through enough,' said Sam. 'If they see you walk in there, no explanation will be good enough to mollify them. Let me handle it. I know what to ask.'

'I know you're right,' said Noah. He sighed as they left the building together. Standing on the sandstone steps of the station house, he scrolled through his missed phone calls, hoping to have one from Caitlin, and saw a whole series of calls from Naomi. He pressed a return call on one of them.

'Noah,' Naomi cried. 'Are you out?'

'I'm out,' he said.

'Thank God. I have to talk to you.'

'I'm going to go,' Sam interrupted him quietly. 'Talk to you later.'

Noah nodded and returned his attention to his sister. 'What's the matter?' he asked.

'Are you with Caitlin?'

'No,' said Noah. 'Why?'

'She brought Travis and Champ over here to the free bookstore about an hour ago. She told me not to let Travis out of my sight for any reason. She said that the police were going to come and talk to Travis. She didn't say why. She even asked Ed, the guy in the booth at the entrance, not to leave us alone with anyone in the free bookstore. What is going on? Do you know? Travis refuses to speak. He's clammed up completely, but I can tell that he's really upset.'

'I don't know, Naomi,' said Noah.

'Why would she do that? She's scaring me.'

'I'm sure she had a good reason,' said Noah. 'Do you know where she went?'

'I don't,' said Naomi.

'Does Travis?' Noah asked.

'I'll ask him again, but he's not answering me. Travis,' she said, her voice muffled but audible. 'Do you know where your Aunt Caitlin was going? Travis?'

There was a silence and then Naomi got back on the line. 'Nothing.'

'Let me talk to him.'

'Travis, your uncle wants to talk to you.' Naomi waited a second. Then she said, 'He's shaking his head.'

'Put the phone to his ear.'

Noah could hear rustling and then the sound of adenoidal breathing.

'Travis, this is Uncle Noah. I know there's something the matter. You have to tell me what it is.'

'Are you in jail?' Travis asked.

'No, I'm out of jail. Tell me about Aunt Caitlin. You were with her today?'

'She said she could protect me,' Travis said ruefully. 'Me and Champ.'

'Protect you from what?' Noah asked. 'Protect you from who?'

'She made me tell her everything and now she's gone,' said Travis.

'Tell her what?' Noah asked.

Travis was silent.

'Look, Travis. I'm worried about Aunt Caitlin. I'm afraid that she might be in some kind of trouble. Do you know where she was going after she left you with your mom?'

Travis remained silent.

Noah tried to remain calm and think, though all his instincts were on high alert. 'Who was she going to protect you from? Maybe that's where she went. To beat that person up.'

'She couldn't beat him up. He's too strong,' said Travis scornfully.

'Who, Travis?'

'Ask Caitlin.'

'I can't, Travis. She's not answering her phone.'

'When she does…'

'What if she can't?' Noah asked.

Travis was silent for a moment. Then he said, in a defeated tone, 'Mr Bergen,' he said.

'Geordie's Uncle Dan?' Noah asked.

'No,' said Travis. 'The other one.'

THIRTY

CAITLIN CAME TO, her face and hair sweaty, her mind groggy. She blinked her eyes and saw…nothing. She was seated on a chair, her wrists fastened tightly behind the chair back with some kind of thin wire, her upper arms burning with pain. Her ankles were joined with the same wire and anchored to the chair legs. She inhaled sharply, overcome by fear, and then understood, as it was sucked into her mouth, covering her teeth and tongue, that a black plastic bag had been tied around her neck. She could feel the wire cutting into her airways when she moved her head. Her head was pounding where he had struck her. How long had she been here? He had left her here to die. He might never come back. It was impossible to breathe and her heart was racing.

Palm trees, she told herself. *Don't lose it now. Someone will find you.* She had left a message for Sam. And Travis had revealed his secret to her. She told herself that it would not be as difficult for him to reveal it a second time. Someone would know where to look, she thought. They had to. She needed to keep calm and try to breathe as shallowly as possible so she did not suffocate from the bag.

Now that it was too late, she realized that she should never have come here on her own. She should have waited, let the police take care of it. She had been too eager to confront him. She had done this to herself.

Between her regrets and the lack of air, Caitlin's heart

beat painfully in her chest. She wondered if she was still in the workshop and thought that she probably was. Westy had surprised her with his strength, but he was probably not strong enough to move her inert body out of the workshop. Not in daylight. Not without being seen.

She tried to move around, to budge the chair, but all around her feet were objects which brushed against her ankles. Her head and shoulders also were also draped with something. She forced herself to be calm and try to think. Heavy fabric, empty sleeves. She was in the closet. She kicked the objects around her feet. Boots or shoes. He had left her in the closet.

Who would look for me here? she thought. But that was the kind of thought which led to despair and she didn't dare think it. She sat still, trussed to the plastic chair, and tried to keep breathing. She thought of Noah and of Geordie. She had the awful, unbearable thought that Geordie might have been held captive like this. Had Westy taken him? Kept him somewhere? Forced on him the same depraved acts that he had visited on Travis? Geordie would never be able to understand. He would panic, hyperventilate. Die.

Caitlin felt tears rising to her eyes but she knew that sobbing would be the worst possible thing to do. Sobbing could hasten her death. She forced herself to stop thinking of anything but those goddamn palm trees. She pictured them and felt her heartbeat slow down a little bit. She refused to imagine the face of her beloved boy. She couldn't. Not if she ever hoped to see him again.

She tried to work her hands and feet free, pulling them apart a millimeter at a time. It was exquisitely painful as the wire cut into her skin, but she didn't really care. What would be the worst that could happen? Her skin would be flayed and she would bleed. So be it. She had to do something to try to save herself. But he had tied her tightly and

her progress seemed negligible. She tried to jerk herself
forward in the chair, but the piles of boots impeded her
and she felt herself end up somewhat off balance, one leg
of the chair caught on the open top of a boot. Angrily, she
tried again, and this time felt herself stuck at an angle, trying to keep her balance.

All of a sudden, she froze. She heard the muffled sound
of voices somewhere outside of the closet. Her heart seized
in fear. Was he back? Had he come back to kill her?

As the door to the workshop opened, she sagged forward in relief. It was a woman's voice. Caitlin could barely
make out the words.

'He's not here. There's no one in here,' the woman said.
'I told you that.'

I'm in here, Caitlin tried to cry out, but when she inhaled the plastic bag filled her mouth, and the wire around
her neck conspired to keep her voice muffled. She tried to
grunt, to make explosive sounds, but the sounds she made
were so strangled that she could barely hear them herself.

'He wanted me to rest. He went back to the hospital.'

Caitlin recognized Paula's voice. She was talking about
Westy. He had gone to the hospital. To see Dan. Caitlin
thought about Dan and then, with a sickening sensation
in the pit of her stomach, she put it together. It was Westy.
He was the one who had attacked Dan. Had Dan somehow found out the truth about his father? Had he confronted Westy?

A man's voice murmured something which Caitlin
could not understand.

Don't try to listen, she thought. *It doesn't matter what
they are saying. There are people in the workshop and
they aren't going to be here for long.* What could she do?
She had to attract attention. Make enough noise for them
to hear her.

She had nothing to rattle, nothing to bang. The only thing she had, she thought, was her own body. She had made a start. She needed to go the rest of the way and hope she didn't strangle herself in the process. She shifted her weight to the tilting side of the unbalanced chair. She leaned over the arm as far as she could, the wire cutting grooves into her skin, and she felt the chair tipping. She was helpless but there was no other choice. She threw all her weight in the direction of the tilt and let the chair, with her in it, fall over.

She landed against the closet door with a thud, her cheek and shoulder smashed against the wood.

'What was that?' the man said, and she knew the voice.

Noah, she tried to gurgle. *I'm here.*

'I didn't hear anything,' said Paula.

'I could have sworn,' he said.

'Look, Noah, I'm just exhausted. I'll tell Westy you were here. What do you want with him anyway?'

Noah did not reply.

'I'm sorry there was a misunderstanding about Dan. But you couldn't blame us for thinking you were responsible.'

Noah murmured something that Caitlin could not understand. The angle that she was now at was causing the wire around her throat to tighten. She could feel black spots popping up in her consciousness. Almost as if she were about to fall asleep.

Was that how death felt? she wondered absently. Like falling asleep. The thought was almost soothing and then it jolted her awake. Her heart was beating wildly and it seemed like it would burst from the lack of oxygen. *Noah,* she thought.

She heard the door to the workshop close. They were gone.

They were gone, and all her hope was gone.

She tried to take a deep breath and the plastic bag filled her mouth and cut off all her air. She thought of Geordie's face and began to let go.

HALEY WAS DOZING in a chair beside Dan's bed, having repetitious dreams of someone chasing her through the hospital corridors, calling out for her to wake up. Finally, she felt the hand shaking her, and opened her eyes. She had a headache and her eyelids felt gritty. She looked up at Sam Mathis, trying to place him. And then she remembered. She felt a little surge of fear.

'Detective, what's the matter?' she said.

'I didn't mean to startle you,' he said.

'That's all right,' she said.

'How's he doing?' Sam asked, frowning at the inert figure on the bed. Dan's complexion remained a yellowish ivory color. He was still attached to several monitors.

Haley looked at him sadly and pressed her lips together. 'We're still waiting for him to come around. He opened his eyes a while ago, but he didn't seem to understand anything I said to him. Then he fell back asleep.'

'Have you been here for a long time?'

Haley rubbed her eyes and nodded. She shifted in the chair and arranged her rumpled clothing. 'Yeah,' she said. 'Caitlin told me not to leave him. I decided to…take her advice.'

'She thinks Dan knows where Geordie is,' said Sam. 'She's terrified that he won't be able to tell us in time to find the boy unharmed. I have to agree with her.'

'You blame Dan too?' Haley asked. 'Dan would never hurt that boy.'

'I don't know about that. But we are pretty certain that Geordie was with him. And Dan had no way of knowing he would end up unconscious in the hospital. So, what happened to the boy? That's the question.'

Haley sighed and studied her ex-husband's features. 'The doctor came by this morning. He said that even if Dan wakes up soon he may have some amnesia. It's not uncommon with a head injury.'

Sam walked around to the side of the bed and bent down. 'Dan,' he said. 'Dan, can you hear me? This is Detective Mathis.'

Dan's eyelids fluttered.

'Dan, you have to wake up. You need to tell us where Geordie is. We have to find the boy before it's too late. Can you do that, Dan? Can you tell us?'

Dan's eyes opened and he looked at Detective Mathis with a puzzled expression on his face. Haley jumped up and joined Sam at Dan's bedside.

'Dan. Honey, are you all right? What happened to you? Who did this to you?'

Dan frowned at Haley, and his monitors reacted to his agitation, their crooked lines jumping up and down. Sam spoke quietly to Haley.

'Miss Jordan. Right now the question we need answered the most is about Geordie Eckhart. We have to get Mr Bergen here to tell us.'

'I'm sorry,' said Haley.

Sam leaned down again so that Dan could see him clearly. 'Mr Eckhart. Dan. Did you take Geordie from his school?'

Dan licked his lips and stared at the detective. Then, slowly, almost imperceptibly, he nodded.

Haley let out a cry. 'No!'

Sam straightened up and glared at her. 'Get out of here. Right now,' he said.

'No, please, let me stay,' said Haley.

'Absolutely not,' said Sam. 'Go.'

'You're trying to pin this crime on a helpless, injured man,' she protested. 'He's not even responsible for what he's saying right now.'

'I'm not trying to build a case against Dan. I'm trying to find a six-year-old child who is missing,' Sam reminded her through gritted teeth. 'That's all that matters at this moment. I have two parents desperate to see their child again. If this man has information, I'm going to question him and I'll hash it out with the attorneys later. Now go. Go wash your face. Go get something to eat in the cafeteria. You look terrible.'

Tears welled in Haley's eyes. 'I'm afraid to leave him.'

'Nothing's going to happen to him. I'm here with him. Officer Wheatley is just outside the door. Now do as I say and get out of here.'

Reluctantly, Haley left the room, stopping several times to look back at her ex-husband.

Sam leaned over the bed again and gazed at Dan. There was a dull, confused expression in Dan's eyes. Then Dan closed his eyes for a moment and Sam feared that he was losing him to another round of unconsciousness.

'Dan,' he said, shaking him gently. 'Don't go back to sleep. Talk to me.'

Haley stumbled out into the hallway and turned in the direction of the elevators. She almost collided with Westy, who was getting off on that floor.

'How's he doing?' Westy asked her.

Haley sighed. 'Detective Mathis is in there with him now. He seemed to be coming around but the detective wouldn't let me stay. He thinks that Dan knows where Geordie is and he is trying to wrest it out of him, even though Dan is still somewhere in outer space.'

'We'll see about that,' said Westy. He raced down the hallway to Dan's room and rushed inside.

'Hey, that's enough. Leave my son alone,' Westy insisted as he entered the room.

Sam Mathis looked up at him. 'Your son knows where Geordie is,' he said.

Westy shook his head. 'Look at him. Where do you get an idea like that?'

'He's trying to tell me,' said Sam patiently.

'NO,' said Westy. 'He's not in his right mind. I won't allow you to try to interrogate him while he's in this condition.'

'Don't you care where your grandson is?' Sam asked suspiciously.

'What kind of a question is that?' Westy demanded indignantly. 'Of course I do. But Dan doesn't know anything about Geordie. He doesn't know what he's saying. You can't question him any further without an attorney present. He may be barely conscious but he still has rights. And while he's in this condition, it's up to me to protect those rights, which is what I'm doing. Not one more question till we speak to an attorney.'

Sam raised his hands in a gesture meant to lower the temperature in the room. 'All right. All right. I'll take a break. But I want you to get that attorney here right away. I'm coming back. He's the only one who can lead us to Geordie. I'm going to try again.'

'We'll see about that,' said Westy angrily. 'Just get out.'

Sam walked out of Dan's room and went down to the elevator. As he stepped into the elevator he tried Caitlin's number again, but there was no answer. He thought about what he had just learned. Dan had admitted to taking Geordie. Only with a nod, but it was good enough. That meant that he knew where Geordie was. Obviously Dan's plan had never been to end up incapacitated in the hospital. He could have left Geordie alone somewhere, or with some impatient co-conspirator. The child might have only limited food or water. That meant that Geordie's life could be in immediate peril. Attorney or no attorney, Sam meant to find out where that boy was being held.

Haley, meanwhile, got halfway to the cafeteria before she realized that she had forgotten to bring her purse. It was still in Dan's hospital room. For a moment she thought she might forget about eating. Her stomach was in such a knot that she couldn't imagine putting anything into it. But she needed something to drink. Something with caffeine. So she turned around and went back up to Dan's floor.

She got off the elevator and walked down to Dan's room. Officer Wheatley was talking to someone on his cell phone, but he nodded to her as she started back into the room. She walked in and stopped dead in her tracks.

'What are you doing?' she cried. 'What the hell are you doing?'

THIRTY-ONE

WESTY LOOKED UP at her indignantly. 'I'm rearranging his pillows,' he said. 'I'm trying to make him more comfortable.'

'No, you're not,' said Haley. 'You had that pillow over his face.'

'Haley, how could you even say such a thing? This is my son.'

Haley shook her head. 'NO, I saw you. Just now, when I walked in. You were holding it over his face.'

Westy replaced the pillow on the bed and came over to where Haley stood. He put a hand gently on her forearm. 'Haley, you have been a wonderful friend to Dan through this whole ordeal,' said Westy. 'I know how much you care for him. Why, if Paula and I had had anything to do with it, you two never would have broken up. I think of you like my own daughter. But now, I think you need to go home and rest. You're suffering from exhaustion. Your mind is playing tricks on you.'

'I saw you,' she insisted.

'You saw me fixing his pillows. I worry that he's uncomfortable. And he can't do it for himself.'

Haley frowned and peered at him. 'Caitlin told me not to trust anyone.'

'Well, consider the source,' said Westy. 'Look, you go home and have a rest. You can trust me and Dan's mother to look after him.'

'Where is Paula?' Haley asked.

'She needed a break, too. But I'm sure she'll be back here soon,' said Westy.

'What about Detective Mathis?'

'He walked out of here just a minute ago. I'm surprised you didn't run into him coming out the door. But there's another fellow guarding Dan out there. Officer Wheatley. Dan's in good hands. He's safe.'

'Maybe you're right,' Haley sighed. 'I'm sorry. That was a terrible thing to accuse you of.'

'We're all on edge,' said Westy.

'I suppose I could use a rest.' Haley walked around to the other side of the bed and leaned down to pick up her purse. She slung her purse over her shoulder and straightened up, gazing down at Dan. His eyes were closed again, as if he had drifted back into the netherworld he had been inhabiting these last few days.

She ran a hand over his hair and then bent down to kiss his cheek. 'I'll be back, Dan,' she said gently.

'Help me,' he whispered in her ear.

THE DOOR TO the closet opened abruptly and the chair toppled over, crashing out onto the floor of the workshop.

'Jesus,' Noah cried.

Caitlin tried to speak but everything went black.

'Don't move,' said Noah. He found a utility knife on the workbench and used it to slice open the back of the bag to let in some air. Then he began to twist open the wires which held the bag tight around her neck. He untangled them to the point where he could pull off the plastic bag off her head.

Caitlin gasped for air, drinking it in like water in a desert. Noah continued to free her from the wires, twisting them free and trying not to dig them any further into her skin as he worked. His hands shook and he was infuriated by the slowness of the task.

'You came back,' she croaked. 'Thank you.'

'Travis told me you were coming here. I needed to think so I took a walk down the road and saw your car in the cul-de-sac. Then I knew you were here.'

'I hid it there when I arrived so Westy wouldn't see it. Thank you for not giving up on me,' she said.

'There,' said Noah. 'You're free.' He began to pat his pockets for his phone. 'I'm going to call an ambulance.'

'No,' Caitlin insisted. 'We can't wait for an ambulance. I'm all right.'

'You're bleeding all over the place,' Noah said, looking at the spots where the wire had sawed into her ankles and wrists.

'Call Naomi. Make sure that Travis is safe. And call Sam. He needs to get to the hospital. I'm afraid for Dan. I'm afraid Westy is going to try to silence him.'

'His own son?' Noah cried.

'Call them,' said Caitlin. She got up and went to the first aid kit with a red cross on the box which was sitting on a nearby shelf. 'Call them right away.'

'What about Westy?'

Caitlin and Noah looked up and saw Paula, standing in the workshop doorway. They looked at one another and then back at her.

'I saw your car was still here, Noah. I came down to see why you hadn't left. What were you were saying, Caitlin? About my husband? What's going on here? You're bleeding,' Paula exclaimed.

'He tied her up with wire and left her in the closet,' said Noah. 'Left her for dead. I'm afraid it was Westy who tried to kill Dan as well.'

Paula shook her head. 'No. That's impossible.'

Noah opened his mouth to speak and then reconsidered. 'There's no time to argue about this,' he said. He turned his back on her and dialed Naomi's number on his speed dial.

'Naomi, it's me. Are you and Travis OK? And Champ.'

'We're OK,' said Naomi. 'Ed's here at the bookstore playing cards with Travis. Travis thinks cards are stupid but…'

'Good. Just keep him there. Stay with Ed. Don't move. I'll explain it all to you later.'

'Travis wants to know if you found Caitlin.'

Noah glanced over at Caitlin, who was wrapping gauze bandage around her wrists. 'Yeah, tell Travis that Caitlin's OK, thanks to him.'

'Put that phone away and answer me,' Paula demanded.

Caitlin tied off the bandage and looked up at her. 'I'll answer you. Your husband is a child molester and a would-be killer. And somehow he is involved in Geordie's disappearance.'

'That's completely ridiculous,' said Paula. 'Westy would never hurt a child. He loves children.'

'Yeah, way too much,' said Caitlin.

'That's disgusting. You have a filthy mind. Why would anybody believe you?' said Paula coldly. 'We know what a liar you are.'

'I don't care whether you take my word or not,' said Caitlin. 'But you better steel yourself for some nasty surprises. Westy is not the man you think you know.'

Noah was speaking to Sam Mathis, whom he reached as he was getting into his car at the hospital parking lot. 'Sam,' he said, 'Westy Bergen tied Caitlin up and locked her in a closet here in his workshop. He's desperate. Don't leave him alone with Dan. Dan is our only link to Geordie. Yeah, we're on our way over there.'

'Dan?' Paula said. 'My Dan?'

'He tried to kill your Dan,' said Caitlin bitterly.

'No. That's preposterous. He adores Dan.'

'Maybe Dan found out about his other hobby. Sexually assaulting little boys.'

'You bitch,' said Paula. 'Take that back.'

Caitlin looked at Paula and she didn't know whether she felt contempt or pity. *How could you be so oblivious? How could you not know this about your husband?* she wondered. And yet, it happened every day. *We all think we know our partners,* Caitlin thought. *We just hope that we are not deceived.* She looked at Paula's carefully constructed façade of calm and competence and saw it breaking apart from this blow. Caitlin couldn't deny that she felt some contempt, but pity won out. 'I can't take it back, Paula,' she said, meeting the other woman's horrified gaze. 'I'm sure you'd rather die than believe it. But it's true.'

Noah ended the call, stood up, and examined Caitlin's bandaging job. 'They're going to have to redo this for you at the hospital,' he said.

'Whatever. We'll worry about that later,' said Caitlin. 'Let's go.'

They heard a door slam and looked up. The next sound they heard was the roar of a car engine. The workshop door was closed and Paula was gone. Noah rushed to the door and looked out.

'She's gone. She took my car,' he said.

'We'll go in mine. We'd better hurry.'

HALEY SLOWLY SET her pocketbook back down on the floor and resumed her seat in the chair by Dan's bed.

'What are you doing?' Westy demanded. 'I thought you were leaving.'

'I changed my mind. I think I'll stay.'

Westy struggled to control his anger. 'You're not wanted here,' he said.

Haley saw his rage and felt strangely calm. 'I thought you were just saying how much you liked me. How much you wished Dan and I had stayed married.'

Westy shook his head. 'Well, I was trying to make you feel better. Actually, I think it's kind of pitiful the way you chase after him now. He's moved on, Haley. Hanging around him isn't going to change anything. You should go. Just go and let him get on with his life.'

Haley placed her hand over Dan's, curving her fingers over his. 'No. I don't think so. I think I'll stay right here like I planned. You can go if you want.' Haley felt the pressure of Dan's fingers squeezing hers.

'Do I have to get the cops to remove you?' Westy demanded. ''Cause I will. There's a cop right outside the door. I'll tell him that you're interfering with my son's recovery,' said Westy.

'You do that. And I'll tell him that you tried to suffocate your son with a pillow.'

Westy glared at her with hate-filled eyes. Haley gazed right back at him.

Suddenly, the door to the room opened again, and Officer Wheatley walked in. 'Mr Bergen,' he said, 'I just received a call from Detective Mathis. There's a young woman making an accusation against you. I'm afraid you're going to have to come down to the station and answer a few questions…'

'What young woman?' Westy demanded.

Officer Wheatley glanced over at Haley. 'You'll have to ask them down at the station.'

'No, I'm not going anywhere with you,' Westy protested. 'I'm staying here with my son.'

'I'm sorry about your son, but this isn't actually a request,' said the officer. 'You can either come willingly or I'll have to arrest you.'

'Arrest me?' Westy cried. 'The world has gone mad.'

'There's no need to make this worse than it is,' said Officer Wheatley. 'Just come along. If we can straighten everything out you will be back at your son's bedside in no time.'

'Don't let him come back,' said Haley in a shaky voice. 'He tried to suffocate Dan with a pillow.'

Westy turned on her in a rage. 'You shut up…'

'That's enough,' said the officer.

Westy shook his head. 'No, I'm not going.'

Officer Wheatley reached out to take him by the arm. Westy batted his hand away and slapped the officer across the face. Officer Wheatley fumbled for his gun and pulled it out. 'All right. That's it. Assaulting an officer. Mr Bergen, you have to come…'

Before he could finish his sentence, Westy seized the gun from Officer Wheatley's hand and fired it at him, point blank.

Haley screamed and then threw herself over Dan, covering him with her own body. Westy fired again. Haley slumped onto Dan's chest, shot in the back. Dan cried out as if he were the one who had taken the bullet. The door to the room opened and several orderlies, a nurse and a doctor tried to enter.

Westy wielded the gun wildly, yelling threats. The people in the doorway jumped back as he commanded, and he pushed his way past them and into the hallway.

'Watch out!' someone yelled. 'There's a gunman.' People dove back into doorways, under desks and behind roll-ing trays. The floor looked suddenly deserted. Westy had it all to himself as he ran for the emergency exit and bolted down the stairs.

THIRTY-TWO

NOAH INSISTED ON driving. As they approached the hospital they could hear the wail of sirens and see flashing lights. Sticking her head out the car window, Caitlin was able to see that a gate had been lowered in front of the main entrance to the hospital and anyone who tried to enter was turned away. The traffic was backed up and at a standstill as people passing in their cars gawked at the commotion. 'I'm going to get out and run,' Caitlin said.

'Are you crazy? There's obviously some kind of standoff going on. Stay in the car. You could get hurt,' Noah said.

'I can't stand this,' said Caitlin. 'What is happening up there?

As they inched closer they could see a raft of police vehicles assembled in the parking lot of the hospital. There were officers with guns drawn and their attention seemed to be focused on one area of the parking lot near the emergency exit. A plainclothes officer with a bullhorn was addressing someone, but what he said was unintelligible.

'That's Sam Mathis!' Caitlin cried. 'I recognize him.'

A uniformed officer in a bulletproof vest loped out into the busy intersection and began to direct the traffic to get it moving. He gestured for the next car in line to pass, and suddenly Caitlin recognized Noah's vehicle.

'That's your car. That's Paula in there.'

Even as Caitlin recognized Noah's car, the driver made

a sharp right turn, floored the gas pedal and ploughed through the barrier, breaking it into pieces as she entered the parking lot.

There was a screech of brakes as the officer directing traffic ran out in front of the oncoming cars and followed her into the parking lot. 'Hey, stop!' he cried.

Noah hesitated and then made a decision. 'Hang on,' he said to Caitlin. 'We're going in, too.' He pulled out of the line of cars and onto the shoulder of the road. He cruised down to the splintered gate and passed through it.

Meanwhile, in the hospital parking lot, Paula was ignoring every warning, every sign, and every barrier. She drove up into the middle of two rows of cars, stopped the car, got out and left it. Noah pulled into an emergency space and he and Caitlin jumped out of their car as well. Paula was hurrying toward the emergency exit of the hospital.

Caitlin heard somebody yell out, 'It's his wife. Don't shoot.'

Noah and Caitlin crouched down and scuttled along behind the parked cars, zigzagging toward the scene of the confrontation. The police were focused on Paula as she ran out in plain sight, impervious to their shouts, seemingly unconcerned by the danger.

'It's Westy,' said Caitlin. 'I knew it. What if Dan is dead? What if we can't find out? What if we never know…?'

'Don't,' Noah advised her grimly. 'Jesus Christ, what is going on up there?'

As if in answer to his question a shot rang out, and everybody in the parking lot ducked except for Paula, who continued to run in the direction of the gunfire.

Caitlin and Noah stayed low but kept moving forward. They could see Westy clearly now. He was holding a gun to the head of a young blond woman in nurse's scrubs, using her as a shield.

Caitlin heard Sam Mathis's voice, calm and deliberate, through the bullhorn. 'Put the gun down, Mr Bergen. Let Sharon go. We can end this peacefully.'

Caitlin, grasping at straws, took comfort from this. 'Maybe no one has been hurt yet,' she whispered to Noah.

'Let's hope,' he said.

Several officers rushed out to Paula and tried to call her back but she waved them off. She continued in the direction of her husband.

'Westy,' she called out in a demanding voice. 'Let that young woman go. She didn't do anything to deserve this. Let her go.'

'Get away from me, Paula. Don't help them,' he called back.

'Let her go. Take me instead,' said Paula.

Caitlin held her breath. She had to admire Paula's courage in the face of Westy's obvious derangement. Although, Caitlin thought, the truth about her husband that she was going to have to face might be worse to her than any hail of bullets.

'Come on, Westy, please.' Paula raised her hands as if to show that she was unarmed. 'I don't care what happens to me anymore.'

'Why not?' he demanded.

'After what you've done?' She let out a bark of laughter that was also a sob. 'What difference does anything make?'

Westy's eyes narrowed and then he shook his head. 'Forty years of this marriage and you don't even give me the benefit of the doubt…' he said disgustedly.

'I tried to,' she protested unconvincingly.

'No, you didn't. You never did. You never respected me. You always treated me like I was foolish.'

A van with a SWAT team had entered the parking lot and rolled slowly toward the scene. Four men in fatigues, holding telescopic rifles, clambered out the side of the van.

'Mr Bergen, you have to give this up,' Sam Mathis called out. 'Let the hostage go. Let Sharon go. No one else needs to get hurt.'

'No one ELSE?' Caitlin cried. 'Does that mean that someone was already hurt? Are we too late?'

'Take it easy. We don't know that,' said Noah.

'Westy, you have to stop this,' Paula said, trying to keep her voice calm. 'Look, I don't know what's wrong with you. But you need help. That much is obvious.'

'I don't need help,' Westy insisted. 'Why do I need help? Because I won't do what you want?'

'They said you molested children!' she cried. 'They said you were the one who hurt Dan.'

'You didn't even ask me if it's true. Right away, you believe them. You just immediately start barking orders.'

'Mr Bergen,' Sam said through the bullhorn, 'Your wife is trying to help you. Listen to her.'

'Help me?' Westy cried petulantly. 'She's ashamed of me. She doesn't believe a word I say.'

'That's not true,' Paula called out to him. 'I do. I do believe you. No matter what they say, I know you would never hurt Dan.'

For a moment, Westy measured Paula's sincerity with his gaze. 'Your darling Dan. You think you know all about Dan. You always thought he was yours. But Dan and I used to have something special together. Something much closer than just father and son.'

Paula shook her head. 'Don't say that.'

'We did, Paula. I'm sorry, but we did. And, in spite of that, he turned on me,' he said. 'He's a traitor. He betrayed me. After all we shared. I am angry. I admit it.'

'What are you saying?' she cried.

'I had to silence him,' Westy said indignantly. 'He was going to put all that we shared out like garbage, in front of the world. I couldn't let him do that.'

'Oh, my God.' Paula doubled over, as if he had struck her. She fell to her knees, rocking back and forth, and holding her arms close to her body, as if to keep her insides from spilling out onto the pavement.

'You bastard!' Caitlin cried, jumping to her feet from behind the parked car. She felt as if her heart was exploding in her chest. 'Where is Geordie? What have you done with him?'

'Caitlin, don't!' Noah cried. He rose also and came after her.

'Get down,' Sam thundered through the bullhorn. 'Caitlin, get down.'

But it was too late. Westy turned and saw Caitlin howling in despair, coming toward him. He held on to his hostage as a shield, but turned the gun on Caitlin as Noah seized her from behind.

'Get back,' Westy ordered her.

Noah tried to drag her back out of harm's way. Caitlin flailed against him, determined to get to Westy.

'You sick, perverted son of a bitch. Where is my boy?' she cried.

'How do I know?' Westy demanded.

Sharon, the hostage, realizing that she was no longer the one under the gun, hesitated, and then seized her opportunity. She pulled Westy's hand close to her face and bit down on his wrist. Westy howled in pain and released his grip on her. The young woman bolted away from the gunman and dove behind the nearest car.

Caitlin shook off Noah's grasp and rushed toward

Westy. Westy wheeled, raised the gun and aimed it straight at her.

'Now!' Sam cried.

The SWAT team sharpshooters, already peering down their sights, steadied their weapons and fired.

THIRTY-THREE

CAITLIN AND NOAH stood on the front steps of the red-brick townhouse and rang the bell. 'The last time I was here,' she said, 'I was convinced that Dan had Geordie in this house. When he let me in I stood in the vestibule and started screaming for Geordie like a madwoman.'

'You were almost right,' said Noah. He took Caitlin's hand and squeezed it. 'It's only a matter of hours now,' he said.

Caitlin smiled at him. 'Thank God.'

The door opened and Paula Bergen stood there. She did not register any emotion at the sight of them. Her face was drawn and haggard, and her eyes were lifeless. 'Come in,' she said, as if she were a servant. 'He's in the living room.'

'How are you doing, Paula?' Noah asked.

Paula shook her head but did not reply. She walked to the living-room door with them. 'Dan,' she said, 'I'm going upstairs. I'm very tired. Call me if you need me.' Without another word, Paula began to trudge up the staircase.

How could you not have known? Caitlin wondered again as she watched her go. *You were so busy paying attention to your beautiful house and your gourmet meals and your executive job that you couldn't see what was happening right there in front of your face.* But then Caitlin chided herself. Paula didn't need anyone else to pass judgment on her. Her suffering would last a lifetime. Obviously, she knew now that her husband had been depraved and had preyed on children, including her own, right under her nose. Paula must have asked herself that question a thousand times in the last few days. *How could I not have known?*

Caitlin and Noah looked in at Dan. He was still bruised and bandaged, but he was sitting up in a recliner in the living room. 'Come in,' he said. 'Excuse me for not getting up, but it's still painful.'

'No problem,' said Caitlin, taking a seat on the couch. Noah sat down beside her and planted his feet widely apart on the floor.

'You look better,' Noah said, and there was an accusing note in his voice.

'I'm getting there,' said Dan.

It was almost as if the death of Westy Bergen had released Dan from the fugue state where he had been suspended since the beating he took at his father's hands. While he was still in the hospital his mind seemed to clear, and the first question he had asked was about the condition of Haley. The bullet had lodged near her spine, and the doctors had at first been worried that she might suffer paralysis. Happily, her surgery was successful and she was expected to fully recover. Westy's other victim, Officer Wheatley, was still in a serious condition in the hospital.

The first question Dan had answered was to tell the police the whereabouts of Geordie. Now Geordie was on an airplane, coming home in the company of two federal agents. Dan and Caitlin had wanted to go and get him themselves but they were told, gently but firmly, that they could not take custody of him until his plane landed in Philadelphia.

That landing was only an hour away. Noah and Caitlin were spending this last hour before their reunion talking to Dan in his house in Philadelphia where he was recuperating, out on bail, facing kidnapping charges. Other than revealing Geordie's location and apologizing to them, Dan had not been able to talk to them since his arrest. This meeting today was tense, but necessary.

Paula was staying in the house with her son, going through the motions of taking care of him, but she was a shell of the woman who had once taken such pride in her perfectly calibrated life. Noah and Caitlin hadn't known whether or not she would be present at this meeting. Obviously she had decided, by going upstairs for a rest, to avoid listening, once again, to her son describe the hellish circumstances that had led to their family's destruction.

'I'm glad you two are here,' Dan said. 'I have been wanting to explain to you what happened.'

'We know most of it,' Noah said abruptly.

'Noah,' Caitlin said quietly. 'Let him tell us.'

'Thanks, Caitlin,' said Dan. 'It's hard to know where to start. First of all, I know that it's going to be hard for you to believe, but I didn't know what my father had done to me. There was a huge gap in my own life. I don't understand how it is possible but I had no memory of any of it. I had completely repressed it. I didn't remember a thing until the birthday party. When Geordie was opening his presents and my father gave him those binoculars, it was like being struck by lightning.

'I watched Geordie opening the present and heard my father say that he was going to take him birding, and suddenly I got the most blinding headache and stomach pain that I had ever experienced. I was reeling when I left the party. I was supposed to go back to Philly but I was in too much pain and I literally couldn't see to drive. I had double vision from the headache. My date went back on the bus and I stayed at Haley's.

'It was the worst night of my life. The images started to

tumble into my conscious mind. I couldn't believe I was having these…disgusting thoughts about my own father. Just the two of us, hiding in the duck blinds and rocking the canoe. I was ashamed of myself for being able to imagine such things. Sometime near dawn, I began to understand that it was real. That this had really happened. To me. That he took me birding and while everybody thought we were out there looking for lifers and making tick lists, he was busy…using me for sex.'

Tears came to Dan's eyes and ran down his cheeks. He did not bother to wipe them away. 'I couldn't tell anyone—not even Haley. I only could think of one thing—he was about to start on Geordie. He was announcing his intentions with that gift of the binoculars. As soon as I set eyes on them it all came flooding back. I had to act. After that sleepless, sickening night, I went to Geordie's school, and I told him that I wanted him to come on a surprise vacation. A special birthday present. And then I took him.'

'Why didn't you just tell us?' Caitlin cried.

'Obviously, I wasn't thinking straight,' Dan admitted. 'I realize that now. I was distraught and I didn't think about the consequences. I didn't think about anything except saving Geordie.'

'You could have called the police,' said Noah.

'And accused my father? Without even speaking to him? Without warning my mother? You know, I never even considered it. I couldn't. I needed time to think. To think about what to do. But I knew I had to get Geordie out of harm's way until I figured it out. I took him straight to the airport. We flew to Puerto Rico. I left him with Ricardo's Ortiz's mother, Soledad. Thanks to Ricardo's success in baseball she has a big house on the beach. It's a family compound actually. Children and grandchildren everywhere. Most everyone in Ricardo's family speaks only Spanish, so I knew they wouldn't be too aware of a kidnapping in New Jersey. Anyway, I've known Soledad for twenty years. I knew Geordie loved being at the beach, and I knew he would be safe in her house. I told her that I needed her to protect him. She didn't ask me any questions. I offered her money, but she wouldn't take it. She always told me, after I helped Ricardo get into the big leagues, that there was nothing she wouldn't do for me. So, I called in my marker.'

'But you let Geordie call me,' said Caitlin.

'I wanted you to know he was safe. I bought the phone in Chicago when I was there for the Phillies–Cubs game. Ricardo is now a coach for the White Sox, so he's based in Chicago. I met him at the stadium and I gave him the phone. He flew to San Juan that night. I told him to let Geordie use the phone for just a minute. I told him how to explain it to Geordie. Ricardo did exactly what I asked.'

Caitlin thought about the plane, which was on its way to Philadelphia from San Juan at this very moment, carrying Geordie back to them. There had been moments when she had lost all hope and thought that she would never see him again. But he was in the sky, right this minute, on his way to them.

'Frankly, I was stalling, avoiding what I had to do. After Caitlin came to my house that day trying to find Geordie, I knew. That's when I came up to Hartwell and met Noah at the cemetery. I wanted to tell you, Noah, but I hadn't seen my father yet so I couldn't. After I left you, I went and I met him in the workshop. That was his idea. I wanted to face him, and that place—another favorite spot for his attacks—all at once.

'Well, you know the rest. First he denied it. But I wasn't going to let him get away with it. My whole life has been ruined by what he did.'

'I thought you said you didn't even remember it. How did it ruin your life?' Caitlin asked.

Dan hesitated and cleared his throat. 'I never understood what was wrong with me. I have never been able to…connect with a woman the way other men do. Sexual acts are something brutal to me. After it's over I feel…anything from distaste to hatred for my partner.'

'This is too personal,' Noah said uneasily.

'No, it's important,' said Dan. 'I took your son. You need to know why. It invades every part of your life. It destroys your…faith. It ruined my marriage to the one woman I really loved.'

'Haley,' said Caitlin.

'Haley,' said Dan.

'She still cares for you,' said Caitlin.

'Obviously,' said Dan. 'She nearly died trying to protect me.'

'Maybe there's still hope for you two,' said Caitlin. 'When you…you know…afterwards.' She didn't want to mention prison.

'That's a nice thought,' said Dan grimly. 'But I don't kid myself. I probably will never be able to overcome it. At least now I know why I am the way I am.'

'Did you tell your father that?' Caitlin asked.

'When I told him what I remembered, my father tried to convince me I had imagined it. When I wouldn't back down and started to walk away, he attacked me with a hammer. He tried to kill me.'

'Jesus,' Noah exclaimed.

'I guess he thought he had killed me. He managed to get me in the car and lug me over to your house so that Noah would be blamed. He left me there in the bushes.'

'He'll never hurt anyone else,' said Caitlin.

'I'm so sorry for what I put you through,' said Dan. 'All

I could think of was that I had to protect Geordie. I didn't want him to be ruined because I did nothing.'

'You put us through hell. I don't forgive you for that,' said Noah.

'I understand,' said Dan.

'I believe you, Dan,' said Caitlin. 'I know you did it for Geordie's sake.'

There was an awkward silence among the three of them. Noah looked at his watch. 'We need to get going. We want to be there waiting when he gets off the plane.'

'Thank you for coming to see me,' said Dan.

Noah did not reply, but Caitlin walked over to the recliner and took Dan's hand. Dan held her hand for a minute.

'Caitlin, come on,' said Noah.

Caitlin and Noah went out to the car. Caitlin got in on the passenger side and Noah drove. As he pulled out of the parking space he said, 'His lawyer is going to claim post-traumatic stress as his defense, you know.'

'Well, if ever anybody had reason to claim post-traumatic stress, it's Dan,' said Caitlin. 'That is as good an explanation as I could imagine.'

'I was hoping he would take a plea so we wouldn't have to go through a trial.'

'Maybe he needs to explain what he did out loud. In the light, so to speak.'

'Hasn't our family been through enough?' Noah cried.

'What would happen if we refused to press charges?' Caitlin asked.

'It doesn't work that way,' said Noah.

'What if he hadn't remembered, Noah? What if Dan hadn't acted and Geordie had become Westy's next victim? I keep thinking about that. We might never have known. Geordie might have suffered like Dan did. Like Travis did.'

'Travis,' said Noah, and there was a tragic note in his voice.

They drove in silence for a few minutes, through Society Hill to Columbus drive. They wound their way through South Philly and out onto Route 95. The highway passed over the gray, industrialized part of Philly which smelled of oil refineries. Caitlin looked over at Noah. 'It was a stupid thing to do,' she said. 'But I believe him when he says that he was desperate. He was trying to save Geordie.' Caitlin turned away from him and looked out at the bleak landscape passing by. 'Maybe I understand it better than you,' she said. 'Having made the wrong choice myself, keeping a secret when I shouldn't have.'

Noah did not reply.

'There's no doubt that Dan has suffered.'

'No doubt of that,' said Noah.

'Did you ever think there was anything…strange about Westy?' she asked.

Noah shook his head. 'I had no idea. God, poor Travis.'

'Don't remind me. When I think how unfairly I treated him,' said Caitlin. 'I feel like I was so impatient with him. So unkind. When I think about the things that were weighing on him. I just hope I will be able to make it up to him.'

'You? I used to ask Westy to pick Travis up for me. Days when I was too busy. I handed my sister's son over to a predator. I will never get over the guilt. If I had paid more attention…'

'Don't, Noah. You couldn't have known. No one knew. Anyway, Naomi tells me that the therapist is optimistic. Just the fact that Travis didn't repress it is good. And knowing that nobody's going to kill Champ has definitely helped.'

'No escaping that mutt,' said Noah, and his voice choked up.

'We just have to start over now,' she said. 'And do better.'

Noah looked at her briefly. 'I really wasn't fair to you. I even accused you.'

'Well, I gave you a good reason not to trust me.'

'Why didn't you just tell me?' Noah asked.

Caitlin had thought a lot about the answer to that question. 'I missed the moment when I should have told you. That critical moment. The first time we met, I should have said it first thing. But I was ashamed and the words stuck in my throat. Before I knew it, we were laughing, you and I. And it wasn't long after that…I knew you were my happiness. You and Geordie. And I wanted my happiness. Selfishly, I just wanted it to last. I thought I could just keep the secret and make it up to you both. Make up for your loss. Make your lives happy again.'

'Penance,' said Noah.

'No,' said Caitlin with a sigh. 'Penance implies sorrow and suffering. All I had with you two was…joy.'

Noah was quiet for a moment. Then he said, 'Me, too.'

Caitlin pressed her lips together and blinked back tears.

'We've all made mistakes,' he said.

'Can you forgive mine?' she asked him.

'I'm not great at forgiveness,' he said. 'Lawyers, you know. We always think we're right.'

They both smiled.

'But I'm trying to learn. I'll start with you.'

'Thank you,' she whispered.

'I'm trying to find a way to forgive Dan,' said Noah. 'God knows, he was a victim, too.'

'So many victims,' she said. 'Emily. Westy was so afraid that she would give away his secret that he chased Emily right out in front of my brother's truck.'

'Does that make your brother a victim, too?' Noah asked.

'No,' said Caitlin. 'I can't say that.'

They sat silently for a moment.

'Poor Em,' said Noah with a heavy sigh. Caitlin had told him everything that Travis confided in her, but he was still having trouble coming to terms with it. 'What a horror…to walk in on that. Her own father assaulting Travis.' Noah shuddered. 'She loved her Dad. She always liked to say that she was a "daddy's girl." What a shock it must have been to her. She must have felt…destroyed. It makes me sick just to think about it.'

'But she was brave,' Caitlin reminded him. 'Emily did the right thing. She took Travis away from there. Travis told me that she was yelling at Westy, threatening to have him arrested. I really think it meant the world to Travis that she stood up for him that way.'

'It cost her everything,' said Noah gravely. 'It cost Geordie his mother.'

It pained Caitlin to hear him say that, even though she knew it was true. Emily was Geordie's mother, and her last act had been to try and save another child from a predator. Someday, Geordie would be proud when he heard that story. She would make sure that he heard it. That he understood what his mother had done. That she had defied her own father and tried to do what was right.

'There's the sign for arrivals,' she said.

Noah took the left fork that led to the airport and they headed for the parking garage. They had talked to Geordie three times in the last two days as the flight home was arranged, and they promised to meet him.

'Did you bring Bandit?' Noah asked.

'Of course,' said Caitlin. 'God, I'm so excited, I feel like a kid at Christmas!'

The arrivals terminal was almost empty. They made their way to the gate where the plane would be landing.

Then, they sat and waited. The plane was scheduled to arrive on time, but every moment felt like an hour.

They were able to see it land and taxi to the gate. It seemed to take forever. Finally, it was anchored to the flyway and the doors were opened.

'Can't we run down there and meet him?' she asked.

'I think we better wait here. It won't be long now,' he said.

'When I think how afraid I have been...' she said.

Noah shook his head. 'I know. Sometimes I thought that I couldn't get through another day of it,' he said. They were speaking to one another and holding hands, but their gazes were riveted to the arrival door for the flight from San Juan.

All of a sudden there was movement at the door. A ticket agent went and opened it, and then they saw three people coming through the door. Two burly men in suits and one small boy between them.

What does your heart say? Caitlin thought. *How do you greet the child of your heart whom you feared was lost forever?* Geordie was wearing baggy shorts and a San Juan T-shirt, and his school backpack was on his back. His glasses were sliding down his nose. When he saw them, his face glowed with delight.

'There's my parents,' he said to the men who flanked him.

One of them nodded and said, 'OK.'

Then Geordie was running up the ramp, and Noah made it to the top of the ramp in two steps. He scooped the boy up in his arms and buried his face against Geordie's shoulder. Geordie hugged him back, hard.

After a minute, he squirmed. 'Put me down, Dad,' he said.

Watching them, Caitlin felt suddenly weak. She knelt

down on the carpet so she would be at his eye level. She
held up the stuffed dog as he came toward her.

'Bandit,' Geordie cried and grinned, showing the spaces
of his missing teeth. 'I thought I lost him.'

Caitlin handed it to him, and Geordie held the animal
close. Then he looked into Caitlin's eyes eagerly. 'It was
fun, Mom,' he said. 'The house was right on the beach.
And they were so nice. Can I go again, sometime?'

'We'll see,' she said softly, drinking in the sight of his
face.

'I missed you, though,' he said gravely.

Caitlin put her arms around him gently, like he was a
butterfly, alighting for a moment on a flower. His skin
was tanned and smelled like bubble gum and soap. His
little frame felt tender, breakable, in her arms. She closed
her eyes and tried not to hold him too tight. 'I missed you,
too,' she said.

* * * * *